BARBARIAN ALIEN

BARBARIAN
ALIEN

RUBY DIXON

BERKLEY ROMANCE
New York

BERKLEY ROMANCE
Published by Berkley
An imprint of Penguin Random House LLC
penguinrandomhouse.com

Library of Congress Cataloging-in-Publication Data

Names: Dixon, Ruby, 1976– author.
Title: Barbarian alien / Ruby Dixon.
Description: Jove trade paperback edition. | New York: Jove, 2022. |
Series: Ice Planet Barbarians
Identifiers: LCCN 2021043265 | ISBN 9780593546031 (trade paperback)
Classification: LCC PS3604.I965 B37 2022 | DDC 813/.6—dc23
LC record available at https://lccn.loc.gov/2021043265

Barbarian Alien was originally self-published, in different form, in 2015.

"Ice Planet Honeymoon: Raahosh & Liz" was originally
self-published in 2019.

Jove trade paperback edition / January 2022
Berkley Romance trade paperback edition / October 2023

Printed in the United States of America
6th Printing

Book design by Kristin del Rosario

*For the readers who are picking up
these books for the first time,
and for the readers who have been telling their friends
about the blue-alien books for over five years now.
Thank you.* ❤

BARBARIAN
ALIEN

PART ONE

PART ONE

Liz

Kira and I watch as Megan and Georgie run their fingers along the panel of the alien ship's hull, trying to figure out how to pry it open and get out the girls enclosed inside. There are six capsules, and each one has another captive girl. Each girl inside has no idea of where she is or how she got here.

"I can't decide if they're the lucky ones or the unlucky ones," I tell Kira.

"Lucky," she says, her soft voice flat. Her gaze is fixed to the blinking lights and the dark wall of the hull. "They don't know what we've gone through for the last few weeks."

I grunt a maybe sort of agreement. I don't know that I agree with Kira, but she can be a real Debbie Downer at times. The last few weeks haven't exactly been a party for the rest of us, but maybe it's better to know everything than to be blind to it.

I guess.

Kira and I are watching the others work because we're too weak to actually help. Of the six of us, Georgie is the strongest still. She's been with the alien guy so she's been getting three squares a day and warm clothing. The rest of us have been stuck in the hull, and Megan is doing the best out of our small group. I'm weak and lethargic, and my toes hurt like mad. Josie has a leg that looks like it's broken in two spots, and no one knows how to fix it. Kira's ankle is swollen and she's super weak. Tiffany is possibly dying, since we can't wake her up out of the deep sleep she's in. She roused for a bit of broth and then fell unconscious again.

We don't need a warning from the aliens that this planet is killing us. Big duh there.

"It's opening," Megan says, and she and Georgie step back. The panel lifts from the wall with a hiss, just like in the sci-fi movies. Inside is a girl in a T-shirt and panties, weird coils wrapped around her body and feeding into her throat.

I shiver despite myself.

Georgie and Megan study the sleeping girl, trying to figure out the best way to free her. Eventually, they just start ripping tubes and cords off of her and she wakes up and begins to gag. A moment later, the new girl is collapsed on the floor and vomiting up the last of the tubes as Megan strokes her back.

Well, that did it. For better or for worse, we have another person.

The girl begins to sob, her eyes wide. She's clearly confused and frightened, and Kira stands up, opening her arms to pull the girl to her. She makes quiet, soothing noises and enfolds the girl in a hug, helping her away from the wall. Without a single person touching them, the rest of the pods suddenly open.

"Shit, I think we triggered something," Georgie says, and they get to work freeing the next girl. In moments, there are several more girls collapsing on the floor. I get to my feet as best I can, ready to help out.

I limp forward, and as I do, I hear the sounds of the aliens talking. I look over even as the girl nearest to me begins to hysterically wail. "What's happening? Where am I? Who are you?"

I offer her my hand. "I'm Liz and I'll explain when we get the others, okay?"

She keeps wailing and I have to bite the inside of my cheek to keep from shouting at her. Look, I feel like shit and am probably a few steps behind Tiffany on the death ladder, but am I squealing and moaning? No, no I am not. I am sucking it the fuck up.

I gather up a second new girl, this one with freckles and bright red hair, and as I do, Squealer starts to make horrified, choking cries. "Oh my God, what is that?" She points a trembling hand in the distance, and I slap it down.

"It's not polite to point," I say, but the other girls are sucking in horrified breaths at the sight of the aliens lurking at the edge of the hull. Another begins to cry, and a third clings to my neck like she's going to climb me for safety. It's making my broken toes hurt like the dickens, and I look over at Georgie. "We have a situation," I tell her. "Do something, fearless leader."

"Right," she says, and hurries over to the aliens. A moment later, they all climb back out of the rip in the hull and it's just us human girls.

"Let's all go sit over here," Kira says, voice soothing. "We have a fire and water and blankets."

"It's cold," whines one. "I'm so cold and I don't have any pants! Where are my pants?"

"That's because the aliens took you while you were sleeping," I say brightly. "No one has any goddamn pants."

Kira bats my arm with a slap, indicating I should shut up. Okay, so I'm not the most patient woman in the world. Sue me.

"Blankets over there," I encourage, and it's more like herding cats—caterwauling, screeching cats—than baby ducklings, but we manage to get them around the fire and tucked under the blankets that the alien guys have provided.

"I'm still cold," one says, teeth chattering, as she hugs the blanket to her.

I just watch her and try not to judge. We didn't even have this much a week ago. Blankets and a fire and food? This is fucking luxury. But again, these girls have been in pods and don't know any better.

"What now?" Kira asks. Why is she looking at me? I'm not the leader, Georgie is. But Georgie's off trying to convince the aliens to keep their scary faces away from us, so I guess I'm . . . Robin to her Batman? Something.

So I take charge. "All right, kids, let's sit in a circle. We're going to do an introduction game like they do at corporate retreats. Any of you work in an office?" When two of the sniffling girls raise their hands, I nod. It's a start. "Then you'll know how this works. We go around the circle, give your name, your age, and what you do for a living. Then you list off three interesting things about yourself. It'll help us get to know each other."

"Where are we?" one weeps.

"We'll get to that," I say. "Soon. Now come on. Let's start with you." I turn to the freckled redhead at my side. She's handling the bizarre situation better than most, which is good. She's staring at me like I'm crazy, but that's okay.

I'm pretty sure I'm crazy at this point, too. Heck, I'm trying to do a meet and greet on a crashed spaceship.

But the girl at my side gives a sniff and scrubs her face, deciding to remain calm. "M-my name's Harlow, and I'm twenty-two, and I'm going to college to be a veterinarian." She blinks for a minute, looking lost and forlorn.

"Add some stuff about you."

"I . . . hate shellfish?"

Close enough. I point at the next girl.

She's the sobber. She weeps and blubbers and her nose runs the entire time. Through a torrent of tears, we get out that she's Ariana, she's born in Jersey, and she's scared. Next to her is Claire, who has big brown eyes and looks frightened. Her voice is barely a whisper, but I don't force her to speak up. Then there's Nora, who looks fierce and pissed off. Marlene, who has a blank expression and a thick French accent, and Stacy, who's weeping but trying really hard not to. I give her props for that. As each person introduces themselves, it becomes obvious that they're all the same age.

Then they get to me. I put a hand to my chest. "I'm Liz Cramer. I'm twenty-two, just like you guys. I was a data entry clerk in a small machine-stamping office. I grew up in Oklahoma and I like hunting and shooting things with a bow. And three weeks ago, I was kidnapped by aliens."

The girls gasp. Ariana sobs harder.

"Way to ease them into it," Kira mutters.

I ignore her. This'll be like ripping off a Band-Aid. Best to just get it all out there and let them process it. "Sit back, kids, because you are about to hear the shittiest campfire tale ever."

And I start talking.

I tell them about how, three weeks ago, I was taken by Little Green Men during the night. When I woke up, I was in a dark, dirty hold with a bunch of other women clad in nothing but their pajamas. That we were going to be sold off at some sort of interplanetary trade station, like cattle. That the aliens had six women stored in some sort of stasis pods in the hold, and me and my new best friends in the pen were the "extras."

From their gasps, I can tell they're starting to put things together. That's right, they were the real cargo. Me and Kira and
the awake girls? Well . . . "You know, when you go to the grocery store for beer and chips are on sale and the next thing you
know, you have a cart full of chips? Just call me Pringles."

No one laughs at my joke. That's okay. I still find it funny.
You gotta find humor in something. "Anyhow, it seems our alien
buddies got greedy and were scooping up as many human
women as they could squeeze into their spaceship. There were
nine of us originally."

Eyes widen. Ariana starts sobbing again. I wish I had a sock
because I'd stuff it in her mouth.

"How do you know?" Nora accuses.

"Know what?"

"That they were going to sell you? Maybe they were taking
you somewhere good?"

Right, and I'm Casper the friendly fucking ghost. I point at
Kira, who's frowning at me.

"That's Kira. Kira's the only one of us that has a translator.
She was 'lucky' enough to be picked up first, so they stapled
some device into her ear and now she can understand whatever
the aliens say to her. That's how we found out what was going
on—that we were going to be sold. With the translator, she was
able to understand what the aliens were saying. That's how we
knew they weren't taking us to Planet Malibu, where we can all
sip margaritas and work on our tans."

"Liz," Kira says softly. Nora flinches.

I know I'm not being understanding. I know, and I'm not
sure I care. "Here's the thing. Those aliens stole us from our
homes. They tagged us like cattle." I point to the bump in my
arm where there's a little metal object that I suspect works just

like GPS. "And they're going to take us to a meat market and sell us like prize hogs to the highest bidder. And while some dudes fuck their hogs—"

"Gross," mumbles someone.

"—A lot of other guys just eat them," I finish. "So you'll forgive me if I'm not willing to cut our captors any slack. The Little Green Men were not nice. They had guards, and those guards raped several of the girls while we were captive. They kept us in a cage. They made us shit in a bucket. They treated us like less than human. So you need to know that, so you can understand where we're coming from when we're smelly and tired and hungry and sick. Okay?"

The girls around me nod. Ariana starts crying again. "Someone's going to eat us?"

"Not now," Kira soothes. She should be talking. She's the nice one. But she looks at me to keep explaining, and so I do.

"Those aliens are gone. For now." I briefly explain our quick rebellion and how Georgie took out one of the guards, just as our cargo hold was dumped planetside. Now we're residents of Not-Hoth, as we've come to name the place. It's cold as hell, snow-covered, and completely inhospitable.

Our landing was pretty fucking rough. No one came out unscathed—two girls died. So did three of my toes, which left me incapable of walking farther than a few feet. But at least I was alive. "Once we'd assessed our injuries, Georgie—our bravest girl and the least injured—headed out in the only piece of warm clothing we had, looking for help. The rest of us got to stay behind and freeze. Did I mention the rest of us were in our pajamas? Not exactly warm."

The girl next to me—Harlow—looks ashamed and offers me her blanket. I shake my head. I'm too tired to bother. And weirdly enough, I'm used to freezing my ass off. This is new to her, so she can keep it.

This last week was a week of huddling into a pile with filthy, miserable, injured women for warmth. It was a week of ignoring each other's smells, abject terror every time there was a sound outside the half-broken hull of the ship, and wondering what was going to happen to us next. Our hair was filthy, our pits stank, and our poop bucket overflowed. But we had no shoes and barely any clothing, so it wasn't like we could just saunter outside and clean up. Because outside it was one constant blizzard. We were trapped. Trapped, and our food and water supplies were dwindling. I fight back the memories.

Every night, I fell asleep wondering if I'd live to see the next day.

"Georgie went off to get help," Kira prompts when I'm silent for too long.

I nod, picking up the story again. "Georgie came back after a few days, with a big blue hulking barbarian with horns, a tail, and glowing blue eyes. His name is Vektal, and he's one of the locals."

I skip the part where Georgie was clearly shacking up with Vektal. I mean, the guy came with food and blankets, so I didn't care if she was giving the Incredible Hulk hand-jobs on the side as long as he took care of us.

"They left us with some supplies and went to get reinforcements for our rescue," I say. "Those are the demon guys outside."

A few faces brighten. "So they're nice?"

"They're conditionally nice." I wonder how much I should tell them.

Because our story is pretty fucking grim and there's not a lot of choices to be had.

Not-Hoth, it turns out, isn't a hospitable planet. In addition to being cold as heck and full of monsters that want to have us for dinner, our new home also has some sort of poisonous gas that's going to kill us slowly. It's already working hard on us. Tiffany's comatose off in the corner, and I'm so exhausted I can barely raise my head. Right now? I just want to fall over and sleep. And it's going to get worse. This element in the air is going to kill us, because we don't belong here.

But there's a fix. Sort of.

The "cure" for the death sentence on this planet? A symbiont that the natives call a *khui* and we humans call a "cootie."

To live? We're supposed to get . . . infected. Now, I admit that I've been pretty gung-ho about a rescue here. I'm the chipper one to Kira's glass is half empty. But I am royally wigged out at the thought of getting some sort of bug to live inside me.

The cootie sounds like it's the answer to our problems, except there's a catch, Georgie has told us.

Because the cootie is interested in propagating species. So when it sees two people that it thinks should be good mates and will make a perfect baby together? There's something called "resonance" that happens. The cootie starts vibrating in your chest whenever you're near your new "mate" and it won't stop until the baby-making happens. And Vektal's tribe of seven-foot-tall blue, horned aliens? They've only got four females.

If we stay, we're getting more than a rescue. We're getting husbands. Georgie's already been claimed by Vektal, and she's pretty happy about it from what I can tell. They can't keep their eyes off each other.

But not only are we getting a cootie, we're getting a man. And we don't even get to pick the man. I'm not sure how I feel about this. So when I say that the guys are "conditionally nice," it's true. They're nice because they want someone to put their baby batter into.

"They're nice," I say again, a tight smile on my face. "And now I'm really tired." I ignore Kira's concerned look and this time, when someone offers me blankets, I take them and curl up.

"What's wrong with her?" someone asks. "She looks like hell."

I'm sick, not deaf, I think crankily. But all that talking made me tired and I decide to let Kira answer.

"She's got the sickness," Kira explains in her soft voice. "We'll all get it unless we get the symbiont."

"Is that why she's so mean?" one of them—Claire, maybe—whispers.

Am I mean? Impatient, maybe. Tired, definitely. And sick. I just huddle down in the blankets. I can't even smell the hold anymore. I can't even feel the cold. I'm just . . . tired. So tired.

"She's having a bad day," I hear Kira say. "Give her time."

It's true. I am having a bad day. To think that despite being kidnapped by aliens and living in a smelly, freezing, broken cargo hold for the last week wearing nothing but a short nightgown . . . I can have a day worse than that? Why yes, yes I can.

The reason for my bad day shows up a moment later. He saunters over to me, where I'm trying to make myself small and invisible under the furs. He ignores the frightened cries of the other women and more or less storms over to my side. Then, he rips back the furs and thrusts a cup of something steaming under my nose.

He says nothing, just waits.

"Go away," I tell him crankily, and try to tug my blankets back.

The alien won't let me have them. Instead, he pulls them farther away, out of my reach. He then pushes the cup under my nose again. It's obvious that if I want my blankets back, I'm going to have to drink that cup of steaming hell he keeps putting under my nose.

He's such a dick.

I take the cup from his hand and glare at him, then try to offer it to one of the nearby girls. "Anyone thirsty?"

He grabs my hand and guides it back toward me with a small grunt, indicating that the drink is for me and only me.

"Who's that?" one of the new girls whispers in a tiny, frightened voice.

"Part of the rescue," I say drily. "The pushy, asshole part." I lift the cup to my nose and sniff it. It smells meaty and like some sort of plant. It also smells like a dirty sock. And there's something peppery in it that makes my eyes water. "I don't want this." I try to push it away. My stomach has shrunken in the last week due to starvation, and the thought of downing this makes me want to puke.

The alien's big hand pushes it back toward me. There's a scowl on his ugly face and he shifts on his feet, waiting. The message is clear: he's not going anywhere until I drink.

Goddamn it.

I take a sip of the broth and immediately start to cough. The aliens have some weird taste buds. Georgie shared some of Vektal's travel rations with us, and it was like biting into concentrated pepper spray. This smells like the sock-flavored hot tea version and tastes even worse. I grimace and push it away, only to have the alien force it toward me again.

"If I spill it, I wonder if you'll make me lick it off the floor," I mutter to myself, but take another sip. It's not as awful on the second taste . . . Oh, who am I kidding? It's rancid. But I drink it, because Tall, Dark, and Brutish isn't leaving until I do. It takes me forever to choke down the sips, and when I get to the bottom of the cup, there's a sludge that makes me gag, but I force it down, too. Then I hand the cup back.

The alien sweeps the furs over my shoulders and tucks them close to my body. He leans in close and I hold my breath. The rest of the ship is utterly silent, and I can feel all eyes on us. He adjusts the blankets, and when I glare at him, says one word.

"Raahosh."

Then he stands, scowls at the others for staring, and storms away.

"What did he just say?" one of the girls asks.

"It doesn't translate well," Kira says, touching her ear where the translator piece is. "Something like 'Angry one who growls.'"

"It's his name," I say, though I'm guessing. "Growly Bastard" suits him. This isn't the first time Raahosh has shown up to say hello. I woke up from a comatose slumber to find him in my face, forcing water down my dry throat. He'd staked himself out as my own personal rescuer, showing up to hand me meat, drinks, and making sure that I am warm.

In short, he's been hovering since the hunters had arrived, and it is pissing me off.

Normally I wouldn't mind when a guy showed up and started giving me presents, especially since I was starving. But these presents weren't freely given. Captain Obvious wanted a mate, and he'd staked me out.

He wasn't doing that weird vibratey thing with his chest, though. Georgie had told me that Vektal had a khui—the cootie, as we liked to call it—and that when it recognized its mate, it would make him purr and make him want to sex that mate up. Vektal had vibrated for Georgie. Raahosh was silent, though.

Which made me thankful . . . and confused. If he wasn't vibrating for me, why keep coming after me? It made no sense. Stupid alien. I licked my lips and then made a face, because they still tasted like the tea.

"He's hideous looking," Claire says. "Do they all look like that?"

"No, Raahosh is scarier than most," I say cheerfully. I'm glad he doesn't understand English, because I don't know what he'd do if he heard me talking shit about him.

Vektal's kind of cute in an overgrown sort of way. He's blue, and Georgie says his skin is like suede. He's got big, arching horns that emerge from the edges of his hairline and curl around his head like a seven-foot-tall ram. He's muscled all over, has a tail, and has these weird bumpy ridges on his arms and across the brow. Most of the other guys have a similar makeup, with only variations in height, coloring, and horns. Just your everyday blue alien people.

Raahosh stands out from the others in a few different ways. For one, he's the tallest. Which isn't much of a thing considering they all stand above seven feet, but it makes him seem to tower more than most. His shoulders aren't as broad as Vektal's, which means he's only enormous, instead of gargantuan. And while Vektal seems to be more of a pure blue, Raahosh is a darker shade, a grayish blue shade that just makes him seem like more of an Eeyore than the others.

The scars don't help that impression, either. One side of his broad, alien face is scarred up, deep gouges over his forehead and eye telling of a past encounter that he lost. They continue down his neck, and disappear into his clothing. The horn on that side of his head is a jagged stump, his other arching upward as a sleek reminder of what he's missing. Add in a firm mouth pursed with dislike and narrow eyes that glow with the weird blue provided by the symbiont?

I think it's a fair assessment to say that Raahosh is scarier than the others, yeah.

The fact that he's staked me out as his property is . . . irksome. I told Georgie and the others that for a cheeseburger, I'd do just about anything. But having an alien lay claim to me feels . . . weird. I don't even get a choice? This is like me saying "I want a cheeseburger" and someone slapping a pickle into my hand and saying "Fuck you, you get a pickle."

And then because I'm thinking of phallic objects, I eye Raahosh again. Not in an obvious way, of course. I'm lying down and my eyes are mostly closed, but I can see him and another alien guy moving at the edge of the ship, packing bags and double-checking things. Georgie and Vektal are nowhere to be seen. I watch Raahosh as he bends over and then stands up.

He has a really long tail. I wonder if that's an indicator of anything going on in another, ahem, area.

Not that I care. Maybe if we have to get this parasite thing, it'll choose someone other than him. Wouldn't that just piss Mr. Pushy off?

I fall back asleep daydreaming of the look on his face when my cootie rejects him.

Raahosh

My khui is an idiot.

It must be. Why else would it ignore the women of my clan and the moment we enter the den of the dirty, ragged humans, it begins to bleat in my chest like a quilled beast? Or that it chose the frailest of the sick humans to select as my mate?

A mate that glares at me with knowing, angry eyes and refuses to eat the medicinal broth that I bring her? That pushes aside my hands when I try to help her to her feet? Who scowls when I bring her water?

It's clear that my khui is full of foolishness.

"Did you resonate for anyone?" Aehako asks at my side. He stuffs a fur into a traveling bag. We are preparing the humans' cave for travel, since they are too weak to do so. Everything must come with us, Vektal says. It does not matter that it is stained and filthy, or useless. The humans have so little that he is sure they will treasure whatever they have, so it must come. Two of the hunters that resonated for females have been sent off to get furs from the nearest hunter caves, because the humans are poorly equipped to face the harsh snows, and they have no khui to keep them warm.

This will be remedied shortly, however.

A sa-kohtsk is near. The large creatures carry many khui, and we will hunt one for its meat and ensure that the humans will not die of khui-sickness.

I think of the hollow eyes of my new mate and how miserable she looks. Most of the human hides are a pale color, but my human is paler than most. That must mean she is sicker. I will insist she be one of the first to get a khui.

Aehako repeats his question. "Raahosh? Did you resonate?"

I don't like to lie, but I also don't want anyone to know, not when my mate is glaring at me as if she is furious.

Raahosh is scarier than most.

Her words cut. She is smooth and pale and weak, and yet I am the one lacking? I shrug and shoulder the pack. "It matters not. We will see what happens when the khui are in the humans."

"I didn't resonate." Aehako looks glum, his broad features downcast. "Do you think more will resonate when they come into season? Perhaps they're not in season." He gives me a hopeful glance.

"Do I look as if I know human seasons?" I snap. "Finish your bag. We need to hurry if we are to get the humans close enough to the sa-kohtsk to hunt it."

Aehako sighs and returns to work. I tell myself he is young. In fact, he might be the youngest hunter in our clan. He will get over his disappointment, or another human will resonate for him later. Or even a sa-khui woman, perhaps one not yet born.

All I know is that I am resonating for one of the dying humans, and if she dies, she takes all my hopes and dreams with her.

I have never had a mate. Never had a lover. Women are few in our clan, and women that want to mate with a scarred, surly hunter even fewer. I never dreamed that I would have a mate of my own.

Now that she is here . . . I'm not entirely sure how to act. So I remain silent and it takes all of my energy to will my khui to remain silent when the humans stand up and begin to ready for the long trek back to the clan caves. Hunters have returned with furs and one is being cut up to make foot coverings. Others are securing their flimsy clothing, and Vektal's new mate, Shorshie—she of the tongue-tangling name—helps another wrap a thick fur cloak around her.

Only a few of the humans are not readying themselves. The one with dark skin and hair like a tuft of sweet-weed lies unconscious under her furs. Vektal says she is one of the sickest. There is another who has a broken limb, and she leans heavily on Pashov for support to stand.

And then there is mine. My human, who ignores everyone around her and resolutely huddles under the blankets.

She is stubborn. My khui chose well in that aspect. I am stubborn, too. Together, we will make very stubborn kits. A bit of the resentment in my heart leaves at the mental image of the human holding my child to her breast. I would have a family after so long.

"Ready all the humans," Vektal says as he passes by, heading for Shorshie. "We leave very soon."

"What about the ones that cannot walk?" Zolaya asks. "Or the one that cannot be woken?"

"Then we carry them. We do not leave any behind."

Shorshie gives Vektal a loving smile and turns to hug him. "You're so good to us. I can't thank you enough."

He touches her cheek. "You are mine. That is all that matters."

I pretend not to see when she playfully nips at his thumb with her mouth. It is fine to be affectionate in public, but knowing that my own sick mate sits in her corner and scowls at me makes it difficult to see. She is not happy at the thought of a mate.

She is not happy that it is me. She finds me hideous.

Raahosh is scarier than most.

I grab one of the furs, angry, and storm toward her. It doesn't matter if she likes me or not. The khui chooses the mate. She will simply have to accept it.

"Wake up," I say as I stride to her side and pull back the blankets. "You—"

Her head lolls and she slumps against the floor. She is not willfully neglecting my attention, then. She is unconscious. Fear strikes my heart and I cradle her against my chest, pulling her against my warmth. Her skin is so cold. Can she not retain heat? How will she possibly survive? For a moment, I panic. This must be how Vektal feels when he looks at Shorshie. Helpless in the face of her fragility. I cradle the woman against me and tap her cheek.

She rouses after a moment, and then recoils at the sight of me. "Captain Obvious. I should have guessed."

I ignore the sting to my pride. I don't understand who this "Captain Obvious" is. A lot of the human words don't make sense. At the ancestors' cave, we received the knowledge gift of their language, but it's clear that things don't match up properly. Sometimes when my human speaks, I don't understand her.

Though I understood her disdain for me well enough.

I prop her up against my chest and help her to her feet. She hisses with pain as she does, and falls back against me. Her small back hits my chest and my khui immediately stirs to life . . . as does my cock.

I close my eyes and concentrate, willing both to remain unaffected. Now is not the time.

The human struggles against me, shoving aside my hands. "Quit touching me! Let me go!"

Let her go? She cannot even stand. I won't let her go. I ignore her slapping palms as I run a hand down her bare legs, looking for wounds. She bats my touch away, but not before I see that three of her many toes are swollen and bruised. They are likely broken, and she does not have a khui to heal her.

And she thinks to ignore my help? More foolishness. I ignore her protests and sling her into my arms. I will carry her to the sa-kohtsk hunt if I must. She will get there. I cannot bear to think of what will happen if she does not.

"Hey! Put me down, you big oaf," she yells in my ear. Her lungs are not suffering, at least. I ignore her bellowing and make sure she is wrapped in the blankets despite her flailing.

"Raahosh," a warning voice says.

I look over—even as the human's hand smacks me on the jaw in protest—and see my friend and chieftain stalking over to me.

"You cannot haul her around if she does not wish it," he says in our language. "Humans must be gently wooed. They are fragile."

My "fragile" human's fist slams into my cheekbone. "Put me down," she bellows again. "You fucking suck!"

I . . . suck? But I am eating nothing.

"Raahosh," Vektal warns. "You know my orders."

I do know his orders. Do not do anything the humans do not want to do. I gently set mine to the floor with infinite tenderness, resisting the urge to crush her against my chest and stroke her filthy hair. "She is wounded," I tell him gruffly. "I wanted to help."

"There will be time enough for that," he says and claps my arm good-naturedly. Of course he's in a good mood. He has his mate. Mine looks at me as if she'd like to bury my knife into my back. "Let her walk if she wishes to walk."

"Fine," I growl out. I make sure the furs are bundled tightly around her and offer her foot coverings. It's the least I can do, and I pretend not to see when she winces and says more vicious, incomprehensible words as she tries to ease one over her swollen foot. She's covered in wounds, this human creature. There's a fresh one on her arm where a "sensor," as they call it, was removed from her flesh. This was from the "bad guys." All I know is that I want to get a khui into her so she can heal and get well.

Mating is not even on my mind at the moment. I simply want her to thrive. My hands twitch, desperate to comfort and caress, but when she shoots me another hateful look, I go to join the hunters.

I cannot be around her and not want to touch her.

Liz

I like to think that I'm not particularly squeamish. I'm really not. My dad was a hunter, and I grew up at his side, baiting fish hooks and skinning the day's catch so we could roast it over a fire. I'm an expert with a bow. I'm not half bad with tracking. I can butcher a carcass like a badass.

But the sa-kohtsk is a creepy mutant motherfucker.

It's been a few hours since we left the ship behind for the last time. I wish I could say I wasn't sorry to see that smelly pit disappear into the distance, but I'm a little freaked out. This planet is an ice planet. It's like Antarctica on steroids, and the sun is setting. There's so much snow that my newly covered feet sink into it like quicksand, and I see no familiar trees or shelter. It's cold as fuck, my toes feel like red-hot pain every time I take a step, and I'm feeling so weak I can barely lift my head. This is not exactly survival mode. At one point, I fall so far behind the others that someone swoops me up and carries me over his shoulder. I don't even have to see the guy's face in the driving snow to realize who it is.

Raahosh. Of course.

Now the girls and I are seated under a few flimsy, willowy trees that shiver with every step the sa-kohtsk takes. The sa-kohtsk is impossible to describe. It's like a wooly mammoth mated with the love child of a brontosaur and a long-legged AT-AT from one of the Star Wars movies. The resulting thing looks like a hairball propped up on spindly legs, and it screeches and moans as the hunters bring it down.

The men crowd around it. Vektal immediately trots over to the women and runs his hands over Georgie. "Are you well?"

She fusses over him, too. Oh, puke. I tune out and gaze at the downed creature. I miss hunting. I haven't done it since my father died, but seeing the dead thing and the scent of its blood on the air brings back memories of hunting together. I miss Dad. I miss hunting.

I look up and see a pair of glowing, intense eyes watching me from a distance. Raahosh again. I hug my furs closer and ignore him, hobbling closer to Georgie and Vektal so I can hear what's going on.

They're busy making out. I watch Vektal kiss Georgie's forehead. "Now, we get the khui. Gather the women."

So sexist. Yes, gather up all the little womenfolk so they can be taken care of. My lip curls at this, but I hate that I'm such a stereotype. Truth is, I'm too friggin' exhausted to do anything other than stare.

Georgie steps forward with Tiffany at her side. Poor Tiff. She's from El Paso and really, really isn't doing well with this weather. Plus, I think she's diabetic, so she's not doing so hot. She's been practically comatose all week. Tiffany stands weakly, and Georgie continues to move forward. "Where are the khui?"

"Inside," Vektal says and points at the belly. "Are you ready, my Georgie?"

Like we have a choice? I let Georgie answer, though, and she says, "Let's do this."

The creature is then sliced open from belly to sternum, and blood rushes out. Weirdly enough, it makes me homesick again. "Just like skinning a deer. No big deal. No sweat."

I look over, and Raahosh is still watching me. My skin prickles with awareness and . . . something else? I might be about to pass out again. I hope not.

At my side, Georgie swallows hard.

There's a cracking sound, and I look over to see Vektal standing on the rib cage of the giant creature, prying it apart with big, straining arms. It gives the loudest snap I've ever heard, and then splits open.

"Really, really big deer," I comment.

Georgie swallows again. Tiffany moans and stumbles away a few feet.

I keep watching, because I need something to concentrate on. I'm afraid if I look away, I'm going to see Raahosh approaching to put his hands on me again. I'm not sure why the thought both annoys me and fills me with a liquid sort of heat.

Vektal takes the heart from one of his men, and it's swarming with wriggling, glowing spaghetti-noodle-looking worms. Okay, yeah. This is not cool in my book.

"I think I'm going to be sick," Kira says somewhere off to my side, and Tiffany makes a hurking noise. But Georgie's watching Vektal like he's about to give her a diamond ring or some shit. They murmur quietly to each other, and then he pulls out his knife.

"What . . . what if it goes to my brain?" Georgie asks.

This is a worm. This is not cool. I am not down with this.

"Like that's any better than your heart?" Seriously?

"The khui is the essence of life," Vektal says in a reverent voice.

And then dumb Georgie takes the worm from him and he cuts a nick in her throat. And I watch the thing wriggle into it like a heat-seeking missile.

Oh, hell no. I am not down with this shit. I have seen what worms do to an animal's heart. Hunters know you don't eat the diseased meat. You certainly don't sign up to *become* the diseased meat. I back away a few steps. Georgie's shuddering and gasping, and she collapses into Vektal's arms. A few other women make cries of distress, and then the men are everywhere, offering glowing cooties to them.

I am so getting out of Dodge. Nope. Nope. Nope. I will figure something else out. There simply has to be another option. I stumble backward to the copse of trees that provide no protection. The other girls look at me curiously, then turn back to Georgie. She's our leader, so they're looking to her.

That's fine. If Georgie jumps off a cliff, it doesn't mean I have to, also. She may be blinded by big blue alien dick, but I am not. There's intense, throbbing pain in my foot but I ignore it. If it's not too late, I can go back to the ship, regroup, and figure something else out. I know I'm panicking. I know this isn't logical, but everything I've ever learned at my father's side is telling me that this is a terrible idea.

Parasites *kill* their hosts.

As I awkwardly shuffle past the others, I see the aliens gently leading the women forward, toward their doom. Gee, that's sweet of them. There's no proof this works on a human, and Georgie went down like a light. That is not normal. Hugging my furs tighter, I waddle away a few more steps.

And stop.

In front of me, slitted eyes glowing, is Raahosh. He eyes me.

"Don't you try to stop me, buddy," I retort at him, though I know it's no good. He doesn't understand English.

But he grabs my furs and tries to turn me around anyhow.

I jerk them out of his grip and continue forward. In the distance, I hear another woman cry out, only to fall silent. I shudder.

Raahosh grabs me by the hips and slings me over his shoulders again.

"No!" I say, pounding a fist on his shoulder. "I don't want it! You can't make me!"

He hesitates, and then to my surprise, he sets me down again. He gazes at me for a moment, and then reaches up to caress my jaw. I allow it, since he's not dragging me back there. His touch is oddly gentle, caressing up and down my cold cheek. Then he gestures at the ground, as if indicating that I should wait here.

"Fine. Whatever. I'm just not going back to that." I sit heavily in the snow, taking my weight off of my bad foot.

He turns and strides toward the dead sa-kohtsk and the group of hunters. I watch him disappear into the darkness and shiver. I'll wait for a few minutes, then move on. Maybe he's going to tell the others that I changed my mind, that he's going to guide me back to the ship.

Maybe this Raahosh guy isn't such a jerk after all.

I close my eyes and rub a hand over my face. It's freezing out here, and I'm so tired I could fall over and sleep, snow and all. My brain's getting foggy. There has to be another option, though. If I could think clearly, maybe I'd be able to come up with one.

My mind goes back to Georgie, and the way Vektal cut her neck. The gleeful wriggle of the thing as it burrowed into her. Her cry and then collapse. I shudder.

A figure appears at the edges of my vision. I just barely realize that it's Raahosh before a gigantic hand goes to my shoulder and forces me onto my back in the snow.

"What?" I sputter.

His knee goes over my shoulder a moment later, pinning me against the ground. His hand is cradled to his chest and I can barely see a glowing, snake-like filament wriggling there.

Then, he draws a knife from a sheath at his waist.

"Goddamn it, motherfucker! No!" I fight him, struggling against his weight pinning me down. But I'm weak and he's huge, and I'm barely able to bat at him as he lays the blade against my neck and carefully makes a cut at my collarbone.

"No!" I protest, but he's not listening. This asshole, this jerk, is forcing the parasite on me.

He's not my friend. Not at all. He's not letting me have a choice.

I fight against his hands as he leans in with the cootie.

"I will hate you forever if you do this," I hiss at him, trying to push him away.

He just gives me a hard look and then leans in. I hear a tiny *hissssss* as the cootie finds my skin, and then it's *wriggling into me*.

And I pass out from shock.

Raahosh

I tell myself that it doesn't matter that she'll hate me forever as I watch her unconscious body shiver and jerk, acclimating to the khui. At least she will be alive. My father and my mother never liked each other. Until the day my mother died, she cursed my father. Their mating was a supremely unhappy one, but they were still a family.

My human can hate me and still be my mate. I'm not going to allow her to choose to die. I won't. I'll keep her safe, even if I must keep her safe from herself.

I heft her small form into my arms and cradle her against my skin. She's so cold. So fragile. I did the right thing by forcing the khui on her. She wouldn't have lasted another day without it. Holding her close, I consider.

If I take her back to camp, when we return, she will be furious. She will tell the others that I forced her to take the khui.

Vektal, my chief, will not be happy. He says we must cater to the humans. Give them what they want.

It is . . . easy for him to say that when Shorshie looks at him with love and affection. Not so easy when your human looks at you with anger and disgust.

Raahosh is scarier than most.

If I take her back to the others now, they will be furious with me. My khui vibrates in my chest for my human, and for the first time in the last day, I let it hum freely. I resonate, and it feels incredible.

They cannot take her from me.

I turn and look back at the others, still huddled close to the sa-kohtsk. They will be there for hours yet. The humans will be asleep for a while. Maybe a day. I don't know how long it will take. There will be meat to carve up and bring back to the clan caves, and humans to escort and fawn over.

They will be distracted.

Instead of taking my human back to camp, I hold her closer and head in the opposite direction, out of the valley.

I'll take her and hide her away, and I won't return with her until she is full of my child and we are truly mated. Then we will return to the clan and be part of it once more.

Until then? She is mine and mine alone.

There's a cave out in the wild I like to think of as my own. Our clan cave supports many mouths and sometimes our hunters must range wide to feed everyone. Thus, we have a network of hunter caves dotted through the wilds that provide a resting place for any hunter who needs to stay out through the night. There are furs, fire-making implements, and sometimes a few other supplies to ease things. These caves are for any hunter to use, so long as they are left in the same condition as when the hunter arrived.

But this cave is mine and mine alone. I found it on a hunt when

I was a small kit on one of my first forays into the wild on my own. The entrance is hidden by a large sheet of glacial ice in the brutal months, but right now it is merely bitter and the path will be open.

It's not far from where we are, and it has been on my mind for hours as I walk. My human weighs nothing in my arms, nor does she rouse. She will just need time to acclimate to the khui, I tell myself. There is nothing to worry about. She has been sick. It will take time. It still strikes fear into my heart, and my steps increase in speed.

My cave is just as empty as I left it. There are signs that a nesting animal stopped in, but it's empty now. I clear debris off the neatly stacked furs in the corner and then lay my human down amidst them. She shivers, her body trembling. The bone-chilling cold is gone from her skin, a sign that the khui is warming her, but still she quivers and shakes. I decide to build a fire, and spend time setting it up, trying to ignore the thrumming of my khui as it sings a song to the unconscious woman in my bed.

My bed.

My mate is in my bed.

I groan, hit by a wave of need so strong it makes me dizzy, and I close my eyes, willing myself to be strong. She will be awake soon enough, and then we can mate.

She moans with pain as she sleeps, and her foot twitches. I remove her coverings gently, then massage her fragile feet. They're dirty and small, without the bony protective ridges that cover vulnerable spots on my own skin. She has five toes where I have three, and at the sight of the purple, swollen ones, I remember that they are broken.

They must be set for the khui to heal them.

She whimpers, her head tossing, eyes flicking under her eyelids. I must do this while she's unconscious so as not to cause her more pain. Strangely, the thought of hurting her makes my stomach churn. I run my fingers over her toes and compare how the bones sit. Then I suck in a breath and set them. I fight back bile as the bones make a snapping noise, moving back into place. She makes a choking sound and slumps.

I manage to set all three toes and then carefully bind them with leather wraps to hold them in place before my stomach rebels. I barely make it out of the cave before I vomit. Then, I kick snow over the patch of sickness, disgusted at myself. I have set broken bones for my clan mates. I have set my own broken bones. Never have I been sick at the thought of causing pain.

Already this female changes me.

My khui hums in my chest, urging me to return to her side. I do, and she looks small and fragile and miserable in my furs. Dirty, too.

I tell myself I should undress her to check for more wounds. That she will appreciate a clean mane and clean skin when she awakens. All the while, my khui thrums and pulses agreement. It wants me to touch her. To claim her. And I cannot resist its siren call.

I set up a tripod over the fire and hang a snow-filled cooking bladder over it. The snow will melt and warm, and then I can clean her. Now to tend to my mate.

Her filthy clothing is strangely made, and it takes me a few moments to pull it off of her body. Once I do, I toss it aside to clean later. There seem to be two parts—a long tunic that reaches her hips, and a tiny loincloth that puzzles me. Is it for protection? It barely covers her hips, and it's clear that the humans cannot handle the temperature extremes of being outdoors. Is that why she is so pale and unhealthy? Does she not go outside?

When she is naked, I see the differences in our bodies more plainly. My khui sings louder than ever in my chest, but I'm not about to fall atop an unconscious, sick woman and mate her, so I ignore it. Instead, I crush soapberries into the warming water and stir. Then I wet my hands and slide them over her skin to clean her.

And if I am being honest with myself, also to touch her. My cock is hard as stone at the first brush of my skin against hers, but I will myself to ignore it. She is filthy, and weak, and tired.

And she hates me.

That enables me to be strong as much as anything else. I sweep my fingers over her pale flesh repeatedly, rubbing at dirtier spots and exploring. She is soft all over, her skin without the distinctive, protective ridges that we sa-khui have over our most vulnerable parts. She is almost entirely hairless, too, which I find odd. My people have a downy fur covering their skin, but hers is open to the cold. No wonder she shivers so easily. The only places she grows a mane is on her head, and between her legs. I remember Vektal telling us of the humans and their strange anatomy. He claimed his Shorshie has a third nipple between her legs. Does this one have the same? Curious, I slide a hand over her sex and push her lips apart with my fingers. Surely enough, a small nub is exposed. It is poised at the top of her slit, and gleams with arousal. Even as I touch her, the scent of her sex perfumes the air.

I need her.

I close my eyes and will myself to be strong. My khui throbs incessantly, full of longing. It reminds me of everything I have never had, and everything I have wanted for what feels like an eternity.

She will be my first everything. My first mate. My first lover. The mother of my children. My hand trembles a little as I release her sex, resisting the urge to stroke the soft folds that gleam with arousal. The khui is already working on her if she responds to my touch, even unconscious.

I hope she will awaken soon.

The thought of my mate awake springs me into action. She will need food and drink, and warm, fresh clothing. She will have questions . . . and she will be angry. For some reason, the thought of her anger amuses me. It's like she blames me for her predicament. As if I could control a khui and choose my own mate. I snort as I go back to scrubbing her dirty skin. Filthy water sluices off of her, and it takes many rounds of washing until her skin is a fresh color that I am satisfied with. I also clean her mane, and it's surprising to me because what seemed dark and unremarkable is now a golden color. It is soft and tangles easily, and I get out a double-toothed pick from my bag and slowly detangle handfuls of the wet locks until they're clean and gleam in the firelight, and run through my fingers like the soft, feathery leaves of a sashrem tree. It's her most attractive feature, I think, because the rest of her is so soft and weak that I don't know what to think. Even her breasts are heavy but tipless. Her nipples are barely noticeable against her skin. It's strange.

I finish bathing her and pull an extra tunic and a skirt out of the bag I had on my shoulder. We took old clothing from the women of our tribe for Shorshie's humans, but when it became apparent that there were eleven humans and not the five we'd expected, the clothing became a precious commodity, and I hid what I could for my mate. I dress her in these as best I can, then let her sleep by the fire as I take a bite of travel rations. The food sticks in my throat. It's difficult to eat when my mate is right there, her legs covered by a long leather skirt. I could easily slide between her legs and claim her, and her body would welcome mine.

And then she would look up at me with more hate in her eyes. I shake the thought away, rub a hand over the bulge of my groin until the ache goes down, and then decide to hunt for my mate.

Fresh food. That will be what she needs. With that idea in mind, I haul myself out of the cave and pick up my hunting spear.

Liz

Everything hurts. I feel like I just woke up from an all-night bender. My head feels swimmy, my skin feels hot, and my foot aches.

But weirdly enough? I'm not tired. Not the bone-deep ache that has been my constant companion since arriving on this planet. I smell something fresh and fruity and turn my head, realizing that I'm lying in a nest of furs, and the nice scent?

It's my hair.

That wakes me up. I sit up and glance around. I haven't been shower-fresh in weeks, and I suppose I got used to my stank smell. But my hair is clean and soft and brushed, and I'm wearing new clothing.

My nostrils flare and my breathing quickens. I'm wearing new *clothing*. Someone fucking undressed me while I was unconscious.

A heavy fur covers my legs, and there's a banked fire with a tripod of something that smells like tea over it. I sit up, confused.

As I do, a big figure enters the small cave and looms in the doorway.

Raahosh. He lifts his chin at the sight of me, awake, and then tosses a fresh kill on the floor of the cave. Then he puts his back to me and works on securing the leather flap that acts as a door.

The sight of him reminds me of why I was unconscious. The cootie. It's inside me. I whimper and my fingers go to the wound that should be at my throat, the wound that Raahosh cut for me when I changed my mind.

It's gone.

It's all sealed up. The thing is in me. I claw at my throat, desperate to remove it.

As I do, Raahosh storms over to me and grabs my hands, pulling me away. As he touches me, my chest starts to rumble. At first I think it's my stomach, but the rumbling gets louder, until my breasts are practically vibrating with the response. I'm purring . . . for Raahosh.

Do not want.

I fight against him, now a mixture of furious and desperate. I don't want the cootie. I don't want Raahosh. I don't want any of this. I kick and snarl and fight against him as he holds my wrists. I try to reach for my throat, but he won't let me. He won't let me claw it out. The alien grabs my jaw and forces me to lock my gaze with his.

Then, he gives a small shake of his head. No, he's telling me.

Well, fuck that. And fuck him. A moment later he releases my hands, testing me.

I slam a fist into the side of his face. "Dress me while I'm unconscious, motherfucker? Bathe me? Fucking force a cootie in me? I hate you!" Each shouted word is punctuated by flailing arms and kicking feet until I'm an unstoppable dervish of anger, beating against him.

His only response?

An annoyed sigh. Then, he grabs my wrists again, wrestles them behind my back, and pushes me into the furs.

"No!" I shriek even as my cheek hits the soft fur.

He mutters something in the alien language and then I feel cords moving around my wrists. The bastard's tying me up.

Just when I think Raahosh can't be a bigger dick, he surprises me. "I hate you so much," I snarl.

He finishes tying me, moves to tie my feet, and then returns to the nearby fire as if it's no big deal.

Panting, furious with anger, my gaze darts around the small cave. Where are we? "Where is everyone?"

He skins the carcass of the small animal and begins to butcher it, ignoring my questions. When he's satisfied, he cuts small pieces and then lays them on a hot rock. His lip curls as they sizzle and begin to cook, and his gaze slides over to me.

My stomach growls. Worse than that, my chest is still thrumming with the reaction of my cootie to him. If this means what I think it means . . .

I just acquired myself an alien husband.

Fuck.

This guy?

I moan, because this is not what I wanted. If I had to have an alien, why couldn't I have a nice smiley guy? Someone with a grin that lights up at the sight of me and treats me like gold? Someone that looks at me like Vektal does Georgie?

Instead, I have the alien version of Grumpy Cat, and he just roped and tied me like a calf at a rodeo. Asshole.

I put my head down on the blankets, trying to calm myself. "Okay," I tell no one in particular. "You're here, Liz. When life gives you lemons, make lemonade. You're alive. You're healthy . . . parasite notwithstanding." I adjust, trying to flex my arms in the bonds. "You've got a new friend, and a nice warm cave. And someone's making you dinner instead of you *being* dinner. It could be so much worse."

I look over at Raahosh.

He glances at me, then calmly turns a piece of meat over with the tip of his knife, cooking the other side. It's clear he isn't paying attention to my talk, which just further emphasizes that he's not one of the aliens that got the language zap. Doesn't surprise me—unfriendly bastard probably didn't want a wife.

"So he doesn't speak English," I breathe, twisting my hands in the ropes. "I'm sure you can communicate with him somehow, Liz. Just use your brain."

I think for a moment. It's an old southern saying that you can catch more flies with honey than vinegar. Too bad I'm all piss and vinegar, but I'll try to be honey for a moment. "Hey, Raahosh?" My voice is sweet as sugar.

He stills next to the fire at the sound of his name. His eyes narrow.

I lift my hands and gesture at them as best I can. "Wanna take these off for me? I promise I won't behave but you don't know that, do you?" I keep my smile encouraging. "Nice alien. Good alien. Come free the nice human."

He blinks.

I lift my hands again and give a wiggle on the furs. The movement causes my nipples to rub against the fabric of my tunic, and . . . oh shit. I have to bite back the moan that threatens to escape me.

I am so freaking aroused. Stupid cootie.

I press my thighs together tightly, willing the thing to stop drumming a beat in my chest. *Stop*, I tell it. *Stop it right now.* Eventually it calms down, and I look at Raahosh again. He's gathering the cooked pieces of meat into a small pouch and then moves over to my side.

"Free me, Raahosh?" I nod at my hands.

In response, he stuffs a piece of charred meat into my mouth.

"I really hate this guy," I say as I chew aloud. "Can't make lemonade when the lemon's such a huge dick."

He simply shoves another piece into my mouth, oblivious to my misery.

After I finish eating, I fall back asleep despite the ties, and when I wake up, it's dark outside. The fire's banked but still giving off low light, and it's rather toasty warm despite the howling snow coming from outside the cave mouth.

Raahosh is gone.

So are the binds on my wrists and feet.

I sit up, rubbing my eyes. I feel better after my second nap, most of my aches and pains gone. I don't know where the others are, though, and I wonder why it's just Raahosh and me. I can't even ask him. Was this part of the plan? I can't think so, because I picture the newly awakened human girls trying to cope with being split off from the group and paired away with a stranger and I can't imagine anyone thought this was a good idea.

"Hello?" I ask.

The cave is silent, near dark. I'm by myself.

For a moment, I think about escaping. Just running away and giving a big fuck-you to Raahosh. But I'm not an idiot. I have no idea where I am, or where he's taken me. I know nothing about this planet and even if he's a dick? He's my best chance at survival for right now.

But I am incredibly glad he's gone for now . . . because I am so damn horny.

I don't want to be. In fact, this should probably be my least sexy moment ever. I'm kidnapped by aliens, forced to eke out a living on an ice planet, and now I'm basically married to Mr. Tall, Dark, and Super Pissy.

Even as I think of Raahosh, though, the mental image makes my cootie start up. It begins to purr in my chest, jiggling my sensitized breasts and making my nipples rub against the thick fabric of the tunic.

I moan and fall back on the blankets.

This feels . . . way too good. It's not fair.

My hand slides under my tunic and I cup my breasts. Oh God, they ache so badly. I feel hollow between my legs, too. I need sex, and I need it badly.

And the only guy around is Raahosh of the tall, lean body and permanently scowling face.

Gee, thanks, cootie. Thanks a lot.

I imagine Raahosh again, though, and my hand slides under my skirt.

My pussy is soaked, my curls wet and slick with need. The lips of my sex feel swollen and achy, and when I graze my fingers over my clit, it's so sensitized that I nearly come right then and there. I moan aloud, and begin to finger myself.

Maybe a quick masturbation session while Raahosh is gone is just what I need to keep the cootie under control. Even as I tell myself that, the mental image of Raahosh fills my mind and I imagine his muscular, tapered shoulders bared as he leans in over me. I imagine his firm, unsmiling mouth pulling back in a hiss of pleasure as he sinks into me and we start to fuck.

Great, now I'm masturbating to the alien. I'm going to blame the cootie for this, too. I don't like the guy. I don't.

I can't deny that the thought of us fucking gets me wet as hell, though. I slip a finger into myself and whimper because it's not enough. I need more. I need him. But for now, fingering will do. I position my thumb over my clit and begin to rub, and arch off the furs.

"Raahosh," I moan, sliding my thumb over my clit.

And wouldn't you know it, the bastard appears in the doorway of the cave as if I called his name.

Which I had.

I'm caught, my hand in my skirt.

Moaning *his* name.

I'm never going to live this one down.

PART TWO

PART TWO

Raahosh

It's late at night when I hear noises outside of the cave, off in the distance. I head out to investigate, spear in hand, ready to protect my human as she slumbers. Being on your own in the hunting lands is always dangerous and a good hunter is always at the ready. It was a herd of dvisti passing nearby. I watch them for a bit, studying the mares. A few do not have young, and it might be a good idea to hunt one when the suns return so that I might fill my small cave with ample food for my mate. The thought is a pleasing one, and I return to the cave in high spirits despite the late hour . . .

Only to find it filled with the musk of sex and my mate touching her strange third nipple between her legs as she moans my name.

The sight fills me with elation, and my cock grows hard with need. My khui sings in my breast. She's ready to mate. She . . . she . . .

I must remember her name.

I stride forward, watching as she pulls her hands from under her skirt with a small cry. She shuffles backward on the furs, but the evidence of what she has been doing scents the air. It calls to me so strongly I can practically taste it with my tongue, and my cock surges and throbs in response.

Her khui resonates in her chest, and I watch as one of her hands goes to her breasts, as if trying to silence it. My own khui sings a response. It feels good. Right. I don't even care that she is small and fragile and not sa-khui. I don't care that her face is flat and smooth. I don't care that she doesn't even like me.

She's mine. My body and hers both know it.

"No," she hisses the moment I step forward, and she puts her hand up and gives a shake of her head. "You don't get to touch me. You can't have this."

Again she refuses me? I snort, incredulous. This human is not to be believed. But I stop in my tracks, watching her. Waiting to see what she does. She is unpredictable.

I . . . am amused by that.

Her fingers stroke over her sex again, and the smell of arousal fills the air. "I hate this," she says as she strokes that strange nipple between her legs and shudders at the touch. "No woman in her right mind would be turned on in this situation. But can I stop touching myself? No! Because the thought of sex makes me ache in ways I can't imagine." Her fingers glide through her juices, rubbing them up and down.

I groan at the delicious sight, and my hands flex. The need to touch her is a palpable thing . . . but so is the scowl on her face. So I clench my fists and hold back, waiting to see what she does. Surely Shorshie did not fight Vektal when he claimed her?

But . . . she's clearly thinking of me. She moans my name as she touches herself. The memory of my name on her lips appeases my frustration and I narrow my eyes, watching.

The breath hisses from her lungs again and she continues to touch herself. "I'm not doing this because I want to," she says. "I'm doing this because I have to. Because this thing humming in my chest won't let me stop." She touches herself again, stroking over that nipple, and then gives me a look so frustrated and angry that I feel a twinge of pity for her. Vektal said the human customs about mating are different. She must feel powerless.

Her head lolls and she bites her small, pink lip. Her fingers work on her cunt and the nipple there even faster. It's clear she's heading toward release, and she has no intention of letting me touch her.

Anger flares in me. Does she think this is fun for me? That I enjoy a mate that rejects my touch? Does she think I do not suffer from the same khui-madness she does? That I don't burn for her touch? To bury my cock in her wet warmth? Does she think she is alone in this?

Or do I not matter to her?

If she insists on taking her own pleasure before my eyes and holding me at length, then I shall do the same thing. I undo the fastenings of my leggings and free my aching cock. It juts out from my leathers, proud and long.

She gasps at the sight, momentarily pausing in her frantic rubbing. "Oh my fucking God."

Her words are nonsense. Something about coitus and spirits, but her expression tells me everything I need to know, as do her parted lips.

In this, I know I am blessed. My cock is the largest in my tribe. I have seen the other males bathing and they do not come near my girth or length. I take my cock in hand, pleased that she likes the size, and I give it a stroke, dragging my hand up and down slowly, letting her watch.

"That is the biggest dick I've ever seen," she breathes. "No freaking way."

I only catch about half of what she says, but she licks her lips, and her fingers slide over her cunt once more. My own breath hitches at the sight. She is going to touch herself at the sight of me touching myself?

A groan escapes me, and my hand strokes over my cock again. I dare her to look. To watch every movement of my hand as I grip my length and flick my wrist. As I move over the crown, then back down to the thick base again. *Watch me*, I silently command her. *Watch me touch myself at the sight of you.*

And all the while, my khui thrums and resonates in my chest, so loud that my blood thunders in my ears.

I hear her khui responding to mine, increasing in volume, and she moans. "Oh God, I feel it buzzing all through me." Her hand quickens, and she rubs the little nipple between her legs with speedy motions. Her gaze fixes on my cock again, and she licks her lips.

I groan at the sight of that. Is she anticipating what I would taste like in her mouth? The thought is a titillating one. I imagine feeding her my cock, the head of it brushing over those soft, plump human lips . . . and her saying my name as she takes it into her mouth. The very image is obscene.

I close my eyes, because it takes everything I have to retain control. To not spurt seed all over the floor of the cave instantly at the thought. I want to see her come first.

She's still speaking, even though she thinks I can't understand her. This human is a talker. I open my eyes to watch her, and see that she's still got her gaze on my cock. "Can't believe you have ridges on your goddamn dick," she says, her hand working her cunt furiously. Her other reaches up under her tunic and cups her breast, and she hisses with satisfaction. "And I don't know what that horn thing is above it, but it's making me fucking crazy." Her fingers slide into her cunt with a wet sound, and then she moans louder. "Fuck, I'm *coming*."

My nostrils flare as I watch her quiver and throw her head back with the force of her orgasm. The cords in her neck stand out and her entire body stiffens, as the scent of sex grows even thicker in the small cave. Her fingers work her cunt harder, and she gasps and makes soft sounds as she brings herself release.

She did that from watching me. Seeing my cock turned her on.

I feel an intense surge of pride and lust at the thought. The need to possess her grows greater than ever, but I remember Vektal's words. Humans have different mating rituals. Perhaps this is one of them. Perhaps I've been reading my human's signals all wrong. Perhaps she's not pushing me away—this is just how she lets me know she's interested. A step in the courting ritual.

I stroke my cock again, harder, as her eyes flutter open and her wet, gleaming fingers leave her sex. In a daze, she watches me pump my cock with my hand, and again, I imagine her closer, so close that I can feel her breath on my skin. She's watching me still, and I want to pull her into this moment, to let her know that this is for her. My cock, my khui, my resonance—it all belongs to her now.

Her.

She said her name earlier, and it reverberates on the tip of my tongue. I remember it now. "Liz."

And I make sure to say it as I come.

Liz

Well . . . that was filthy.

I hadn't expected him to catch me touching myself. Moaning his name? Just double the humiliation. It had angered me, and I'd started to masturbate as a deliberate show of independence. To show him that he didn't own my body like he thought. That the cootie wasn't the boss of me.

And what had he done? Whipped out his enormous dick and came along for the ride.

Worst of all? It had been incredibly sexy. The sight of that enormous hand deftly stroking up and down his length, showing me just how he likes to be touched? It had made me wetter than ever before.

I blame the cootie. I should be appalled. I should have stopped touching myself the moment he caught me. Instead, we mutually diddled ourselves into a frenzy. Now, I lie back, panting and exhausted. His seed is splattered all over the floor of the cave, and he is staring at me, a challenge in those glowing blue eyes.

I curl up on the blankets, tucking my legs closed. "If you

think I'm cleaning that up, you have another thing coming to you." But it reminds me that my hand is wet with my own juices, and I don't want to wipe it on my nice clean clothes—not after weeks of rolling in my own filth. I stare down at my hand, frustrated.

To my surprise, he approaches, buck naked. I gasp and back up against the cave wall. "Don't touch me! Don't—"

He grabs my hand and bends down, sniffing it. Then, with his gaze on me, he licks my palm and my fingers.

"Oh my God," I moan. "You are straight up nasty kinky, aren't you?" I try to pull my hand away, but it's locked tight in his grip and he tongues every inch of my palm and fingers. All the while, his enormous alien dick is inches away from my face, and it's hard all over again. He is so not getting round two. I squirm out of his grip, hating that his tongue on my flesh makes the cootie start up again. He eventually releases me and I jerk away from him. "Pervert!" This is a man who undressed me while I was unconscious and isn't shy about making claims on my body. It's freaking me out . . . and it's freaking me out that I'm also getting aroused by it.

Still blaming the cootie.

I push at his stomach, trying to get him to take a few steps back. "Go away. Ever heard of personal space?"

He stares at me, and his dick is seriously right at eye level. It gives me a good look at the "extras" in his anatomy. I mean, he's an alien so I don't expect him to be like the guys at the clubs back at home, but I'm a little pissy that Georgie never mentioned anything like this when she mentioned these guys were looking for wives. He's got a fricking horn of some kind above his dick. It's not pointed like the horns on his head, but it looks almost like another thumb sticking out above his junk, and I have no idea what the hell that's for. Worse than that, his dick—not that I'm scrutinizing, mind you—has the same ridges along the top of it that his arms and chest have.

It's so *weird*.

I am so not turned on by it.

Not at all. Nope.

The cootie in my chest thrums, and I smack it to silence it. Fucking cootie. I grab at the furs under Raahosh's feet. "Can I have these, please?" To my relief, he steps aside and I grab the blankets and tuck them close around my body, grumbling as I close my eyes and try to go back to sleep. The cootie in my breast just keeps purring away like an asshole, and I'm cranky and not at all feeling an afterglow.

It's like the masturbating made things worse rather than better. Which . . . really sucks.

I'm still utterly exhausted, though. My body's telling me it needs more sleep. Well, actually, it's telling me it needs sex and then sleep. But I can give it sleep. I close my eyes and try to ignore Raahosh moving around at the far end of the cave. I don't think he'll try anything; if he wanted to, he could have already. So even though I'm alone in a cave with a crazy alien and we just mutually had an angry masturbation fest, I drift off to sleep.

When I wake up in the morning, I'm not entirely surprised to feel a big warm body pressing up against mine. Raahosh isn't exactly Mr. Boundaries, but if all he's doing is sleeping, I can live with that. I yawn and sit up, scooting away from him.

His big arm automatically goes around my waist. He grunts and pulls me back against him, then nestles farther down in the blankets.

Typical man. I pry his arm off of me. "Some of us have to pee." I slide out of his grip and wobble to my feet. My legs feel shaky, but I feel strong. I wiggle my toes, and they're dandy, too. Huh. Maybe the cootie isn't the world's worst. Then again, it has terrible taste in men.

The floor of the cave has been swept clean, and the fire has low, warm coals on it, which tells me that Raahosh hasn't been sleeping for long. I yawn and look around for shoes, but the only thing I see are his boots. I shrug and stick my feet in them, then clomp out into the snow to do my business.

I don't go far, because I'm not stupid. This place is alien and completely foreign and could be full of all kinds of dangerous things. I don't stray far from the mouth of the cave, and I'm not surprised when I turn around to see Raahosh there, a sleepy look on his face, spear in his hands, ready to protect me.

Or, you know, hunt me down.

"I'm not going anywhere," I tell him. "Not unless there's a Starbucks around the corner." He gestures at the cave mouth and I roll my eyes, heading back inside. "Seriously, where do you think I'm going to go? I have no idea where I am and no clue what direction everyone else is in. Do you think I'm just going to pick a direction and decide to wing it? After all I've been through?"

When he just stares, I sigh. "Never mind. I'm clearly talking to a brick wall here. Thanks for kidnapping me, by the way. Props for making a shitty situation even worse. I sincerely appreciate that."

He glares and gestures at the cave mouth again.

"Right. I was heading in that direction."

I move inside the cave and plop down near the fire. It takes me a moment before I realize that I'm not . . . shivering anymore? Either I'm completely numb to the cold in this place or the cootie is doing its magic. I mean, it's brisk and I could use a nice warm jacket, but it no longer feels as if my feet are going to turn into blocks of ice. I sit down on the furs and pull his boots off, offering them to him again.

He takes them with a narrow-eyed look. Then, he examines them carefully, as if I've somehow booby-trapped them in the three seconds that have passed as I removed them from my feet. I snort. "Make me some shoes and I won't steal yours." I push a lock of hair out of the way. It's still clean and shiny and smells good, but it's also a wavy mess from drying in tangles. I need to braid it and get it out of the way. I try to sit cross-legged and my long leather skirt hinders my legs. Pants, too. I need pants. Pants, shoes, and something to pull my hair back. "I don't suppose there's any coffee in this joint?" I ask him, knowing very well he can't answer. "If you plan on keeping me captive, I'm going to be the most demanding, bitch-ass captive you have ever dealt with, so just be ready, barbarian dickhead."

Raahosh moves into the cave and crouches near the fire, oblivious to my insults. He takes one of his bone knives and drags the point through the coals, stirring up the fire and making it higher, the flames flickering to life. Then, he moves to the back of the cave and grabs a few bricks of what I hope is peat and not poop. He adds them to the fire and stirs it again with his knife. All the while I watch him. I'm trying not to notice that when he walks, he's got this graceful sort of movement, almost like a dancer. Or that his leggings are made out of some weird leather rigged together as if it's attached to a loincloth, and it delineates some rather interesting equipment that I saw up close and personal yesterday. His leg muscles flex with inhuman beauty as he squats near the fire again, and his tail thumps on the ground, flicking like an annoyed cat. Is he annoyed with me? Or does that mean something else?

"You are kind of like a cat, now that I think about it," I tell him. "You've got a pissy tail, and I bet if I pet you, you purr. Ha. Now if I could only get you to go chase a mousie and leave me alone."

His eyes narrow at me again.

"I'm talking about food," I lie, keeping my expression bright. I pantomime eating. "How about some yum yums for my tum tum, Whiskers?"

He grunts and stands, and I swear I'm not creeping on him or those big, rock-hard thighs. I'm not. I'm *not*. He moves to the far side of the cave again, where he has a small pack of his belongings stored, and pulls out a waterskin. I've seen the type before. My dad used to love to go old school when he went hunting, and he had one very similar to this one. I reach out for it.

Raahosh gives it a little shake, letting the water slosh around the bottom. Then, he lifts it toward his mouth.

"You dick!" I say, outraged. "Are you fucking with me?"

Just before he's about to take a swig, he looks down at me, and a devilish grin crosses his face.

I immediately start to purr, and my pulse begins to pound between my legs. Dammit, cootie, now is not the time.

"You are totally fucking with me," I grumble, but he hands me the skin and then caresses my cheek, indicating that it's all mine. I'm not amused by his playful side. I'm not. So not. I'm totally not smiling, either. My lips are jerks because they're not listening very well, though.

I drink down the water, a little disappointed that it's not coffee, and save him some because I'm not a jerk. He sips it, then returns to the mouth of the cave, packs the now empty skin with snow and ties it shut, then hangs it off of a small ledge on the wall.

As I watch, he puts his boots on.

"Oooh, are we going hunting?" I say, excited. I straighten my clothing and get to my feet. "I used to help my dad with the hunting. I'm a great shot with a bow. Of course, I don't have a bow right now, but I've got good aim. If you can lead me to some wood, I can probably make one. I made one in shop class in high school, you know."

He says nothing, simply pulls on one boot, tightens the laces right under the knee so his entire lower leg is covered, and then repeats the motion. He grabs his spear, and then without a look back to me, heads outside.

I gape. That dick. He just totally ignored me and went hunting without me. Furious, I storm after him, barefoot . . . for about three feet. Then I give up because even the cootie can't keep my toes warm. I shiver and head back into the cave, irritated with my captor.

If he thinks this is the way to woo me, his head is as broken as this so-called relationship.

I stomp my way back into the cave to sit by the fire and wait for my jerk of a captor to come back.

Raahosh

She's a talker, my Liz. Even when she thinks I don't understand her, she rambles and speaks, carrying on a one-sided conversation. It's strange to me, as I've always been a silent one. Even my tribe jokes that I like silence the best.

But . . . I don't know that I do.

She mentioned hunting as I left the cave and seemed disappointed when I didn't take her with me. Does my woman hunt? The thought is unusual to me. It's not that our women are not capable, but they are so few and precious that we dare not risk them on a dangerous hunting trip. Perhaps when she has given in to the khui-bond between us, we will go on hunting trips together. We will track kills together, and bunk down in caves and make love during the long winter nights . . .

And Liz will yammer the entire time and scare off all the game.

The idea still fills me with joy. To think I can have a companion after so long. I have my tribe, but I have always felt . . . alone. On the outside. Perhaps it was because I never had a mate, or a lover. I assumed no one wanted me.

Then my spirits sink. No one wants me still. Liz does not. Angry with myself, I stab the butt of my spear into the snow and use it as a walking stick. She will change her mind. She must. I . . . don't know what I will do if my own mate spurns me despite the khui in her breast.

The thought makes my very soul ache with loneliness.

The game is scarce near the sheet of ice, and it takes me a little time to find a meal that will be large enough for both of us. I sneak up on my prey and stab it in the throat before it can run. Then, I bleed the carcass and slit it from rump to throat because I don't want the blood to clot before I can make it back to my mate. I take out the offal and use it as bait for a snare trap that I will check tomorrow. The rest of the tasty organs, I snack on as I jog back to the cave, since Vektal said the humans are picky and won't eat the best parts of the kill.

When I return to the cave, the human's hair is wet as if she's bathed herself again. The waterskin is full of snow once more, and she's sitting on the furs without her skirt on. I pause at the sight of one delicate bare flank, the curve of her buttock making my khui thrum mercilessly in my chest.

She shifts and delicately pulls the furs over her loins, hiding them from my view, and her face turns an interesting shade of pink.

"So nice of you to return," she says.

My heart thumps. Does she mean that? My cock is stiff and aching with the need to claim her, but her expression doesn't say she is happy to see me. It's confusing. Is this more of the human mating rituals I don't understand?

Why did Vektal not tell us more about human courting? I'm at a loss.

I watch as my female uses a bone knife to punch a hole in her skirt. Actually, it's not a skirt any longer—it looks as if she's making leggings. That's clever. Her hair is woven into a crown atop her head and I'm impressed at her ingenuity.

I'm also a little worried—I'm deliberately keeping her without shoes because I suspect she'll leave the moment she has them. I'll have to watch her closely.

A growl fills the cave, and for a moment I think it's her khui . . . then I realize it's her stomach. She's hungry.

I move toward the fire and use a few twigs to create a spit. The humans like their meat burned, so I'll do this for Liz. I skin the creature and notice that Liz is watching with interest. She's not revolted like I thought she would be.

"Is that a porcupine?" she asks as I toss aside the skin of the quilled beast. "It looks like it mated with a cat and a platypus."

I don't know most of those words. I work on cutting long strips of the juiciest flesh off of the creature's flanks and spear them on twigs so they can cook in the fire. She continues to watch, commenting occasionally.

"I can't smell the food as much as I thought I'd be able to," she says. "It's weird. It's like my nose is stuffed up but it's not. I just can't seem to smell things like I used to." She lifts one arm and sniffs under it. "Even my own BO is practically nonexistent. Is it the cootie? Or a physiological sort of thing? Does a girl in the forest stink if there's no one around to smell her?"

Her incoherent talk continues and I eventually take one of the strips off the fire, sniffing it. It looks awful . . . which probably means that it's done. I hold it out to her, wanting to feed my mate.

She reaches for it, and before she can take it, I pull it away.

Liz frowns at me. "Really? Are we playing this game again?" She gives me a disgruntled look and puts her hand out.

Fine. I can just as easily examine my mate when her hands are full. I give it to her, and when she takes it, her hands are occupied.

I lean in and put my fingers on her face, examining the blue of her eyes. Even though she tries to bat me away, I'm pleased with what I see—there's a strong blue shining from her eyes, which tells me her khui is healthy. The resonance that starts in her chest at my touch tells me our bond is bothering her as much as it is me.

Good.

I sit back on my heels and watch her nibble a piece of meat. She has a look of frustration on her face as she chews. "It doesn't taste like anything."

I eat another piece of raw meat and watch her. Her small, flat features screw up and she grabs another piece from one of the skewers and eats it. "Why can't I taste it?" She watches me as I take a raw piece of meat and pop it into my mouth. She licks her lips, and my cock responds as if she were licking it. My khui resonates fiercely, and hers responds. She ignores it and focuses on my food. "Can I try some of yours?"

She points at the raw meat I've been cutting off the kill. I'm surprised. Didn't Vektal say his mate was squeamish about raw food? But Liz's eyes are wide and curious, and she's watching my mouth in a way that makes me imagine the two of us mating, my mouth pressed against her soft, pale skin.

I will give her anything she asks for. Anything. Everything.

I cut a thick, meaty chunk of flesh from the quilled beast for her. When she reaches for it, I brush her hand aside. If my mate wants my food, I will feed it to her. She gives me an irritated look when I try, but I'm used to that by now. After a moment, she dutifully opens her mouth, waiting for me to feed her.

A low groan of need escapes me.

She closes her eyes. "You are such a pervert," she says in a husky voice and her mouth opens a little wider.

I delicately place the bit of meat between her lips. The thoughts

I'm having about my mate are carnal and wrong, because I'm picturing her pink mouth moving over my skin, caressing the ridges along my arms and stomach . . . and then moving lower.

I'm not entirely sure if that's done, but now that the image is in my mind, I can't get rid of it. My cock strains behind my breechcloth, desperate to claim my mate.

She takes the meat and chews slowly, considering. Then she nods and opens her eyes. "Better. Much better. Now I see why you guys eat the raw stuff." Her hand goes to my knee and she gives me a wide-eyed, innocent look I have seen on young kits trying to coax a parent. "Can I eat yours?" She points at the meat I've laid aside for my own meal.

And then to emphasize her point, her thumb strokes my knee.

I am being coerced by wide eyes and a simple touch. I know it's all to manipulate me, but I find I don't care. If she keeps her hand there, I will feed her every scrap of meat in the cave. I cut her another chunk and feed her again, fascinated by her small mouth working, the pleased expression on her face.

The hand on my knee. I'd give anything for it to be under my breechcloth, stroking my cock.

I feed her bit after bit, and she takes it from my hand, her own khui thrumming. I've forgotten all about food. My mate's nearness has taken over all my senses.

Eventually she sighs and pats her stomach, and waves me away when I try to offer her another bite. I get up, though, to find the waterskin and offer it to her, so I can be close to her for a few minutes more. She drinks, her mouth wet and glistening, and I'm fascinated by it.

When I first saw the humans, I thought they were ugly, their faces strange, and their skin too soft. They have no hard ridges along their arms and chest like we do to protect muscles and organs. They have no horns or tail. They are utterly defenseless. Even her small face is different than my own people's, with its flat forehead and pale hair unlike any color I have ever seen.

But it is burned into my dreams. Now, when I imagine happiness, I imagine her face. It doesn't matter that she is different— she is mine and I am hers.

"You're staring at me," she says as she puts the waterskin down. "Always staring, dude." She sighs a moment later, before I can look away. "I wish you spoke English so I could tell you how weird I find all of this."

I feign ignorance and reach out to touch her face again.

"Newwwp," she says, and I don't recognize the word. It's obviously a dismissal, though. She raises her hands and shakes her head. "Enough with the kissy-kissy stuff for now. We need to talk. Language lesson time." She puts a hand to my chest. "Raahosh."

I put a hand to her chest in the same spot. "Liz."

Her face goes crimson and she slaps my hand away. "Not the boobs!"

What did I just do wrong? I reach for her again, and she slaps my hand away once more. Her khui is thrumming, and I see her nipples hardening under the thin leather of the tunic. Ah. This arouses her? Unable to help myself, I brush my fingers over one of her nipples.

She emits a shriek and slaps me across the face. "No means no, dickface!" Then she gets up and storms away.

I reel, touching my cheek. Her little smack on my jaw didn't hurt, but I'm more stunned that she struck me than anything.

She's fierce, my Liz. I like that.

And if she thinks she's going to scare me away with a slap on the cheek, she is very wrong. I grin to myself as she grabs the blankets and huffs away, deliberately turning her back to me. I can still hear her khui thrumming. It gives away how much she liked my touch—as does the scent of arousal on the air.

My mate's arousal.

This must be more of the curious human mating rituals. Maybe that's what *newwwp* means. I mentally repeat the word to myself so I can tell her the same thing at the appropriate time.

Liz

Dumb, dumb Liz. Your communication skills need some serious work, I tell myself. I put my hand flat on his chest and said his name. He knew my name, though. He gritted it out between those big fangs when he stroked himself off.

I'm not getting hot thinking about that. I'm not. I'm not. I slap my chest to make sure my khui is listening.

So of course he put his hand on my tits. It's the same spot, just on me. Except I forgot how sensitive my body is thanks to the cootie, and I nearly leapt out of my skin at his touch. I might have freaked a bit. Just a bit. Because one more touch after that nipple grab? I'd have been shucking my barbarian version of panties—

Oh wait, that's right. I don't have *any*.

I'm pantsless under the blankets, my half-finished skirt-now-pants still needing more stitches. My hand is desperate to press between my legs and relieve my need . . . except I know it won't. And I don't know what I'll do if he grabs himself and starts stroking his ginormous cock again. I don't trust my cootie-crazy self to not just, like, shimmy on up to him and start tonguing him everywhere and anywhere. *Oh, is that your ear? My bad, it's so sexy. That elbow, too. And dig those eyebrows. They're just begging to be licked.*

Actually, I'm so horny that even the thought of a good eyebrow licking is making me wet. Then the word "horny" makes it worse, because now I'm picturing his big horns and what it'd feel like if I licked those. Or, you know, straddled one and rubbed my girl parts on it for a bit.

Stop it, Liz! You suck!

I do suck. I sigh. I need a game plan. The longer I'm in this cave with no one but Raahosh and my cootie, the harder it is to deny the urgings my body is singing with. I need a plan of escape. I'm not sure where to go, but I know I can't stay here. I mentally catalog the things I'll need for survival. Food. Drink. Weapons. Shoes. Warm clothing. Shelter.

My dad and I used to go on hunting trips back in Oklahoma, back before he died. I know how to build a fire. I know not to eat the yellow snow. I've got clothing and these blankets will do just fine as wraps to keep the coldest winds out. I know how to hunt, so food can be had if I have a weapon. Shelter might be tricky but I can't plan for that, really. I just have to hope for the best.

I'm really down to shoes and weapons. I can make shoes with leather from my pants and one of the blankets here—I just need to do it when Raahosh is out hunting so he won't notice.

As for weapons . . . I could steal Raahosh's spear, I suppose, but it's huge and heavy, and my muscles are wimpy. I don't know that I'd be effective with it. What I really need is a bow. If I had a bow, I'd be able to rock this survival shit. I've got mad skills with a bow and arrow.

So. Shoes first, then I can look for stuff to make a bow. Once I have a bow, I can get away out into the wild white yonder.

And do what? Not entirely sure, but it's a plan. Sometimes all you can do is run with what you've got.

Raahosh

My mate's too quiet.

Liz, who talks endlessly even though she knows I can't under-stand her, Liz, who would talk to a stone if it had ears, Liz, who even talks in her sleep—is silent. She awoke from her nap with a cunning look in her glowing blue eyes, and watches me as I pre-pare to go hunting again.

I'm out for most of the day, getting food for my mate, and when I return, she's still silent, but her mood is pleasant. She lets me feed her raw bits of food and doesn't even push me away when I caress her cheek.

I sense a trap.

But she yawns sweetly and smiles at me when she crawls back to the furs for sleep, and I'm drawn to her anyhow, my khui thrumming with need and want. Is this . . . part of the human mating ritual? Do I tell her newwwp now? Will she fall into my arms and part her legs for me so we can mate and become one?

I have no experience in this. I lay down in the bed with her, unable to stop from caressing the shoulder and back turned in my direction.

She flicks my hand away, and oddly enough, that makes me feel better. That is familiar. I wait until she goes to sleep, and then I drift off as well.

Sometime just before dawn, I feel her small form tense next to mine.

I keep my breathing even, so I don't alert her to the fact that I'm awake. I'm curious to see what she's going to do. Run? Try to kill me? This isn't like before when she rolled out of bed and smacked her lips noisily before heading out to relieve herself. This time, she's trying to be sneaky. She slowly, carefully removes my hand from her waist and lays it flat on the furs. Then she carefully peels the furs back and wiggles her way out, trying not to disturb me as I "sleep." When she's out of the furs, she looks over at me, but I'm still feigning, my eyes closed, breathing peaceful. Satisfied, I hear her take a few steps away and I open my eyes a slit, peering at her through my lashes.

She's moving to the corner of the cave, and as I watch, she takes my boots and slides them onto her smaller legs. I watch as she rolls the leather up to her thigh and then secures it with the ties, and the picture is breathtaking in its eroticism . . . despite my curiosity as to what she's doing. My cock's hard as stone by the time she puts my other boot on. My khui hasn't stopped thrumming all night due to her nearness, and the ache in my body is becoming a palpable thing. I need to possess my mate.

She looks at my spear, considers it, and then glances back at me to see if I'm still asleep.

I remain still, waiting to see what she does.

Liz turns away and pads out of the cave on quiet feet, my spear in her hand.

Well, now I have to see what is going through her mind. I roll from the bed and decide to follow a safe distance behind. The snow's cold on my feet, but I ignore it. My skin's used to the harsh conditions and I can stand a little ice, unlike her fragile human flesh. I notice she's also finished her leggings while I was gone. I admire the curve of her bottom as she moves through the snow, clearly struggling in my larger shoes. The snow near the ice wall is up to my knee, and goes to her hips. She mutters unhappy words in her human language as she struggles forward, every footfall sinking into the powder. Perhaps she'll get tired and turn around.

But my human is made of sterner stuff, and I suppress a smirk as she struggles onward, muttering human words under her breath that I can't quite catch.

To my surprise, she heads for the distant trees. Is she hungry? The leaves are inedible, and the bark is only medicinal, good when steeped in hot water for long hours and left to soak overnight. Curious, I follow a safe distance behind. What is she up to?

I wish the khui let me read her thoughts, because my human mate is impossible to understand.

Liz

There are trees not too far from our hidey-hole. I make a beeline for them, slugging through the heavy snow. I have to be fast, because if Raahosh discovers that I'm gone, he's going to lose it. I'm not trying to escape—not yet. I'm looking for materials for a bow. I need some elastic sort of material for the string, but rawhide will do if I can twist it into a tough, flexible cord. Raahosh has been saving the pelts from our kills, and I have plans for them. I can even make a string from fibers or even my own goddamn braided hair if I have to—I'll figure something out.

But I haven't seen a lot of material that would make a good bow itself. It has to be a long length of something wood-like. It needs to flex a bit, and bend, but not too much.

I spent a lot of time studying Raahosh's spear, because it's nearly seven feet long and has a bit of flex to it, but it's too heavy for what I need. I need lighter, stronger.

So I trudge through the snow, heading for the trees. They don't look like any sort of regular tree that I know of. For one, they look more like eyelashes or feathers than actual trees. They whip back and forth in the bitter winter winds, and the leaves look like pinkish, fluttering floss. Still, they're the closest thing I can think of to wood, so I head toward them.

I make it to the trees and the snow shallows out a bit, which is nice. It makes it easier to trudge along, and I head for the first tree, running my hand along the bark. At least, I think it's bark. But it feels spongy and slightly sticky, which squicks me out. The trunk itself is maybe as thick as a can of soda, and as another breeze rises, it flaps and flutters in the wind. Damn it. This probably won't work. I use the big stone spearhead on Raahosh's spear to cut into the side of the bark. Maybe if I get past the bark, the core itself is solid and usable?

But as I saw into the wood (and really, calling it that might be a joke), it just seems to get more gelatinous and mushy, and begins to ooze pink stuff that smells terrible and sticks to my fingers. I wipe my hands on the snow and wrinkle my nose.

That is not going to work for a bow.

I sigh and stare around me, miserable. There has to be something on this damn ice planet that will function as a bow. Seriously. I know that Raahosh and Vektal's people are super low-tech due to being as stranded here as we are, but come on. Bows are basic.

Then again, I haven't seen anyone here with a bow, either. They all had slings, spears, and knives.

Dammit.

I haven't been gone that long, so I trudge onward in a straight line. I'm not sure where I'm heading off to but fuck it. There's a big giant glacier of ice behind me that I know the cave is at the base of. I'll just follow it home if I get lost. I crest a hill or two when I see . . . something. I trudge through the snow a bit more—while it's nippy, it's not bone-chilling cold like it was before, and I know my cootie's probably the one to thank for that. It's adjusting my body to the environment, adapting me.

I'm still a little bitter about that shit, no matter the benefits. I can't smell like I used to, I can't taste things like I used to, and it's matchmaking me with the surliest alien imaginable.

With the biggest junk. Not that I'm thinking about that. Dammit. Or his hand slowly stroking down the length of it, taunting me.

My cootie immediately starts purring, jiggling my breasts with the force of its intensity. "God, cootie, you are such an asshole!" I tell it, thumping my chest again to try and make it calm down. Not that it works, but I do it anyhow.

Then I pause, because in the distance I see a dark, threading line in the snow. Curious, I step toward it, and as I get closer, I realize that it's a stream of some kind. There are some pole-type bamboo-looking things sticking out of the water. They look lightweight and stiff. I wonder if I could use them. Encouraged, I slog forward. I can check it out, haul one out of the water, and then head home before Raahosh wakes up. I'll hide my prize in the snow at the mouth of the cave and he'll never know that I'm secretly constructing myself a nice, handy weapon so I can escape his ass.

The suns are coming up on the far side of the sky, leaking a milky-pale color into the world that will never be bright enough to melt the snow. Even though there's two of them, they're such small lights in the sky I imagine that Not-Hoth (as I've taken to calling the planet) is a lot farther out in its solar system than Earth is from the sun. Maybe that's why it's always so cold here. When I get to the stream, I can smell a faint hint of rotten eggs in the air—sulfur. It's a hot spring, which explains why it's running water and not a block of ice. Georgie mentioned seeing others when she was traveling with Vektal. I should be glad that it's warm enough, because otherwise this planet would be that much more inhospitable.

The banks of the stream are muddy but smooth, and I slide down to the edge of the water. The scent of sulfur is thicker here, but the water is blue and pretty. I wonder if I should swim. The bamboo shoots are at least ten feet tall and push out of the water like random toothpicks and I lean over the blue surface, reaching for the closest one. I'll pull it out and see just how sturdy the material is. If it's lightweight like I think it will be, it might just work—

"*LIZ!*" a familiar voice bellows, and I slide forward on the bank, almost into the water.

Raahosh. And he almost made me do a face-plant into the stream, that jerk. "Can you not fucking yell at me when I'm standing over the water? I—"

I gasp, my angry words dying in my throat. There's a horrible face with bulging eyes and big, jagged teeth on the other end of my stick. It looks like one of those monstrous creatures from the deep, dark parts of the ocean—except it's about a foot away from my face.

A scream rips from my throat and I stagger backward, clutching my bamboo.

The creature comes along with the end of the bamboo, to my shock. It sticks to the end of it, thrashing and splashing wildly.

I scream again, and fling it onto the snow. It hisses and starts moving toward me, and I glance around, looking for Raahosh's spear. It's a few feet away, where I must have flung it. Meanwhile, the thing thrashes and hisses on the far end of the bamboo, its mouth snapping angrily in my direction.

Something big appears out of the corner of my eye, and I watch as Raahosh stalks toward the thing I've pulled out of the water, blade in hand. He looks extremely pissed off as he grabs the thing by one of its flinging flipper-things and slams it to the ground. Then, with an ease that astonishes me, he thrusts his knife into its eye.

The thing's flippers flail, blood spurts onto the white snow, and then it stops moving. As I stare, wide-eyed, he glances over at me and flings his blade to the ground, then stalks toward me.

I crab-walk backward a few feet. "I didn't know! Like I was supposed to know one of those things was attached to the end of the bamboo? All I wanted were some supplies!" My babbling doesn't make him pause an inch. Of course not. He can't understand me. My fast talking is futile.

The big alien stalks toward me as if I'm his prey. I scoot backward again, terrified—and a little aroused by the hard look in his eyes. My cootie immediately starts thrumming as he looms over me, to my horror and chagrin, and my nipples get hard.

Fucking cootie.

His nostrils flare and his eyes narrow as he gazes down at me.

"I'm not turned on," I say in a shaky voice, even though I can feel my blood pulsing and thrumming in my veins, my cootie purring in my chest. I'm a shitty, shitty liar. I want nothing more than to reach between my legs and stroke my clit again. Maybe it's adrenaline. Maybe it's the way he's gazing down at me as if he can't decide if he wants to rip my clothing off or turn me over and spank me. Both mental images make me a little crazy.

Whatever it is, my body is acutely aware of him, and the cootie is going wild. I'm panting as I sit in the snow, and I realize a moment later that my legs are sprawled open.

I watch as his nostrils flare. A low moan escapes my throat. Why is that so fucking hot? God, I hate this cootie.

"Liz," he growls, the word feral in his throat.

"I totally don't want you," I pant, my cootie purring so loud it practically drowns me out. "My cootie is full of lies."

He reaches a big hand down to me, to help me up.

I slap it away, annoyed at both him and myself for being all aroused after nearly getting my face eaten by a stream-Cthulhu-on-a-stick. "Go away."

Angry, he bends down and grabs at the front of my shirt. I know he's about to haul me upright since I won't take his help, but the moment his face nears mine?

I lose all sensibility. I grab him by the one horn jutting from his brow, my fingers curling around the broken stump of the other, and I drag his face toward me for a kiss. I'm sure I'll regret it later, but right now, my hormones are singing and my body desperately wants his mouth on mine. I barely hear his small gasp as I take his lower lip between my teeth and gently bite down.

Raahosh makes a low, rasping groan in his throat, and then he mashes his mouth against mine.

It's clear the guy doesn't know how to kiss. That's okay—my cootie's purring so hard I don't think I could stop if I wanted to. A soft whimper escapes my throat, and then I begin to show him how a kiss works. My lips caress his, slow and sensual. He freezes against me, his big hands down along my sides, his body looming over mine, and he's stiff and unyielding. So I continue to coax him with my mouth. "This is how you kiss, big guy," I murmur between pecks of my mouth against his, letting my lips caress the hard line of his mouth.

For a long moment, he's tense above me, and then his lips part, letting me in. I slick my tongue over the seam of his mouth, and it brushes against his fangs, a reminder that he's an alien. I shiver, and start to pull away.

That's when Raahosh kisses me back. At first hesitant, his movements grow bolder when my tongue meets his, and I make needy little noises in the back of my throat. His tongue has bumps on it, much like the ridges that cover his body. It drags over my own tongue, sending unique sensations skyrocketing through my body. Oh . . . wow. Georgie didn't mention this. She didn't mention anything even remotely close to this. I wonder if he's got the amazing bumps in other fun locations.

He's taking to kissing well, his lips caressing mine and then his tongue dragging against my own, until my cootie is rumbling so loud that I can barely think, and it feels as if my entire torso is vibrating with need. My pussy aches with a similar need, and I feel, for a moment, as if I might die if he doesn't touch me soon. I break away from him, panting.

He immediately captures my mouth with his again. His tongue flicks against mine, a silent question.

"I don't want this," I breathe, even as I grab his horns and drag his mouth against mine once more. My moans of pure delight are swallowed against his tongue, and I wrap my legs around his waist, feeling him stiffen against me in surprise. "I totally don't want you tonguing me," I hiss at him, and then proceed to tongue his mouth all over, like a wild woman.

Raahosh breaks away from my kiss and stares down at me, eyes as feral as I feel. He leans in and captures my mouth in another breathtaking kiss, and I nearly lose my mind when he sucks on my upper lip. This man is a fast learner. Maybe too fast. I feel as if I'm losing control of the situation.

Of course, I'm assuming I ever had control of the situation.

I pull my mouth away from his again, and I drag one of his hands from the snow to my breast. "I don't want you to touch this," I tell him, fierce and just a little bit angry. Truth is, I am angry as much as I'm aroused. I'm not sure if this is me or the cootie, but I know I can't stop. And when he squeezes my breast through the thick fabric of the borrowed tunic, I fling my head back and moan again, my hips undulating against the snow.

I need him so *bad*. It's like my body has been half asleep and now that we're touching, I'm alive. My senses are awakened, and my body is singing—

And I need sex like I need air.

He rubs his thumb over my nipple through the leather, and my breath hisses from my throat. That should not feel that good. It should not. And yet, I want more than just that. He bares his teeth in a snarl, and I gasp at the sight of those sharp fangs. I must be sick in the head, because they're arousing to me, too, and I give his head a little push.

"I don't want you to lick my pussy," I tell him, nudging him lower to emphasize just what it is I want despite my words. It's okay, anyhow, because I'm babbling like a crazy person. "I don't want your mouth on me at all," I tell him, even as I lift my hips and use one hand to start to pull my newly made pants down.

Even though he can't understand me, he gets the idea, and his hands go to my pants, tugging them down to my knees. He gives me a hot look that makes me melt, and my nipples feel like hard, aching points of agony under the leather. They're dying to be touched, so I reach up and toy with them myself. My cootie's humming so hard my entire body feels as if it's vibrating, and I'm hurting with need.

My pants get caught up around my knees and he jerks at them for a moment, frustrated. Then, he grabs the fabric and hauls my legs forward, pressing them against my chest. My ass sticks out into the snow and I'm bare from my waist to my knees.

And trapped.

I suck in a breath and wait.

Raahosh stares down at me, at the pink part of my flesh that I imagine is slick with moisture and feels as if it's throbbing with aching need. He looks up at me, his glowing blue eyes slitted, and I can't tell what he's thinking. Then, I feel him touch me. His fingers trace over my sensitive folds, exploring me.

I nearly weep with how intense it feels. Breath shudders from my throat, and I make a low, keening sound. I want more than just that exploratory touch. I want—no, crave the feel of his mouth on me. "I don't want your mouth on me," I grit out, even as I tug my legs forward so he can get a better look at what I'm presenting. "Not at all."

Raahosh ignores the lies I'm spewing and studies me for a long moment. I watch his nostrils flare, and he runs his finger up and down my folds again. I cry out and buck against him, and when he pulls his big hand back, it's gleaming with my juices. He studies his wet thumb and fingers, and then brings them to his mouth for a taste.

"Oh goddamn, that was dirty. You are so dirty," I tell him, hotter and more turned on than ever.

He licks his fingers with an almost reverent expression on his face, as if the taste of me is better than the finest chocolate. And that just makes me quiver with lust, seeing his delicious, big, bumpy tongue scraping over those fingers, licking them clean. It's driving me crazy, just watching him lick his hand. It should be me he's licking.

Wait, no it shouldn't. "I totally don't want any of this," I spit out at him, furious with myself and him for my body's fierce need. "I don't want you. I don't want your mouth on my pussy, licking me until I come." The very thought makes me shudder with how intense the visual image is.

And because I *don't* want it so bad, I reach between my legs and spread my pussy lips for him to see.

I watch as his eyes flare with need, and then his head pushes between my legs. I feel his big hands bracing my thighs, separating them, and I feel the jagged, homemade seams on my pants give under the stress of my spreading legs. Don't care. Raahosh pushes my thighs apart and gazes down at my spread, slick pussy. I feel scorching hot, aching and swollen. I'm about to touch myself when he bats my hand aside and then drags his tongue over my flesh.

A scream bursts from my lips.

Oh my *God*.

I grab his horn and the stem of the other one and push his face against my heated skin. I'm wild with urgency, and when his tongue—God bless that bumpy, bumpy tongue—swipes over my skin, I scream again. I drag my hips up and down even as he grunts and licks at me with his mouth, his own desire as intense as my own. His tongue is moving everywhere, licking and pushing against my softest parts, and I feel it flicking over my clit with every lapping taste. Then, he nuzzles my clit.

He nuzzles it.

And I come so hard I'm seeing stars. My cries echo in the snow, and I'm grinding my sex against his face, working every last bit of my orgasm out from under him. He doesn't seem to mind the fact that I'm using his horns like a steering wheel, driving his mouth this way and that, demanding more from him. He's all too eager to comply and lick me into oblivion. I keep coming with every flick of that tongue over my sensitive parts, until I feel a second orgasm ripping through me, and I'm practically writhing on the ground, my juices covering his face.

When I come down, I collapse in the snow, wheezing. My cootie rattles a bit, and then settles into a softer thrum, temporarily content.

Raahosh's cootie is grumbling so hard it sounds like a motor, though, and when he licks me again, I push his face away, because I'm too sensitive right now for another round. "Not yet," I whimper. "I can't."

He looks up at me, his face feral, eyes glowing with an unholy light. His hard, sexy mouth is wet with the taste of me, and as I watch, he bares his fangs and gives me a look that makes my nipples perk all over again.

"Mine," he growls, and buries his face between my legs again.

He begins to lick me again, and I squeal. I lie back, ready to be all his like he just said and—

Wait a fucking *moment*. Was that *English*?

I sit up on my elbows and stare down at the alien licking me out. "What did you just say?"

PART THREE

Raahosh

A small hand jerks on my horn before I can bury my face between her legs again and drink the sweet nectar that flows from my mate's body.

"What did you say?" she repeats again. The look on her face is utterly furious.

I narrow my eyes at her and try to dip my head again, but she twines her fingers in my hair and jerks instead, and I snarl at her. I want nothing more than to taste her again, to lick her for hours and hours until she's trembling beneath me. Then, I will slide my cock into her warm, waiting well and we will be together as mates. As it should be. But the hand in my hair is insistent, and she snaps her knees together, trying to push me out.

"You spoke fucking English."

"I did," I say, and force her knees apart again. I want more of her thick, sweet honey. I want to lose myself between her legs for hours. The men of my tribe say that there is no taste like that of a resonance mate on the tongue, and they are right. I never knew what they referred to until now. Now, I want to taste nothing but her for the rest of my days.

Her cunt can be my sustenance. All else is unworthy of notice.

I dip my head again, determined to lick her. She likes it when I lick her. Was she not pushing her slick, wet petals against my face moments ago? Demanding more? I will give her more. My cock aches, as hard as the stone in my spear-tip. I long to bury myself inside her, but I want more of her on my tongue first.

She gives an angry screech and slams a small fist into my eye. Then she cries out in pain and shakes her hand. "Damn you! Why is your head so hard?"

That gets my attention. My mate is hurt. I sit up and take her small hand in mine, only to have her try to hit me again.

"Stop touching me," she bellows in my ear. "I am so stinking pissed at you! You speak *English*!"

"I do." I catch the hand that rises to strike me before she can connect with my forehead again. It's not that her hits hurt—it's that she's going to damage her soft little human hands. My brow is plated, and her tiny fists are weak.

"You lied to me!"

That makes me angry. She thinks I willfully deceived her? For what purpose? "How did I do such a thing?"

"You never told me!"

"You never asked," I counter, my irritation rising. "You simply talk and talk and assume I don't understand you. You never bothered to ask me if I could."

Her pink face flushes, and I watch as she pants, her breath puffing in the cold air. "You are a dick."

"I do not know what this word means."

"Oh really?" Her voice is a sneer. "Here I thought you were the expert on the human language."

"There are words you speak that have no match with what I have learned."

"Funny. I thought 'dick' was the language of your people."

I frown down at her. "I do not know this word, dick. I am sa-khui. That is my people."

Her eyes roll and she pushes at my chest again. "It's called sarcasm."

"I do not know this word, sarcasm—"

"Never mind," she bellows, clearly furious with me. "God!"

She's mad at me? I saved her. If she'd have fallen into the water, they'd have torn the flesh from her bones in an instant. The thought of her suffering—dying—fills me with an incoherent rage. I straighten and stare down at her, naked legs still sprawled in the snow. She's scowling up at me, which makes it easier to resist her beauty. "You shouldn't have run from the cave."

"Running? I wasn't running."

She can lie to herself, but not to me. I step forward and grab the front of her tunic, then haul her to her feet. She slaps at me, but I right her anyhow, and then she tugs on the hem of her tunic, a fierce frown on her face. I lean in close to her. Her scent is in my nose, making my khui resonate with hunger. I want nothing more than to press my mouth to hers and mate with it again.

But not while she is looking at me as if I am filth. My heart hardens a little and I lean in. "You belong to me, female."

She smacks a hand to my shoulder, angry. "I don't belong to anyone."

"There is no place you can run that I will not find you and return you to me." She doesn't realize that every day she ignores the call of her khui, it will grow worse. There is no reasoning with it, or changing its mind. It simply wants what it wants.

And it wants Liz to be my mate.

I want that, too. She's mine, and I'm going to claim her yet.

"God, you are such a stalker," she mutters, crossing her arms over her chest. "And if you must know, I was looking for materials for a bow."

"A bow," I repeat. This word is known, but the thing it calls to mind is not familiar to me. "It is a weapon, yes?"

"Yes," she says, and gives me a challenging look. Her chin lifts. "I know how to shoot a bow. I can hunt, too."

I grunt. Part of me is pleased that she wants to hunt, and part of me worries. The women in our tribe are so few that they do not participate in the hunting treks. They stay close to the caves, because we have lost many in our tribe over the last few years, and if we lose more, we cease to exist. But I see the determination on Liz's face and know she will not like that answer.

So . . . a grunt is what she gets.

"What is that supposed to mean?" She gets right in my face and tries to reach for one of my horns, no doubt to tug me down to her height and get my attention. My Liz is brave. I have respect for that, even if it's infuriating.

I stand at my full height so she can't pull any more of my hair or tug on my horns. "You belong to me. If you need something, you come to me. My job is to provide for you."

"Well, great," she says in a testy voice. "How about you provide my friends to me, hmm?"

I ignore that. I'm not taking her back until we are mated. Instead, I head over to the face-eater I killed for her. If she wants it for her bow, she'll have it. "Come. You need to go back to the cave. Your human flesh is still weak despite your khui."

"Gee, you didn't think it was so weak when you grabbed me and ripped my pants off."

I turn to give her a quelling look. Was she trying to pretend that she didn't like it when I touched her? Her cheeks are bright pink, which is curious. I study her for a moment more, and she squirms under my hard gaze. "You did not seem to mind my touch."

Her face turns even redder. "Oh, just throw that back in my face, why don't you."

Her words make no sense to me, but the color in her cheeks tells me plenty. She is embarrassed. I find it charming, even more so when her hands move to cup the tiny tuft of hair between her legs and shield it from my gaze. Does she think that protects her? I licked every inch of her mere moments ago. I study her bare thighs, her feet still covered in my boots. My own feet are barely aware of the cold, but I see her soft human skin is prickling with the cool temperatures. I must ensure that she is warm and taken care of.

But Liz is a fighter, and she's choosing to fight me. So I grab the dead face-eater and the long tube they use as a lure, and sling it over one of my shoulders. "Are you coming, or do I carry you?" I ask her.

She scowls darkly at me. With a jerk, she scoops up the torn halves of her pants and storms ahead of me. "You are such a dick. I hate you."

"Do you ever stop talking?" I ask.

She raises her middle finger in the air in my direction. I'm not sure what it means, but I can guess it's not pleasant. "I guess I'm walking back pantsless. Thanks a lot."

"Do you want my loincloth?"

Her face turns that bright red again, and she gives me a scandalized look. "So you can be naked? No thanks."

Her refusal just further emphasizes how unattractive she finds me. It stings. "Whatever will silence you," I jab back.

She makes an outraged noise, and then storms ahead of me.

Liz is silent as we make our way back to my secret cave. I let her walk in front of me, so I can guard her . . . and so I can watch her small, pert bottom as it flexes when she walks. She has no tail, so the view is a curious one . . . but still arousing. I mentally picture bending her over, spreading her bottom, and then licking all of her wet female parts again until she screams her pleasure once more.

By the time we get back to the cave, my khui is resonating and my cock aches fiercely. It strains against my loincloth, the ache almost unbearable. Is she not suffering, too? Why does she fight this?

A resonance mate is always final.

Liz heads into the cave without a backward glance at me. She's still angry—it rolls off her in waves. That's fine. Let her resist if she thinks it will make a difference. She is mine. She was claimed the moment her khui resonated for me.

Nothing she does will change this.

As if she can sense my turbulent, possessive thoughts, she grabs one of the furs and wraps it around her waist, then turns to me. "I know what your goal is, here."

My brows draw together. My goal? I have no goal other than to claim her as my mate. So we can be one.

"You're going to hide me away until I'm pregnant, right?" She sounds defeated, the look in her eyes miserable.

"And what if I am?"

"Once again, I'm being held hostage for my vagina." She sighs. "What is it with you aliens? Can't a girl just make her own decisions for once? Is that so freaking hard?"

"The khui has decided," I tell her.

She gives a small shake of her head. "It's always someone else's decision. When's it going to be mine?"

I watch her, frustrated. There is no decision to be made. The khui has decided. And yet . . . I don't like the way her words make me feel.

Or the defeat in her voice. Liz is a fighter. I don't want her to give up.

Liz

Things are uncomfortable in the cave when I come back. I ignore Raahosh and concentrate on sewing my pants together again with a few scraps of leather that I use as thick ties. I knot my pants every few inches instead of using one long thread in the hopes that things hold together better, and I blush the entire time I work on them.

Raahosh putters around the front of the cave, getting water and melting it, gathering more dung chips for fire fuel, and then butchering the thing that we killed at the river. He saves the bamboo for me, and then takes the bits of the creature with him, mumbling something about "bait for traps" under his breath.

I say nothing. I'm still pissed at him. Actually, "pissed" is not the word. I'm frustrated. Frustrated beyond belief. I know it's not his fault that our cooties decided to become friends, but can the guy throw me a bone and freaking help me out instead of acting like I'm the problem? Excuse me if I don't want to automatically jump in the sack and demand that he squirt me with his baby batter.

My face grows hot as I remember our little throw down in the snow. I think of him ripping my pants off, and my cootie starts vibrating and I get wet between my legs again. Gah. This is so frustrating.

I don't know which is worse—the endless horniness the cootie brings, or the fact that Raahosh has let me yammer on and on without telling me that he understands English. I try to recall all the things I've said and draw a blank. Truth is, I ramble, and I don't remember what has come out of my mouth. Ugh.

A few hours alone lets me fix my pants, and when I put them on, they're a lot tighter, but they still fit. The downtime away from Raahosh also puts me in a better mood and gives me some perspective.

Really, he's just as trapped as I am. And maybe it's the orgasms talking, but he did a lot of giving and very little taking in our, ahem, snow incident. Maybe I'm being too hard on him. He is right about one thing, though—I never bothered to ask him if he spoke English. I just assumed he was an ignorant alien . . . which makes me a jerk.

I sigh. I'm not sure if I'm ready to apologize, but I do know I'm mentally exhausted from fighting with him all the time. It's getting me nowhere. My dad used to tell me I could catch more flies with honey than vinegar.

Lately, all I've been doing is spewing vinegar. No wonder I'm not getting anywhere.

And while Raahosh and I still have opposite wants—he wants a wife and baby-carrier, and I want to be left alone—we can still act like adults.

It'd be nice to have a friend again, I think wistfully. The girls I was captured on the ship with? Those were forced friendships. If we hadn't been stuck together, would we have ever spoken two words to each other? I miss home. I miss my friends. I miss my dad, gone for five years now.

When sunset approaches, I take stock of the cave, knowing Raahosh will appear soon. I've tried to make things as presentable as possible. I've gotten extra water, braided my hair to keep it out of my face, repaired my clothing, stoked the fire, and started working on a cord for my bow. The bamboo we've gotten is different than what I expected, but it's hollow and has a bit of give to it, not unlike bone. I'm going to try wrapping it in leather at certain spots to reinforce it, and hope for the best.

He enters the cave shortly, two smaller creatures hanging from his hand. Tonight's dinner.

"Welcome back," I tell him.

Raahosh pauses and frowns at me, and I can see the wheels working in his mind. He's trying to figure out my angle. Like I have an angle other than trying to be a decent human being? I sigh. "Look. We started off on the wrong foot, all right? You forced me to get the cootie, and I've been making you pay for it ever since. Can we call a truce for a bit? I'm tired."

He grunts and kneels by the fire, stoking it.

"You're not a chatty sort even on the best of days, are you?"

He glances over at me. "And you would talk to the walls if they would listen."

My smile grows tight. "You're making this whole 'truce' thing hard, dude. Fair warning."

I expect another grunt from him. Instead, he nods. "That was not kind of me. I apologize."

I sit back, surprised that he caved. "Well . . . okay then." I move toward the fire and sit across from him. "You want help with dinner?"

"Dinner?"

I gesture at the kills. "Dressing those? Skinning? Making it food?"

He gives me another narrow-eyed look. Not an angry one, I think, but more along the lines of trying to figure me out. "It is my job to provide for my mate."

"Ah." I think for a minute, and then hug my knees to my chest. My bare feet wiggle near the fire. "Can we save some of those skins for boots for me?"

He nods.

"Thank you," I say softly. "I'm not going to run away, just so you know. There's nowhere for me to go."

Again, he nods. I stare into the fire as he begins to skin his kills. I need to get him talking, if only so I can crack open the hard shell that seems to be around his mind. He's a hard man to figure out, this Raahosh. "So tell me about this place."

He looks up at me. "This is my cave."

"No, not this place specifically," I say, gesturing at the cave. "This planet. This entire world. I don't know anything about it other than that it's cold."

Raahosh grunts, and for a long moment, I think he's going to ignore my questions. Then, he pulls out a smaller knife than his skinning one and begins to cut the meat into smaller, bite-sized chunks. "This . . . is the warm season. We say it is the bitter season, and the colder months the brutal season."

My eyes go wide. I sputter. "But there's three feet of snow on the ground!" How can this possibly be warm?

His mouth curves slowly, and I see a devastating smile spread across his face. It makes the breath escape my lungs and turns his hard, blade-sharp features into something deadly sexy. "You will just have to get used to the snow."

"Snow. Right." I ignore the throb of my girl parts in response to that smile. My cootie starts up and I mock-cough, thumping my chest to try and shut it up. "So this is . . . summer?"

He cocks his head, mentally searching through words, I imagine, and then nods. "What you call winter is a time of very little light. The suns barely show their faces and there is much darkness. It grows much colder and game grows scarce. That is why it is so important to hunt so much during the warm months."

I nod, digesting this. Okay, if this is about as warm as it'll ever get, I'll live. I won't like it, but I'll live. "And you're a hunter?"

He nods and offers me a bite of red, bloody meat. I take the bit from him and pop it into my mouth, raw. A burst of flavor sweeps over my tongue and I moan. It's so good this way.

His hands jerk against the kill, and as I watch, his breechcloth gets tight over his groin. Oops.

"Um, it's tasty. Sorry."

"Do not apologize." He cuts into the meat viciously. "I am pleased that I can feed my mate."

Yeah, I can see that he's pleased. There's no hiding that fact. I eye the enormous length from under my lashes for a long moment. He hands me another tiny chunk, and I lean forward and take it into my mouth directly from his fingers without thinking. His glowing blue eyes flare, and my cootie starts up all over again.

Stupid cootie, always fronting me out.

Raahosh watches me chew, and when he holds another piece of meat out to me, he pulls it away when I reach for it with my fingers. He wants me to eat from his hand again. I lean in and let my tongue graze his fingertips, just because it's cruelly fun to tease him.

And it turns me on. Just a little.

His bloody fingertips trace my lips before he pulls back again, and then he shifts on his haunches. His cock is a hard bar against his leg, bigger than any dude's junk has the right to be.

"So, what is that creature called?" I ask him, rubbing a hand up and down my arms to stop the goosebumps from rising on my skin. I'm totally turned on right now, damn it. Raw meat and an asshole captor should not be making my girl parts juice but I can't seem to help myself.

He glances down at the raw meat and cuts another piece for me. "We call it two teeth." He pulls back the lips of the creature to show me two gigantic fangs. It's like a beaver. Kinda. A vampire beaver. With a row of spikes along its back and fuzzy, fluffy feet.

Okay, so it's nothing like a beaver, but my brain feels better associating it with Earth animals.

"You're not eating," I point out to him as he holds another bite out for me.

"My mate comes first," he says, and gives me another scorchingly intense look as he pops the meat into my mouth and then brushes my lips with his thumb. "I will eat when she is sated."

I squirm a little. This is the most bizarrely sexualized meal I've ever had. I shouldn't be enjoying myself half as much as I am. "Tell me about your tribe? Your family?"

The hungry, aroused look on his face vanishes, and I see his expression tense, becoming a mask of indifference. "I have no family."

"None? But what about your parents?"

"Dead." The look on his face is closed off.

"I see. No brothers or sisters?"

He shakes his head. "My younger brother died not long after my mother did."

"Ah." Raahosh seems lost in thought, so I continue on. "Do you have close friends in your tribe?"

"Vektal."

Getting this guy to open up is like prying teeth. "I met him. What about the others?"

He eyes me. "Why do you wish to know?"

"Because I'm going to be living there soon? They're going to be my tribe, too?" Saying it aloud makes me a little heartsick. "What if they don't like me?"

His thick, ridged brows draw down, as if he doesn't quite grasp this. "You are my mate. There is no like or dislike. You will be part of the tribe."

"Easy for you to say," I tell him. "You grew up with them. You're the same species. I'm a weird outsider who won't stop talking, remember?"

He gazes at me for a long time, expression inscrutable. Then, after what feels like forever, he offers me another chunk of meat. I take it, and he says, "There are two kits in our tribe currently. With Shorshie's kit, that will be three. And if the others resonate, that will be more."

I absorb this information. "And women? How many women?"

"Without the humans? Four, if you do not include the kits."

I blanch. That leaves a lot of unsatisfied men. Maybe it's a good thing that Raahosh hid me away in this cave for a bit. I wonder if the other girls that didn't resonate are going to be fought over like scraps at dinner. "How many men?"

"Twenty-four of us are left. Twenty unmated."

"Left?"

He nods, carving another piece of meat away. "Life here is difficult. We lost many of our tribe several years ago on a bad hunt. Four of our men were killed and one female before we could bring down the *ta-li*." He shakes his head. "It was a bad time."

"Sounds dangerous."

"It is why the women no longer hunt. It is not that they cannot, it is that we will not risk the life of the tribe by putting them in jeopardy."

I open my mouth to reply and he immediately pops another

bite of meat into it. This feels like a shushing tactic, so I chew quickly and then continue. "But you have the human chicks now. That means that you're no longer one big sausage party. That'll bring the tribe up to . . ." I count for a moment. "Twelve humans and thirty of you guys means there's forty-two of us. Plenty of hunters."

"Not many will wish to risk their mates on a hunt," he says, offering me another piece of meat. I refuse it, and he eats it instead, his expression thoughtful. "Many will no longer want to hunt at all."

"Why not?"

"Hunts are very solitary by nature. We go out for long periods of time into the snows. We might be gone a full turn of the moons before returning home."

"Like a month?"

He shrugs. "Most hunt alone. It is easier to cover more ground that way. We hunt smaller game in many different directions and cache the kills under the snow so we can recover it later, when the land is forbidding and all the good game has gone to hibernate to get out of the ice."

"So hunters . . . are alone a lot? It's probably not the worst thing in the world, given that you've only got four girls back at home," I muse. "Is that what you do?"

He nods. "I am a hunter. I spend more time out in the wild than at the tribal caves."

"Why?"

"Why what?"

"Why spend more time alone than back at home?"

His glowing blue gaze neatly pins me in place. "There is nothing for me there. At least in the wild I can provide for my people. At home, I only see what others have that I do not.

Sometimes it is . . . difficult." The look he shoots me is utterly possessive once more, and I know he's talking about mates.

I swallow hard. So he voluntarily exiles himself for long periods of time so he's not around all the happy couples? My heart twinges with pity. No wonder Raahosh is crappy being around people. "Dammit, don't make me feel sorry for you."

He grunts and savagely cuts another bit of meat off the kill, then chews it, the expression on his face bitter. "I do not want your pity, woman."

"Pity's all you're getting from me tonight," I quip.

He bares his teeth in a snarl. "Your words are not amusing to me."

"I wasn't trying to amuse *you*," I point out. Then I get to my feet, irritated. "Ugh. I don't know what to do with you."

"I want my mate," he grits out, still at the fire. "That is how this works. The khui has decided that you and I shall be mated. Nothing in that can be changed. You will be mine, and that is all there is."

"Is that so?" I turn back to him and put my hands on my hips. "I want to go hunting. How do you like them apples?" He cocks his head, and I realize he's trying to analyze my words. "It's a human saying," I snap. "I want to hunt and provide for myself. And you know what? I'd like to decide for myself, too. When do I get to decide what I want, damn it?" I fling my arms wide. "Everyone around me thinks they know what I should be doing, but you know what I want? No, you don't, because no one asks me."

"You want to hunt," Raahosh says in a flat voice.

"That'd be good, for starters."

"Very well. I will take you hunting in the morning."

I blink at him in surprise. His mood seems dark, but he's . . . going to let me join him hunting? "Really? Just like that?"

"Provided . . ." He pauses and gives me another heated look.

"Oh, here we go," I mutter, then wave at him to continue. There is always a catch, isn't there? "Lay it on me."

"I will take you hunting if you lay with me tonight as mates do."

"If you think I'm going to bone you for the privilege of hunting—"

"Not sex. Boning?" He looks at me curiously. "Not boning. Just touching. Holding each other."

My guilty little heart twitches again. He's lonely. God, I am such a dick. Poor Raahosh, to get stuck with the most stubborn woman ever. I soften. "I can handle that, I think."

Raahosh gives me a silent nod, and then straightens. "We should clean the cave and prepare for the hunt tomorrow if we will be out."

"Let's do it," I say, hiding my excitement. Truth is, I'm a little nervous and fluttery at the thought of sleeping in his arms tonight and letting him touch me. My mind goes back to the fierce pussy-licking from earlier and a pulse of need rocks through me. My cootie immediately starts purring so loud it sounds like a chainsaw. *Dammit, cootie. Show some restraint, girl.*

We putter around the cave for the next few hours and it's surprisingly companionable. Raahosh makes me a pair of shoes with some scraped leather hides he's been saving for the past few days. I know he treated them with a mash of innards and crap he used from the critters themselves, and the result is a tough leather with a bit of fur on the inside to keep my feet warm. They are little more than mittens for my feet with drawstrings at the ankles, but I'm pleased with them nevertheless. I work on my bow, and when I tell Raahosh about the kind of material I need for the bowstring, he produces something from his traveling pack that's a lot like a thick twine. I string my bow and hope for the best, and then set about making arrows. I have to use bone for those, and the ribs and wing-bones from something unnameable that looks like an ostrich with shorter legs—four of them, mind you—ends up being perfect. I now have arrows that are a little bit shorter than I am used to, but lightweight and deadly as needles at the tip after a good sharpening. I sharpen and fletch my arrows for what feels like hours, until the fire dies down and I'm nodding off with the knife in my hand.

Raahosh takes the arrow from my grip as I struggle to stay awake. "It is time to sleep," he tells me.

"Oh, but I've only got four of them," I tell him with a soft protest. "That's not a lot of hunting."

"We have spears and knives as well. You can learn more ways to hunt," he says, voice low and tender as he carefully puts my bow and arrows aside. "Come and undress for bed, my mate."

I should have protested that I wasn't his mate, but all that comes out is a yawn. "I can sleep in my clothes."

"Not if we are sleeping as mates," he murmurs. "This is what you have promised to me."

So I did. I'm too sleep-drowsy to protest, and I don't realize just how exhausted I am until he stands me up and my legs feel like Jell-O. When Raahosh leans me against him and begins to undo the laces at the neck of my tunic, I realize he's warm and oddly soft, despite the hard protective ridges along his arms, chest, and other parts of his body.

My hand goes to his pectorals and I rub them under his vest. "You're soft," I murmur. Touching him is like touching . . . suede or doe-hide. There's a fine layer of fur on his skin that I didn't notice until now, but it's soft and oh-so-warm and I can't stop petting him. I actually don't mind the thought of sleeping naked against him if he feels like this.

My cootie purrs an agreement, the little whore.

"Arms up." His voice is a soft rasp, and I sleepily raise both of them before I can stop to think. In the next moment, my tunic whisks over my head and then I'm topless in front of him. My cootie's humming in my breast, and my nipples harden, even as I yawn again. "Pants," he says, and he's not grabbing at me or making me feel weird, so I obediently step out of them and hand over the clothing. I watch with sleepy eyes as he turns away and carefully folds my things, setting them nearby. Then, with his back to me, he begins to undress.

That gets my attention. I watch his arms flex as he undoes the laces in the front of his chest and then removes his own tight-fitting tunic. Then he's down to his tall boots and his breech-cloth. I'm totally creeping on him at this point, watching his ass flex as he undoes the ties on his breechcloth and it slides to the ground. He steps out of it, lifting one leg with casual grace, and I see the sway of his balls from between his legs. Then his ass flexes again and his tail lashes, and I just stare.

Why is a tail sexy to me? Why does the sight of it flicking over that taut ass do terrible, nasty things to my girl parts? He glances over his shoulder at me, and the look is so heated, I get all aroused and squirmy. I'm not sure if us being naked together is a good idea, but I also don't think I could stop even if I wanted to.

And . . . I kinda don't want to.

He turns to face me again and his cock juts forward from his body, long and obvious. He's completely erect, and I try not to stare at his different anatomy. I'm no virgin, but Raahosh has a mon-strously huge dick, and to top it off, it seems to have . . . ridges along the top, the bumpy, rough plated areas like his arms and chest have.

That will either feel really awesome or really awful.

I frown as I stare at the blunted horn a few inches above his cock. I remember it from last time, but the sight of it baffles me as much with a second viewing. "What's that for?"

He steps forward and his hand caresses it in a way that makes me feel filthy with lust. "My spur?" He shrugs. "It is part of my body."

"Yes, but does it have a purpose? I mean, other than to freak out Earth girls?"

Raahosh takes my hand and moves me toward the nest of furs. "Do your men not have such things?"

"Yeah, that's a big no."

"Do I frighten you? Is that why you turn me away?" He looks almost hopeful.

Weird. "I'm not scared of you."

His expression blackens. "Then you turn me away for other reasons."

"Reasons like, oh hey, it's not my choice? That's enough reason for me." I thump to the blankets and slide into them, scooting to the far edge of the nest. The blankets make a nice, snuggly bed, but they don't make a very large one.

He doesn't get into bed next to me, and I hike the covers up to conceal my breasts, suddenly embarrassed. I'm the only one, because he squats next to the bed and studies me, and his cock sticks out like a third leg as he rubs his chin and muses. I try not to make eye contact with, ahem, his small head.

"Is it because I am ugly?" he asks after a long moment. "Is that why you hate being mated to me?" He rubs the scars on the side of his face thoughtfully.

I frown up at him. "You're not ugly."

"I am scarred. Surely you have noticed."

I snort. "I'm not blind. It's a little obvious."

His expression closes off and he gets to his feet. I've hurt his feelings. Damn it, the man's more prickly than even I am. I clasp his ankle to stop him, and he gazes down at me with those narrow, blade-sharp eyes that seem to hide all emotion. "You misunderstand me," I say. I don't know why it matters to me that I don't hurt him, but it does. "I think it's obvious that you're scarred. You're missing a horn. But I didn't say it was unattractive." I lick my lips. "I kind of like it."

His eyes narrow again.

My fingers slide over the soft suede of his ankle, caressing the hard tendons under his flesh. There's not an inch of him that is soft with fat. He's all lean and wild and . . . well, even if I didn't have a cootie, he would probably be my type. "The only thing I don't like about this situation is the fact that I don't have choices. It's not you. It's me. Does that make sense?"

He squats again, and his cock comes precariously near my hand. I try not to notice, "try" being the key word. "There is no choice when it comes to mating. The khui decides. It is what makes strong children."

"Back where I am from, the woman decides." Okay, that might be a little broad, since a lot of women don't get to decide, but I'm running with it. "The man courts her and she lets him know if she appreciates his efforts."

He flings his arms wide, gesturing at the cave. "Do I not court? Is this not all effort to show you how I can provide?"

"Kidnapping me from the others and then pretending like it's courting doesn't count, no," I snap. "You know what? I give up on trying to be nice. You're determined to take everything I say the wrong way. Forget it." I lie back in bed and pull the covers up, then turn on my side so my back is to him.

He lies down next to me. Of course he does. The man wouldn't know the word "no" if it bit him in the face. I ignore him anyhow, determined to go to sleep. He wants to lie down like a couple? That's fine—this can be his first experience with the wifely cold shoulder. *Welcome to married life, Raahosh.*

I roll my eyes at nothing when he reaches for my arm and strokes it. "Did you change your mind?"

"Change my mind?" I don't turn to look at him, because if I do, he might get a fist in the face.

"About hunting? Do you not want to go in the morning?"

My jaw clenches. "You are such a blackmailing jerk."

He pauses. His hand strokes down my arm, eliciting a response that ticks me off almost as much as his next comment. "I do not understand these words. What is a jerk?"

"Your people. Next question?"

He grunts, and I can't tell if he's annoyed at my snide commentary. "Black . . . mail? What is this?"

"That's when you force me to do things I don't want in exchange for something that I do want."

This time he makes a sound of disbelief. His long fingers trail up and down over my skin, and it prickles in response. My pulse beats hard between my legs, and I can feel myself getting wet just at that small touch. "You say you do not want it. The only thing that says you do not want this is your mouth."

"It's allowed to have its say, too."

"It says plenty," he comments sourly.

"And see, shit like that is why you don't get laid." I pull away from him. "Quit touching me."

He chuckles and leans in, his mouth brushing over my skin. "Ah. More of this mating ritual? I remember it from before."

And his hand covers my breast, squeezing my nipple.

I sputter and flick his hand away even as my cootie starts a symphony with his. "What are you doing?"

His hand returns to my breast, his big arm pinning my flailing ones. He caresses and cups my breast while holding me down, and begins to nibble along my shoulder. "I am courting you as you have shown me. You tell me not to touch you . . . which is human mating talk for me to pleasure you."

"It is *not*!" But then I remember holding his face down between my legs, grinding against him with my pussy. *I don't want you to touch this.*

Well, damn. I have been sending this boy some mixed-up signals, haven't I? Time to explain. "Raahosh, I think we need to have a little talk. I—" My words cut off in a surprised yelp when his fangs score my shoulder, and my nerve endings go wild. That should not have felt as good as it did. That should not have made my entire body sing. But my cootie's gone mad with delight, and when he nibbles on my shoulder again and drags his tongue over my neck, I don't fight. And when his hand goes between my legs to cup my mound?

I'm wet. I'm so wet.

And I moan, unable to resist.

"You see," he murmurs, his tongue brushing against my ear. Oh, it's ridged. I keep forgetting it's ridged, too, and the rasp of it against my flesh makes me wild. "I am learning how to court you, my Liz." His fingers glide through my folds, and then dip, seeking my slick heat. One caresses the opening to my core, and I arch against him, wishing for more than just a finger. I feel the hard, impossible length of his cock against my back, and I want to be filled with it.

"No sex," I breathe out. Truth be told, if he rolled me onto my stomach and pushed into me from behind, I'd probably be just fine and dandy with it. But a girl's got to hold on to her standards.

"I am still courting you, my mate," he says in a low voice, his throat humming with the ferocity of the cootie resonating in his chest to match mine. "Allow me to lick and pleasure you for tonight, as we promised."

Well, that doesn't sound so bad.

Oh, who am I kidding? I want his touch *yesterday*. I need his hands all over me. I need him to keep exploring my body and stop with soft touches and get down to some dirty, dirty business. "Raahosh," I moan, reaching back to touch him. My hand slides into the thick mane of his dark hair and I find a horn. I clutch at it, happy for the handlebar as he strums my body with his fingers, his chest purring hard against my own.

"Your nectar fills your cunt for me," he murmurs into my ear, and then tenderly licks the shell. "Shall I sip it and taste of my mate?"

"That is so corny of you," I breathe, but damn, his corny lines are getting me all squirmy with need. His finger keeps circling my aching core, and I want nothing more than for him to push it deep and start fucking me with his big fingers instead of just teasing me.

"Corny?"

"Just another saying," I tell him, and then make a weird mewing noise when he dips his finger inside me. "Oh God, keep touching me like that."

"Do you want my fingers?" He buries his face against my neck, and I feel the rasp of the hard ridges on his brow against my chin as he nuzzles my throat. My breasts ache for his touch, and I begin to play with my nipples, rocking my hips against his finger that feels just barely inside me. "Or do you want me to lick the nipple between your legs until you scream my name?"

A horrified giggle escapes my throat. "Did you just say n-nipple? Between my legs?"

That gets his attention. He sits up and frowns down at me. "Is that not what it is?"

"No! Nipples are on breasts!"

His hand leaves my pussy and slides to my breasts, and I moan when his wet fingers begin to trace a circle around one areola. "These are nipples, yes?"

I nod, unable to speak. His touch feels too good.

"Humans are so soft," he comments, flicking his big thumb over my taut nipple and then rolling it between his fingers, fascinated by the hard nub of it. "We are not built like this."

"No?" I shift until I'm on my back instead of my side, and I'm gazing up at him. I reach up and boldly caress one of his pectorals, sliding my hand over his nipple and feeling it. Sure enough, it feels like a rock. My fingers flick over it, and I'm surprised. "Wow. That's . . . different."

The breath hisses from his throat at my touch. Encouraged, I keep rubbing my thumb over his nipple—even though it's already hard, I can tell he's enjoying my touch.

He caresses my breast a moment longer, and then his mouth dips toward mine. I meet it, even though I tell myself that kissing him is not smart. That it's going to lead to nothing but false expectations. I can't help myself, though. The moment that velvety skin brushes against mine and his lips meet my lips, I'm a goner. I kiss him back, reveling in the feel of his hard mouth. He licks at my tongue, even as his hand caresses my breast, and I push against him. My arms twine around his neck and I pull him down against me, feeling his big, heavy chest against my breasts. The ridges along his skin—rough, hard patches on his arms and the center of his chest—feel odd mixed in with the plush suede of the rest of his skin, but when I rub my nipples up against him, the dichotomy feels incredible. I moan again, lost in the sensation.

His cock prods my abdomen, and I feel the hot beads of pre-cum drag against my skin, leaving wet trails. He continues to kiss me, his tongue dancing against mine, and his hand moves down my side and rests on my hip. "If it is not a nipple, then what is it?"

I chuckle against his mouth, amused by his alien lack of understanding about female anatomy. Really, I suppose it does make sense to think it's a nipple. "It's called a clitoris. Or a clit, for short."

His hand slides to my pubic hair and he drags his fingers through it before finding my clit again. He brushes the tips of his fingers over it in a careful exploration that makes me grip him against me, hard. "And what purpose does it serve?"

"It, um, just feels good." I don't know if the clit has any sort of anatomical purpose. It's not like a kidney or anything. My breath explodes when he circles it with his finger again. "Oh God. Really, really good."

"Mm? So you like it when I touch it?"

I cry out and my fingernails dig into his skin when he continues the indolent, aggravating circles around the small patch of sensitive skin. I lift one leg and wrap it around his hips, and my pelvis bucks against his touch. "God, yes. Please . . ."

"Will you say my name, Liz?" He presses light kisses to my mouth even as he continues to touch my clit in maddeningly slow, grazing motions.

I lick my lips, whimpering with his touches. "Why?"

"Because I want to hear my mate say my name when she comes for me," he murmurs, and nips at my chin.

Another whimper escapes my throat. "How . . ." God, it's getting hard to think. I just want to grab his hand, shove his big fingers inside me, and ride until I'm coming like a madwoman. "How do you know . . . I'm about to come?"

"Are you not?" His teeth graze my chin, and then he begins to lick down my neck. "Shall I drink your sweet nectar from the source until you do?"

"Oh God," I moan. My fingernails dig into his shoulders. His filthy, weird words are going to make me come like crazy. I'm so close as it is. "Raahosh . . . I need a finger inside me. Fuck me with your hand."

He groans against my throat, and his tongue flicks against the cords of my neck. "Say my name again and I shall give you whatever you want."

"Raahosh," I cry, and one big finger brushes against my core again. This time when I arch against him, it sinks deep. I bellow his name again, and my cootie gives a long, hard shiver of delight in my chest. "Just like that! Oh God!"

"Say it again," he demands, and thrusts into me with his finger.

I buck against it, clinging to him. "Raahosh! Raahosh!" My cootie purrs so loud I feel as if it's drowning me out, and then when he thrusts again, his thumb grazes my clit. My body explodes and I repeat his name with a keening cry as I come.

The breath hisses from him as he continues to pump into me with his finger, over and over again. "I feel that," he says, voice soft with wonder. "I feel you clenching against my fingers."

A hot blush heats my cheeks and I push at his hand, since I'm starting to feel oversensitized. He ignores my attempts to brush him away and keeps thrusting into me, a fascinated look on his face.

"My mate," he says reverently. "My Liz."

Oh dear. I have a feeling if I don't distract him away from his shiny new toy, I'm not getting out of this without him "claiming" me for real. Of course, the thought sends another shiver through my body and my thighs clench around his hand, which doesn't help. His cootie purrs even louder in his chest, and both of them sound like a cacophony in my ears.

"Let me taste you," he says, and begins to move down my body.

Wait, wait, wait. I'm not ready for that again. Not with my legs still quivering like noodles. "Actually," I say, latching on to an idea. I slide a hand down his big arm and then move boldly to his front and cup that big, enormous cock. "It's my turn to play with you. That's how humans court."

He looks up at me and frowns. "This is courting?"

"In some circles it is," I tell him, and wriggle away from his grip. His finger slides out of me, and for a moment, I feel so empty I want to flop right back onto my back and let him fuck me. That's probably just the cootie talking, though. And I'm determined not to be ruled by it, so I slide my hand up and down his cock to get his attention.

It does the trick. The breath hisses from him and his hand covers mine. "Wait—"

"It's okay," I tell him, releasing my squeezing hold on his cock a little. "Have you not had sex in a while?" That's a legit concern, considering there are four women in the tribe, and two have babies. "We can go slow."

His jaw clenches and he looks away from me, removing my hand.

"Um. A really, really long time?"

"Does it matter?" he growls.

Oh boy. I have myself a bona-fide alien virgin. I regard him for a long moment, and then my heart squeezes with sympathy. No wonder he thinks he's ugly. If no one in his tribe has ever touched him, he has to think it's because of how he looks. A tribe with only four women would mean those ladies have their pick of men—until they get cootie-mated, of course. I guess Raahosh has never had that sort of experience.

Poor guy. Never to have a loving touch? A caress? Fooling around just for fun? He's missed out on so much. I feel like a bit of a dick suddenly for constantly pushing him away. I'm probably the culmination of a bajillion dreams for him and for me to turn him away has to hurt.

I'm starting to get an idea of how lonely his life has been . . . and what I must mean to him.

Suddenly, I want to make this good for him. It's no longer about distracting Raahosh so he'll stop teasing me. It's about making some heavy petting fun for him, too, so he can see that he's sexy and desirable and someone wants him after all.

"Do you trust me?" I ask him, placing my hand flat on his chest, over his heart. It's a safe spot, for all that it's rough and ridged there like the skin over his brows.

He hesitates for a moment and then nods, his jaw clenched.

"Then lay back," I say in a soft voice. "And let your mate pleasure you a little. It's all part of the human rituals of mating."

For a long moment, he tenses, and I think he's going to refuse me. Then, he turns and flings himself onto his back in the furs, his cock jutting into the air. He props up on his elbows so he can watch me, his eyes glimmering slits of intensity.

I'll need to go slow to make this last a bit. I rack my brain, trying to think of ways to extend an orgasm for a guy that's inexperienced. I'll just have to play it by ear. He'll get embarrassed if he blows his wad too quickly and blame himself, and I don't want that to happen.

So I put my hands on his thighs and wait. "Is this okay?"

He watches me with a hot gaze and, after a long, tense moment, nods.

"Can I explore you?"

His cock twitches, and more pre-cum beads on the head. As I watch, he grits his teeth and nods again.

Maybe I'd better take the edge off first. So I slide forward, pushing my arms against my sides so my breasts (while not impressive) push together. "I'm going to make you come," I tell him, dragging my nails down one thigh lightly. "And then I'm going to take my time with you. All right?"

"Do what you must." There's tension in his words. Poor thing. He's probably about to blow and feeling a bit awkward about it. My cootie continues purring like a mad thing, and his rumbles even louder when I lean forward.

I grip his length in my hand, and my fingers don't quite meet. That's . . . interesting. He's also hard and ridged along the top, and my thighs clench together again at the realization. He's not circumcised, and I grip him by his foreskin and then drag it over his cock as I pump him once.

He gasps, and then hot semen spatters over my hand, erupting from the big head of his cock. His body jerks, and I place my hand flat on his thigh again. "It's okay," I tell him, and then when he's gazing down at me, I lean in and lick the head of his cock clean of semen.

I've never been a big fan of the taste of cum—there's a bleachy sort of taste to it that I just can't get used to—but with the cootie adjusting my senses, there's no hard flavor to him, only a mild sort of musky taste that is actually . . . quite nice. It's a pleasure to lap at him and clean his cock, and his muffled groans and hisses of breath are making me feel pretty good, too.

When I'm done tonguing him clean, I look up and give his cock head another swipe with the tip of my tongue. "Can I play with you now?"

His nostrils flare and he inhales sharply, then nods.

"If you come again," I warn him, "it's all right. But I'll try and be gentle with you." I give him a wink as the look on his face turns incredulous.

Then I drag my fingers up and down his thighs, exploring the ways he's different than me. I'm your average girl—average height, average weight, average boobs. Raahosh, in comparison, is over seven feet of slate-gray muscle. There are the ridged plates on the sides of his big thighs, a line of ridges that goes all the way down his chest to where a happy trail would be if he had hair on his groin, and ridges on his arms and shoulders. I suspect if I ran my hand down the small of his back his spine would be ridged, too.

Of course, I have more interesting things to look at, like his junk. My hands slide back down to his cock. It's impossible to resist it, because the darn thing is just gorgeous. Long, thick, with a heavy, deep-blue crown, he feels more velvety here than anywhere else. His balls are an impressive size, his sac tight against his groin.

Blue balls. I giggle. Never has the phrase been more true.

He frowns and bats my exploring hands away.

"I wasn't laughing at you," I explain, biting my lip. "Just at a saying we have among humans about blue balls."

"What is the saying?" His breath rasps in his throat as I bend down and take him in my hand again, then begin to nibble up and down his shaft.

"It's not important." I drag my tongue down one thick vein and then back up over the bumpy ridges. "How does that feel?"

When he doesn't answer, I look up from my ministrations.

His glowing blue eyes pin me with an intense gaze. "Why are you stopping?"

I giggle. "Because I asked you a question?"

"It feels like . . . nothing I have experienced before." His voice is husky with need, and even as he says the words, more pre-cum beads on his cock.

"Good enough answer." I return to licking and nibbling on his length, figuring out which touches he likes. I seem to get the most reaction when I drag my teeth along his tender skin, or when I squeeze hard at the base of his cock.

So naturally, I do both quite a bit, until he's thrusting into my hand and there's sweat on his brow. His gaze hasn't moved from me and my ministrations, though. If another alien ship landed outside, I doubt he'd look away. He's utterly fascinated with my mouth.

I continue my exploration of his body with a few licks across the top of his shaft, the hard, ridged portion, and then move on to the thumb-like protrusion above it. "What do you call this again?"

"It is a spur."

"Is it like . . . a clit? Does it feel good if I touch it?" I drag my fingers over it experimentally. It feels different than his cock. Where his penis feels like velvet over hard muscle, his spur feels . . . strange. A bit like bone, but covered with skin and flesh. It doesn't deflate or grow any bigger when his cock does, and when I trace my fingers over it, Raahosh doesn't seem to react like he does when I lick his cock.

He shrugs. "Everything you do feels good."

"But this doesn't feel like . . . hmm. Like lightning strikes when I lick it?" I lean down and give it an experimental lick, watching his face.

His cock bobs in response. "Feels good," he murmurs.

But I want him going crazy. So I move to his cock, squeeze the head in my fist, and then lick the slit. "And that?"

Before I can even finish my sentence, he's bucking into my hand, panting. His eyes close and he falls back into the furs, groaning.

"Yeah, that feels better. Okay, good to know." I return to my licking and sucking of his cock, because it never hurts to stick with what a girl knows. I'm actually kinda glad that his spur isn't a major pleasure point, because I know how to work a cock. I don't know much of what to do with that. I suck on him for a moment more, and then an idea hits me. I lean down and tongue the base of his spur while working his cock with my hand.

His entire body jolts. Raahosh gives a shout, and then my hand is covered in hot, sticky cum as he crests once more.

I continue rubbing my tongue along the underside of his spur and he continues to come, his hips shuddering. I can tell he's doing his best not to move so he doesn't stab me with the thing, but I'm pleased that I made him come so hard. I lift my head and admire the cum shining on my fingers. "Guess you're sensitive there after all."

He stares at me for a long moment, and then grabs my hand. "I shouldn't have—"

"No?" I interrupt before he can get all moody on me. "You wanted to come in my mouth?"

Raahosh's nostrils flare again, the only sign of his acknowledgment of my words. Aww. He's shy. I give him a blissful smile and then yawn. "I'm gonna grab some of the water and clean us up, and then we can go back to bed. 'Kay?"

The purring in his chest—and mine—has gone to a low rumble. His cootie is sated for now. Mine, too. I'm surprised when he gets up, though, and caresses my cheek. "Wait here."

I do, and he returns a moment later with a small, soft pelt and the waterskin. He takes my hand in his, and with the water and the fur, cleans me free of his cum. It's a thoughtful gesture, and I can't help but watch with appreciation when he cleans himself off, too.

Even if I don't like the man a lot of the time, he's sure pretty to look at.

He puts the waterskin back in its place on the shelf and then returns to the bed. His cock is half-mast now—I don't know why I keep looking, but I do—and there's a softer expression on his hard face. He touches my cheek again. "Sleep now? We have an early day tomorrow."

I blink and suddenly realize how tired I am. I guess the post-endorphin glow is wearing off quickly. My cootie hums a song to his as I nod and lie back down in the furs. As soon as I lie down, he is at my side, and pulls me against him. My body nestles against his and he's warm, his arms hugging me to his body. He nuzzles my neck and his hand cups my breast.

I worry he's going to think too much of our fooling around. "This doesn't change anything, you know," I tell him. "I still haven't accepted you as my mate."

"More of your denials," he says in a smug voice. "Say what you want. I will play along with this courting ritual."

Gah.

Raahosh

Has any sa-khui hunter ever slept as well as I did last night? I wake up with my cock hard, pressed against the soft, tailless bottom of my sleepy human mate and know a contentment like none I've ever felt before. Liz mumbles something and burrows farther under the blankets, so I run a hand along her shoulder and back, admiring her soft human body.

The things she did with her mouth last night . . . my own mouth goes dry in remembrance. Surely those sorts of things are not done between mates? Maybe humans are more inventive. Whatever it is, I am glad for it—and for her. We must be reaching the end of the strange human courtship, and my cock aches to be sheathed deep inside her. Even now my khui begins to resonate at the very thought of her, and hers answers, singing in her chest.

I let her sleep for a few minutes more, and relieve myself outside of the cave, then return to stoke the coals of the fire. We will be out hunting for most of the day, but I want the fire pit to be warm for when we return, so I can make her a tasty broth out of bones. She's still pale and thin, my fragile human mate, and even with eating good raw meat and a strong khui inside her, she's still more delicate than I would like. I'll feed her like a sickly kit, then. Many hearty meals and lots of marrow-filled broths to make her cheeks flush with color.

Even if that color is a strange pink.

I put on my breechcloth and my boots, and shrug on my tunic. She will need to dress warmly if we will be out all day, and I will have to watch her closely. Liz is not the type that will admit if she cannot keep up. She will protest and snarl and demand, even if she is staggering with weakness.

I admire the strength of her will, but out in the wild, it is better to be safe. A cautious hunter is a successful one.

I kneel beside her sleeping form and pull the covers off. Her pale human body is all soft curves, the gentle swells of her ass calling for my touch. I admire her rounded thighs and the curve of one half-hidden breast, and imagine what delights she will show me tonight.

Perhaps she will welcome me into her cunt, protesting the entire time as part of her bizarre human rituals.

And I will be home.

I nudge her when she doesn't awaken. "Come, my mate. The hour grows late and we need to start the day."

She groans and rolls over in the blankets, offering me a tantalizing glimpse of her breasts and the thatch of soft fur between her legs. "Not your mate," she yawns. "Last night was just for funsies." Then she grabs the furs and pulls them back over her.

I scowl. Not this again? It doesn't matter if she took me into her body or not. Our khui have decided. She took me in her mouth and made me erupt. Of course we are mated. Irritated, I rip the blankets off and toss them aside. "If you are not my mate, then I do not need to be soft on you, do I? Get up or you will be welcoming a face full of snow, as I would any other lazy hunter."

Her eyes open and she scowls at me. "Seriously? Who peed in your cornflakes? You're in a foul mood."

"And you're being slow. Did you wish to hunt or shall I go without you?"

"I'm coming, I'm coming," she gripes, sitting up. "Dick."

"The song of my people?" I reply back to her, remembering her words.

"You got it."

Once Liz gets moving and out of bed, she picks up speed and I no longer have to wait on her. We bank the fire and leave the cave behind, and I begin to show her how a sa-khui hunter moves in the wild. If it was just me, I would tie a few branches to my tail and whisk them through the snow as I walk to cover my tracks. But because I am traveling with Liz, I want the tracks to remain, in case we get separated. I want her to be able to find her way back to the cave.

Also? She has no tail.

We move through the snow and Liz suggests something called snowshoes. She is smaller than I am and the larger snowdrifts go as high as her waist. At her suggestion, we head to the trees and get a few slim stalks so my mate can play around with her shoe concept when we return to the cave.

She's happy to be out and about. Her cheeks are ruddy, but her eyes are glowing bright and there's a smile on her face. She's proud when she demonstrates her bow, too. I sit on my haunches and watch her practice a few shots. It's a strange weapon, a bit like a sling that fires darts instead of stones. She pulls on the string to launch her darts, and mutters unhappily when it falls a few feet away. She makes some adjustments to the bow itself and adjusts the tiny feathers in the fletching, and then tries again, and this time she's able to hit a tree with some speed a short distance away.

I'm impressed. "It's an interesting weapon. You are quite clever."

She beams at me. "I used to hunt with a bow all the time as a teenager. This isn't quite the same, and I'm having to adjust as I go, but it's close. I think I can get it to work." Liz pats her waist. "Now I need to make an arrow pouch to go here."

I nod. "I can help you with that when we get back."

She bites her lip, happiness on her face, and my khui begins to sing. She's beautiful, even with her flat, strange human features. Her khui responds to mine, and her smile falters a little.

Ah yes. More of the strange human rituals. Denying a mating. I ignore it and gesture at the twin suns, now high in the skies. "Are you ready to hunt then? We can head to the water."

"Water?" She brightens. "Is it another heated stream? I could use a bath." She lifts her tunic and wrinkles her nose. "I'm a little sweaty."

Her scent is like perfume to me, but I shrug. "We can bathe, or we can hunt."

"Let's hunt. Maybe we can bathe later tonight?" Her expression is innocent. "If we catch something, I might even let you wash my back."

I will find her the slowest, most sluggish creature in all the snows so she may fill it with her darts.

Liz

Hunting with Raahosh is kinda fun. The air is crisp, and even though the snow is heavy, the twin suns are shining and it feels good to get out and explore. I've been cooped up too long in that cave. Raahosh isn't the most patient of men, but I can hold my own. My bow is a work in progress, but I'm confident I can get it to work after a few test shots.

"There," Raahosh says as we crest a craggy hill. He pulls a strand of hair from his head and releases it, checking if we're upwind or not. He grunts and then gestures over the horizon. "Do you see the tracks?"

I squint. "How the hell can you see anything from this far away?"

He grabs my chin and tips it down. "You're not looking at the snow."

I pull away from him and peer down over the ridge. Sure enough, there are tracks in the snow. They head off over the next crest. "So we're heading in the right direction?"

"We are," he agrees. "You look at the snow . . . or you can follow your nose."

"My nose?"

"The smell of the water that comes heated from the earth."

I sniff and he's right—there's a faint whiff of rotten eggs in the air, which means there's water nearby. "Gotcha."

He arches one heavy brow at me, which is impressive because his forehead is damn near unmovable with all that plating. "What kind of hunting did your father show you?"

"If that's a crack aimed at my dead father, I will kick your ass—"

He reaches for my chin again and tips my head toward him before I swat his hand away. His hard mouth is curled at the edges in amusement. "So defensive. I meant nothing by it. Your weapons are different. I assumed you had different hunting methods."

Oh. I relax a little. "Well, my daddy owned some land out in the sticks. He had a deer blind and we'd set up near the trails." I sketch out to him with words what a deer blind is, and he nods understanding. "And then, of course, there's the deer corn or the salt lick."

"Deer corn?"

"Yeah, you kinda feed them in the same spot every day and stuff. Then when they're nice and fat and used to handouts, they come to you instead of chasing them down."

He grunts acknowledgment and then shields a hand over his eyes, gazing down at the snow. "We have kits that do that to a few two-fangs back at the home caves. But we call those creatures 'pets.'"

"Hey," I say defensively, thwapping him on the arm. "Not every family can afford a freezer full of fresh meat, you know.

You do what you have to in order to survive, Mister Judgey." Of course, I remember saying the same thing to my father back when I was younger. Pot, kettle and all that. "If it puts food on the table, it's hunting."

"Wise words," he says. "But now you must learn to track."

He's right, of course. "Lead on, O wise one."

We cross over the hills and I slog through the snow, following him. About fifty yards away, I see the bubbling pool of water, bright blue against the snow. Which is great . . . except that there's a cliff about five feet ahead of us, and it's a sheer drop for at least twenty or thirty feet. Drinking at the water is a shaggy, pony-like creature that looks like a cross between Bambi and a sheepdog.

"Dvisti," Raahosh says.

"Okey-doke. Looks like good eating." I pull up my bow and nock an arrow, then aim. The wind is against me, and we're pretty far away. I'm still not used to the pull on the bow and my needle-like bone arrows are iffy at best. "I don't think I can hit him from here. How do we get down there?"

"Wait here," he tells me, straightening. "I'll find a path down." Raahosh saunters away, spear in hand, and I might ogle his ass a bit.

Just a bit.

I relax my arrow and glance down at the creature, watching it to see if it leaves. I'm so intent on watching it, that I almost miss the *chirrup* I hear from behind me. But then it happens again.

I glance over my shoulder.

There's a friggin' Ewok. Ohmigod.

Okay, so it's not really an Ewok. It's a fuzzy thing that looks more like an overgrown Furby with long arms and legs, but the round eyes blinking at me are adorable. It chirrups again and then dashes forward a step or two, then moves back. It blinks at me, then repeats the motion and runs in a circle.

Is this a game? For all of its hair and beaky face, it looks young. Maybe it's the big, liquid eyes. When it *chirrups* at me again, the hairs on the back of my neck prickle.

This might be bad. Like, finding a happy, roly-poly bear cub bad, only to realize that Mommy bear is a few feet away. "Raahosh? You still here?"

It cocks its head and scampers away, and I slowly replace my arrow back into firing position. The chirrup sounds again—

And then is repeated by another creature's deeper voice. And another. And another. As I gaze out at the snowy ridges behind me, they seem to emerge from everywhere. More of the tall, furry creatures with dirty, matted hair and bulging eyes.

I was right. This one's a baby. The others don't look nearly as friendly.

"Raahosh?" I call again, raising my arrow as one of the biggest ones moves toward me. "Help?"

"Liz," Raahosh says in a low voice, off to my side. I look over at him, heart pounding, and see he's several feet away, spear at the ready. He's in a stare-down with three big, nasty versions of the things. He doesn't look over at me, and his stance is one of battle. He's ready to attack the moment anyone moves a muscle.

"What are these?" I hiss. One takes another step forward, and I step backward, only to remember that I'm on the edge of a cliff. Shit. Shit. Shit.

"They are metlaks. And where there is one, there is a hundred."

"Well, I see a hundred," I say, exaggerating a bit. Just a bit. There's probably only two dozen or so. Gee. That's all.

"My mate," Raahosh says in a low voice. "When I say run, you must run. Do not argue."

What is he talking about? Is he going to distract them so I can run away? "What? No! I—"

"Liz," he says again, warningly. I look over and his hand clenches on his spear. "Do not argue with me. Now—go!" With that, he gives a battle cry and surges forward.

Fuck that noise. I aim my first arrow and let it fly just as the first creature opens its mouth and lunges at me with a snarl.

PART FOUR

PART FOUR

Raahosh

The scene before me is something out of my worst nightmares. Liz's small form stands on the edge of the cliff, her strange weapon clenched in her hands. Metlaks—the wild, unpredictable creatures—surround her. I have seen them tear a hunter limb from limb in a matter of seconds, and I have seen them walk past another as if he did not exist. They are impossible to understand, and savage when provoked.

And a cub stands near Liz's leg, which definitely counts as provoking.

"Run," I command her again, but the stubborn woman doesn't listen. Instead, she raises one of her bone-sliver arrows and aims, waiting. A protective fury comes over me when one of the metlaks bares its big, yellow teeth in my direction. They think to hurt my mate? To take her from me after waiting for so long? I will snap their bones and crush their filthy pelts under my boot before I let them touch her. A feral snarl escapes my throat and I pull one of my deadly bone knives free from its casing, my spear in my other hand.

Liz takes another step backward, ever closer to the edge of the cliff. My heart hammers in my breast, and a wave of pure fear moves over me.

"Liz," I bark out as one of the metlaks prowls toward her. "Run past me. Go *now*. I will distract them. Quickly!"

"I'm not leaving you," she calls out, not looking away from the metlak closest to her.

"Don't be foolish," I growl as it paces ever closer to her. Two more steps and he'll be able to reach her with his long arms. She needs to move fast. "Come, Liz—"

My heart stops as it lunges for her. I cry out and surge forward, my spear flying. It flies through the air and slams into the side of the metlak reaching for my precious mate. It staggers and then falls forward, still reaching for her. I cry out in anger and storm through the snow, moving to stand in front of her.

Another creature bellows and begins to beat on its chest, sending a furious call forth across the snows. The other metlaks respond, and one charges forward. I've seen these tactics before. They will rush us to the edge of the cliff and pick off our carcasses later, once they know we are dead. I refuse to fall back.

Ssssthok.

One of Liz's bone needles flies past and appears in the eye socket of one of the bigger males. It groans and falls into the snow, twitching. Her shot is beautiful, and I see the potential for the weapon.

"Watch your arm," she calls to me as she raises another arrow and aims it. When another metlak leaps for us, she shoots again, and again her bone needle hits its mark. The metlak is dead before it can hit the ground.

It is a thing of beauty to see, and fierce pride in my mate surges inside me.

Then, the remaining metlaks scream and charge forward all at once.

My instincts honed from years of hunting, my need to protect fierce within me, I surge forward with a yell of my own. I hear Liz gasp, but it only encourages my ferocity.

They will not get near her. They will have to storm over my dead carcass first.

I launch into the first one with a fury, my bone blade slicing against its wooly neck with such ferocity that it's nearly severed. I lunge for the next, and instead of fighting me, it ducks away. Another lands on my back, pulling at my hair and clothing. Sharp teeth sink into my shoulder and I hear Liz scream. I jam my knife into the one in front of me, even as the one on my back slides to the ground. I look down and see another one of Liz's thin bone arrows jutting from its throat.

"I've only got the one left," she cries out behind me, even as two more jump onto me and a third attacks from the front. One on one, they would be no problem. But metlaks are savage, ripping creatures. Already their claws and teeth are sinking into my skin, tearing at me. I growl with pain when one slashes across my face, and blood veils my sight. "Raahosh!" she cries from a distance. "You're moving too close to the ledge! I—hey! Get back!" Her warning voice changes to one of fear, and I snarl and turn toward her. Three are heading for her, pacing in her direction, their large teeth bared. The one on my back bites at my neck furiously, and I feel shock waves go through my arm even as my blade sinks into the chest of another.

Must save my mate.

The thought rings in my head over and over again.

Must save Liz.

She is everything.

With a brutal cry, I grab the two metlaks in front of me. My fingers sink into fistfuls of shaggy fur and I pitch toward the cliff.

"Raahosh! Look out!" she cries.

But she does not realize my plan until too late. I hear Liz's scream of anguish as I topple over the side of the cliff, taking five of the brutal creatures with me.

I will even the odds this way. Maybe she can escape the two or three left.

The memory of Liz's face swims before my mind moments before I hit the ground with a sickening crunch, and all goes dark.

Liz

I scream in horror as Raahosh's long body goes flying over the edge of the cliff, several of the creatures flying over with him. I rush to the side where he went over and look down. It's at least a thirty-foot drop and Raahosh is on his back, crumpled in the snow. One of his legs is at an odd angle and he lies atop a dead metlak. The others are strewn around him, not moving, and the snow is spattered with blood. I can't tell if he's alive or dead.

I can't be alone out here. I can't.

I can't lose him.

Hot panic rushes through me. I only have one arrow left and there's three of the creatures remaining, along with the young one that still frolics and plays in the snow as if this is all a game. I don't know what to do. They continue to advance and I see wicked claws tipping each finger, and their Furby-like faces look more and more ominous as they approach.

And they killed Raahosh. These fucking *dicks*.

My last arrow trembles in my hand and then I get an idea. I fling my bow aside and grab the metlak youngling as it frolics close, and I jam the arrow under its jaw and pin it against my body. A hostage is the only chance I have—but I don't know if the creatures are smart enough to realize what a hostage situation is. They look vaguely human-like, but I could be all wrong. They could just stare at me and then come and rip my throat out anyhow.

But they cry out and stop when I grab the young one. It wriggles and squirms in my arms, and its claws sink into my arms, but I hold the arrow against its jaw, grimly determined. I take a step to the side, and they watch me, their eyes wild. They make weird crooning noises in their throats, and the one in my grip responds.

This . . . might work.

I glance over the edge of the ledge, desperate for a way down. I have to get to Raahosh. Have to. In my head, if I can get to him, I can save him. Let him know that I don't really hate him, that I'm just confused and unhappy, but that his smiles make the world not so bad . . .

I pace against the edge, watching the other metlak-things as I creep around the cliff, looking for the way down. I spy something that looks like a footpath and head toward it, my hostage squirming and clawing in my scratch-covered arms. I look at the others, to see if they're staying back. They hunch in the snow, watching me with predatory eyes. "Raahosh," I call out, hoping he'll answer and is fine, and my eyes are just mistaking things. But there's nothing but silence.

I call his name desperately again as I slide down the steep path. "*Raahosh!* Please! Answer me!"

The "path" gives out a short distance from the bottom and both I and my captive tumble the last few feet to the ground, only to land in thick snow. The breath is knocked from my lungs and I pant, flat on my back. Next to me, my captive gets up and darts away, heading away from the cliff instead of back toward its parents. It disappears over another snowbank and I consider going after it, but pick myself up and grab my lone arrow and then rush to Raahosh's side.

"Raahosh?" I press my hand to his chest. There's blood tingeing his mouth and his eyes are closed. There's a small puddle of blood where his head was and a sob escapes me at the sight of it. I press against the armored skin over his heart and hear it beating, slow and steady.

Oh, thank God. For a moment, I want to fling my arms around his big blue neck and cry my brains out, but I look up the cliff, my arrow clutched in hand, waiting to see if the others are coming down after me and the child.

But there's nothing. For several minutes, there's nothing and I sit alert at Raahosh's side, waiting. I can keep waiting, or I can help him. I focus on the fallen man at my side. I run my hands over him, trembling, trying to assess the damage. His leg is at an odd angle, and his breathing is shallow, but I can't tell if he's broken ribs or worse. I try not to think about that. His cootie starts up at my touch, and I hope that's a good sign. "I'm going to get you out of here," I whisper to his unconscious body. "You can count on me. It's going to be all right."

I wish he'd wake up and smile at me. Or frown. Or something. But he's so still.

One of the metlaks twitches and makes a wounded sound. I gasp and turn to it, my hands scrambling to find a weapon. The only thing I have is my last arrow, and my bow was left atop the ridge.

But it's not getting up. It makes a pitiful cry and jerks on the ground, as if trying to get itself up but can't. Its hips are at an odd angle, and as I look around, I see another metlak is moving, just a little. I look at the top of the ridge to see if the others are going to return, but there's no sign of them.

I think these wounded ones have been left for dead.

My heart gives an uncomfortable little squeeze. Even I wouldn't wish this kind of pain on our attackers. The sounds they're making are horrible, and I glance around and spy Raahosh's bone blade a short distance away. I grab it and stand over one of the wounded creatures. There are five of them in total, but only two are moving. I don't know that it was a big enough fall to kill them, and I don't know what I'll do if they wake up and attack again.

I'm low on options. So I kneel beside the first one. "I'm sorry," I say, and cut its throat. I remind myself that it's a mercy killing. That it's kill or be killed out here, and that it's wounded beyond its ability to get up and limp home. It still doesn't make me feel any better. It was easier to do this when they were attacking and there was no time to think or process. I move to the next creature. It's unmoving, but I cut its throat anyhow, just to be sure. By the time I finish the last one, I'm spattered in blood and crying.

I move to Raahosh's side and touch my fingers to his cheek. Does he feel cool? Oh God. I don't know what to do. "Please don't die on me, Raahosh. Please, please." I lean over him and give in to girly tears for a bit longer, sobbing. Then, I sit up and wipe my eyes, because tears won't make it magically better.

I have to get him home to our cave.

"Okay, think, Liz," I tell myself, and glance around, sniffing. "You have a big honking alien you can't carry and can't walk, and you need to get him home."

I look over at Raahosh and wonder if my cootie has made me stronger. Can I drag him? Our home cave is up the cliff and a few miles away, but there's got to be a way back up that doesn't involve the shitty footpath I came down. There has to be another way around. I just have to find it. I stand up and examine Raahosh, then grab his arm and tentatively tug on it.

The fucker is heavy. I pull harder, trying to move him. He makes a low groan of pain and I immediately stop. "Shit. Sorry!" I examine his other arm to see if it's any better and I can see the bones sticking out of a break near his wrist. Fuck. I can't tug on that one. It's just as well, because that test-tug only told me that he was super heavy.

I need a better way.

Desperate, I look around. In the distance are the pink, whippy trees that bend and move with the breeze, and I grab Raahosh's bone knife and head for them, an idea in my head. When my dad shot a deer, we'd normally tie the legs to a pole and then shoulder it, but there's no one to hold the other shoulder for me this time. One time, though, I was being a whiny kid and my dad got pissed and made himself a travois out of two branches and a tarp, and dragged the deer home behind him while I blubbered at his side.

God bless me being a shitty kid. I can make a travois and drag Raahosh home.

It takes me nearly an hour to chop down one of the flimsy trees, but they'll suit my purpose just fine. The "trunk" is big enough for me to grip comfortably, and even though it's sticky and spongy to the touch, I should be able to carry it just fine. I chop down another, and by the time I drag them back to Raahosh, I'm trembling with exhaustion and I worry I've ruined his bone knife by dulling it.

There's no time to worry about that, though, because a fine snow is now falling and the skies are overcast. If I don't get Raahosh home, we're going to be in deep shit. So I kneel to the ground and shrug off the warm cloak he gave me this morning, and begin to tie it down to the poles to make the base of the travois. I use some of the ties on my leggings to tie the cloak down, and by the time I'm done, I'm shivering in the cold, my clothing is wrecked and half gone, and the snow is coming down in a thick blanket.

"Raahosh?" I call softly, tapping his cheek to see if he's awake. No response. In a way, I'm glad. This will hurt less if he's unconscious. With an apology in my brain, I grab his good arm and drag/roll him toward the travois. He groans with pain but doesn't rouse.

I grab the poles, clench the knife between my teeth, and begin to drag my makeshift travois after me. Fuck. It's heavy, but I'm out of options. I'll just have to suck it up. We can't stay here. I bite my lip and begin the long, slow, drag home.

It takes me hours to find the way out of the canyon, but once I do, I'm able to see the remainder of our footprints as dips in the falling snow, and the glacier's in the distance. I can make it home. I can. My fingers feel like bricks of ice and I have blisters on my hands, but there's a light at the end of the tunnel.

As I give the travois another tug, Raahosh groans. I gasp and set it down gently, then rush to his side. "Raahosh? Are you awake?"

His head tosses, and then he gazes at me with a pain-glazed stare. I'm not entirely sure he's aware of where he is. "Liz," he breathes, and tries to reach for me with his hand. His face contorts in agony and he falls back against the travois.

"Don't move," I tell him. "I'm getting you out of here. It's going to be fine."

"Leave . . . me . . ." he pants. "I am too wounded."

"Bullshit," I tell him, though he's voicing my worst fears. "You're fine! You just need to rest and recover for a few days. Let the cootie do its work!"

"You're . . . not . . . safe." His eyes slide closed again.

"I'm fine," I bellow a little louder than I need to. I lean forward and grab Raahosh by the collar. "Are you listening to me? I'm fine, and you're going to be fine. Don't you die on me!" He doesn't answer, and I panic a little. I shake him, eliciting another wounded groan from him. I don't care. If he's groaning, he's alive. "Don't you fucking leave me, Raahosh." I release him and smooth his clothing down, then lean in, putting my hand over his chest. His khui vibrates at my touch, and I decide bribery is the best weapon I have. I place my mouth close to his ear. "If you come out of this alive, Raahosh, I'll fuck the hell out of you, so help me God."

Raahosh

My mind is a blur of red pain and black dreams. Sometimes my khui resonates in my chest, and everything feels better. Sometimes there is a jolt of dark pain, and I sink further into the blackness. I need to focus, to concentrate, but my mind won't stay alert.

But I have to, I remind myself. I must protect Liz.

"Liz," I breathe. "My mate."

"I'm here," a soft voice says in the darkness. Tender fingers brush my cheek, and I fight against the tide of pain that threatens to pull me under. My eyelids feel as if someone is sitting on them, they are so heavy. "Relax," she says, her breath sweet. I feel her lips kiss my cheek, and then she caresses me again. "You're safe. Just heal, okay?"

I lick my dry lips. "Metlaks—"

"Taken care of. I've got a fire and meat drying, and I've re-sharpened your knife." Her hands smooth down my chest and my arms, and I feel a fiery bolt of pain surge as she does. A hiss of breath escapes my throat. "You're healing well. Really fast, actually. I had to set your bones. I'm sorry. I know it must hurt. Just relax, okay?"

My khui thrums in my chest, and I hear hers respond. Even though I am grievously injured and awash in pain, my cock stirs in response. We are taking too long to answer the call of the resonance, and my body reminds me that we must obey soon. "Do not leave me . . ."

"I won't," she says in a soft voice. "Just live. Sleep." Her fingers brush over my lips. "Sleep," she repeats again.

And I do.

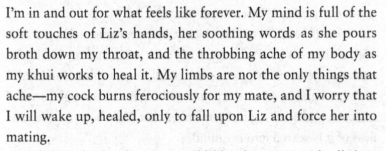

I'm in and out for what feels like forever. My mind is full of the soft touches of Liz's hands, her soothing words as she pours broth down my throat, and the throbbing ache of my body as my khui works to heal it. My limbs are not the only things that ache—my cock burns ferociously for my mate, and I worry that I will wake up, healed, only to fall upon Liz and force her into mating.

I do not think a human would like that. Not with all their rituals of denial.

But my choices are not my own. My body must have time and rest to heal, and so I slip in and out between dreams.

At one point, I wake up, surprisingly clear-headed. There is an ache in my body like a rotten tooth, lingering but not overly painful. I'm able to open my eyes without it feeling a chore, though, and I look over to the fire.

Liz is there, my leather tea-pouch boiling over a tripod placed over the fire. She sharpens my knife against a rock, and as I look over, I see strips of dried meat hanging from a net of woven reeds placed against the wall. Her bow—no, a new one—is placed against the far wall, and a companion to it lies unstrung nearby.

My mouth feels as if it is leather. I lick my lips and try to sit up, thirsty. I am weak, and my khui throbs and hums with hunger.

Liz looks over at me with surprise. "Raahosh!" She moves over to me and puts a hand on my chest. "Don't get up. Seriously. You're still weak."

I ignore her fussing and sit upright, testing my body. It aches but nothing grates out of place in my chest. I lift one hand and flex it. There's hot pain in it, but it is straight, a makeshift splint around it.

"I had to set the bones," Liz explains, tucking blankets around my body. "Does it feel okay?"

"You did well," I tell her thickly. Her nearness makes me ache with a different kind of hunger. My cock aches and my khui resonates as she leans in to press her small fingers to my forehead. I grab her hand and kiss the palm, wishing it was wrapped around my cock and stroking it. I remember that from before—the rawness of it is seared into my mind.

"Are you thirsty? Hungry?" she asks, her eyes wide and searching. She pulls her hand from my grip and gets up, moving toward the fire. "I made you some broth. You need to keep your strength up."

When she brings the small cup of broth to me, the scent of her warm skin is more appealing than the drink. She lifts her arm to hold the cup to my mouth, and I caress her round, lovely breast through her clothing. Liz trembles and my khui resonates in time with hers. "I see you're feeling better," she says in a shaky voice, and pushes my hand away. "No hanky-panky right now."

"Hankeepahnkee?" I ask. I do not know what this word is. Nor do I particularly care. Liz's hair is braided back from her face, displaying her beautiful neck, and I want to bury my face there. I want her small body against mine, to feel her heart beating, to scent her arousal and touch her and claim her.

"That's right," she says, and her voice is breathless. I hear her khui resonating in her chest. "It's not the time right now. You're not really well yet."

My fingers brush her cheek, touch her jaw, her throat. I touch her everywhere I can before she moves away, even as she puts the cup to my lips and forces me to drink. When she pulls it back, I lean my head against the cave wall, my eyes closed. I'm tired, but touching her is making me feel better.

She puts the cup aside and peels the blankets off my legs. I hear a muffled snort. "Well, it seems part of you is working just fine," she says.

I open my eyes and glance down. My cock is at attention, thrusting up from my body. It aches, and for a hopeful moment, I think she will take it in her soft human mouth again and tongue it. It is not to be, though. Liz is all business and checks my bandages, clucking at my wounds. "You're on the mend, but still not better."

"My khui does not care," I tell her. She's bent over and her face is close to my cock even as she fusses over my bandages. "It wants me to claim you."

She makes a humming sound in her throat, but I can't tell if it's agreement or not. "Tell your khui now is not the time."

I watch her as she gets up and moves about the cave. Her body is graceful and lean under the shapeless leathers, and her eyes are bright. She smells like the richest honey, and my senses are starved for her. I shift in my pallet. "I recall . . . a promise you made."

Her face flushes and she moves toward the fire, tucking one of her braids behind an ear. "When you're better, I intend to keep my promise. But for now you need to sleep." She rubs one of her eyes and I realize that she's got dark rings on her pale skin. She looks hollow and tired herself. Her clothing is dirty and ragged, and her hair has not been washed in many days. She's thin, too, like when she was sick before.

"How long have you been caring for me?" I ask, humbled. While I have been lying here sleeping, letting my khui heal itself slowly, she has been hard at work.

She moves to the wall of the cave and touches it, and I see hash marks chalked onto the stone. "Nine days," she counts, then picks up a chalky stone and adds another mark. "Ten, really."

No wonder my body is reacting to her nearness. I've never heard of a couple avoiding a resonance mating for this long. I also wonder if this has to do with how long it is taking my body to heal. With the healer Maylak's help, a break can be healed in a matter of days. If I have been mostly unconscious for nine, I worry that my khui is overtaxed and unsatisfied.

Soon, it will stop asking and start demanding. I wonder if Liz realizes this.

***

Now that I am conscious again, my khui has decided it must claim Liz, and must claim her now. It does not matter that my body is yet healing, or that Liz is exhausted. All that matters is the mating the khui demands. Liz resonates every time she gets near me, and sometimes when she returns to the cave, she smells of sex on her hands, as if she has pleasured herself. I know she is not unaffected by the need between us. She must be hiding her desires, thinking my body more fragile than it truly is.

The only thing that is fragile is my control.

Every night, she curls up against me, exhausted from a day of hunting and tending the fire, and then tending to me. She tenderly bathes me and feeds me chunks of dried meat from kills she has made. All the while, she is busy making weapons or melting more water or emptying out my piss-pot, since she insists I need to stay off my leg.

It is becoming impossible to resist her. When she moves past me, I reach for her automatically. When her body fits itself against mine in bed, it takes every ounce of strength I have not to push her to the ground and fuck her.

And when she comes back with her hands smelling like her sweet cunt? I must close my eyes and remind myself that control will win my human, not brute strength.

But control only goes so far, and I worry it will flow through my hands like water.

Liz

It's a lot of work to rough it and take care of Raahosh. The day seems like a never-ending list of chores. Clean cave, bathe Raahosh, shake out blankets, melt water for drinking, eat, check traps, smoke extra meat, melt more water, fix weapons, tend to Raahosh, melt even more water, and so on and so on. Raahosh is a terrible patient, too. He's healing faster than anything I've ever seen, and I suspect that's the cootie's work. Too bad it's not helping his mood any. He's grabby despite his injuries, and cranky when I push his hands away. He's healing, which means fooling around is a terrible idea, no matter how good it sounds to me.

Truth is, I'm indescribably horny.

I've never felt this way in my life—like I need to jump Raahosh's bones or I'll die. But Raahosh's bones are newly mending, and I just can't. He needs to save his strength. And truth is, I'm tired and I don't feel very pretty. I'm grimy and sweaty from all the work I've been doing around camp, and my leather clothing is stained with Raahosh's blood, mine, and the metlaks I killed, along with the game I've been hunting.

But this afternoon, it's snowing fiercely and there's plenty of fuel for the fire. There's dried meat for dinner and Raahosh is napping in the blankets, his long legs sprawled in the furs. He watches me sometimes and then pretends to sleep. Right now, though, I think he's truly asleep. I scratch at my itchy scalp, and my tightly braided hair feels dirty. I look at the fire and wonder if I can have myself a quick hot sponge bath while he's resting.

As soon as the idea enters my mind, I'm all for it. I fill the cooking skin with snow, and when it melts, add more handfuls of snow until there's a good amount heating over the fire. I find the soapy berries that Raahosh explained to me were for cleaning and not eating, and smash a few of them between my fingers and add them to the water. While it heats up, I strip my leathers off and stretch near the fire.

I stay clothed around Raahosh, mostly because I don't want to tempt him. It's not that I don't want to have sex with him anymore. Nearly losing him made me realize that, okay, yes, I do want to have hot, nasty sex with the man—er, alien. I was only torturing myself by denying it. I'm not sure I'm ready to deal with the "mates" and "babies" aspect, but one thing at a time, and right now I'm fixated on sex. Sex, sex, sex. Masturbating quietly outside the cave hasn't been scratching the itch, and I can hardly wait for the man to start walking around so I can jump his ass.

Metaphorically speaking, of course.

But while we're in physical denial, a nice quick sponge bath sounds awesome. I take a tiny bit of rabbit-ish fur and dip it in the warm water and then begin to bathe myself. Grime streaks off of my arms as I do, and I bite back a moan of pleasure. My sponge bath feels amazing already. Quickly, I wash my body, running the fur over my skin, across the back of my neck, and under my arms. My breasts are sensitive and I whimper when the wet fur glides over them. I'm half-dreading, half-anticipating how it'll feel to wash my girl parts. When I get to that section, though, I screw my face up and give it a quick, vigorous wash, trying not to touch myself more than I need to. No sense in getting worked up only to have zero release. I dunk the bit of fur and then start to wring the water out into my braids, wetting them in the hopes of cleaning my hair a bit. When it feels a little cleaner, I squeeze my braids to remove the excess water and then all that's left are my legs.

I bend over to swipe at my calves.

Warm hands grip my ass, startling me. "Raahosh?" I glance over my shoulder to see him press his mouth against my hip, the look on his face one of sheer and utter bliss. He's naked—he's been naked and in bed for days. And he's completely aroused.

And my pulse goes wild, as does my cootie.

"You shouldn't be up," I tell him, sounding as breathless as I feel.

He presses kisses on my damp hip, and his hand slides up the inside of my thigh. "I can smell your arousal, mate. Can smell it on your hands when you return to the cave. Do you think I do not notice?"

A hot blush steals over my cheeks. "I was, um, keeping things under control."

"I have no control where you are concerned," he murmurs, nipping at my skin with those long, inhuman fangs. I have no idea why the sight of them gets me so hot, but it does. Damn, does it ever.

"You're not feeling well—"

"My greatest ache has nothing to do with bones," he says, and his fingers brush over the folds of my sex, insistent.

A whimper escapes me.

"Bend over." His breath tickles my leg. "I would taste my mate."

I clutch the bit of wet fur I've been using as a washcloth, and then toss it aside. My entire body is flushed with heat, and while part of my brain is screaming that I shouldn't give in to what the alien wants, my cootie's humming a delicious song in time with his, and I'm so full of need that I could crawl out of my own skin. So I slowly reach down and put my hands on the backs of my calves, like I'm in gym class and stretching. Except I'm naked, so naked, and turned on.

I feel Raahosh spread my cheeks and then his mouth is on my sex, tonguing with a ravenous ferocity that makes my knees weak. I cry out and immediately stumble forward, too close to the fire. Only his strong arm around my thighs keeps me from tumbling in. Instead, he swings me around until I'm facing the blankets, and then he pushes me forward, his arm still locked around my thighs. It forces me into the furs, my cheek moving to the floor, and my ass is in the air.

And still, he devours me with single-minded intensity. My toes curl and cries escape my throat as his tongue, bumpy and thick, spears me deep inside my core. Oh fuck. This is too much for me to handle. It feels too good.

He groans and pauses, and I catch my breath. "So sweet." That's the only warning I get before he dives in again, and my legs tense with the aching need of it all. Oh God. I am *this* close to coming already, and all he's done is slam his face into my pussy and start licking. Of course, the visual of that makes me crazy, and I squirm against his mouth, bucking backward and trying to ride his face.

"Mine," he growls into my flesh, and then thrusts his tongue into me again.

I scream and fist my hands in the furs as I come, my legs tight with the orgasm ripping through me. I feel my body spasm with the force of my orgasm, and wetness floods between my legs.

It makes Raahosh lose his mind. He snarls and then grabs my hips again. Before I can breathe, he has me flipped to my back, and my legs are in the air. He takes his cock in his hand and then he thrusts into me.

And I scream again. It feels as if I've been hollowed out from the inside, he's so big. It feels downright amazing. I've had sex before but I've never felt every inch of a man as he was inside me. Normally it just feels vaguely full.

This feels like intensity. I can feel every ridge of his cock, every rough bump, every vein. And I for damn sure feel the spur above his cock. The moment he thrust inside me, it slid between my pussy lips and brushed against my clit, gliding like another finger.

I'm overwhelmed with sensation.

He freezes over me, his glowing eyes narrowing as he gazes down at me. He's utterly still, not even breathing. I can't read his expression.

"Liz?" He asks. "Did I . . . are you hurt?" His hand drags over his mouth, and I realize the carefully veiled expression on his face is hiding worry.

"I'm good," I tell him, and lift my hips. "Please, don't stop."

He growls low in his throat and the feral look returns to his face. He leans forward and plants a hand on my hips, and then he slams deep into me again.

And I cry out once more because, God, how can I not? It feels like he's fucking me inside out. It's the most amazing thing I've ever felt. His hair is hanging close to my face and I grab it by the fistful, holding on to him as roughly as he's holding on to me. "Don't fucking stop," I snarl back at him. "Don't ever stop!"

His nostrils flare, and then Raahosh hammers into me harder than ever. I'm screaming as I come, yanking on his hair, and raising my hips to meet his eager thrusts. It's like my orgasm that I had a few moments ago never went away. It just keeps rolling through me, and I scream and scream as it goes on and on. With every thrust, Raahosh's spur drags against my clit, and I feel as if I'm coming apart at the seams. I can't handle this much pleasure. I can't.

Raahosh's body jerks, and for a moment, I think he's going to complain about his knee or a muscle cramp, the look on his face is so utterly surprised. But then his breath hisses from his tight lips, his body jerks, and I realize he's come, too.

Raahosh

I am utterly reborn.

Every muscle in my body, every tendon, every organ—it no longer belongs to Raahosh. It is all Liz's to dispose of. I am completely and utterly hers.

I collapse on top of my mate, spent from our furious coupling. It hasn't been very long at all, and my cock is still twitching despite the fact that it's buried deep inside her, and I've come. But the resonance isn't going away. If anything, it's growing stronger with each passing moment, our khui united in a song.

Liz's hands slide from my hair and she grimaces at the sight of the long strands on her fingers. "I . . . might have pulled out a handful or two. I'm sorry." She offers it back to me.

I take the strands of hair and toss them aside. "I have more." She can pull it all out if she likes. I care not. I just want to remain buried inside her. I roll on my side and tuck her against my body, pressing her face to my chest. I have never felt so . . . much.

She is mine. All mine. Even now, she is full of my seed. I can feel her cunt gripping me tight, hot spasms working through her body. She gives a little gasp with each one, and I suspect they are pleasurable for her. I stroke a hand over her pale braids, wet from her bath. "My mate," I murmur. "My Liz."

My human makes a little sound that is half moan, half sigh, all pleasure. She nuzzles against my chest and her hand strokes down my arm. I do the same to her, enjoying the difference in textures of our bodies. She does not have the soft fuzz that covers my people. Human skin is different, but . . . I enjoy it. It feels decadent to the touch, and it reminds me of licking inside her smooth cunt.

It is a good memory, and it's something I want to do again, immediately. My fingers move to the base of my cock, still seated deep inside her, and I run my fingers along the edges of her opening, where she is gripping me tight deep inside her. Her folds are stretched taut.

She sucks in a breath. "What . . ."

"I like the feel of you when I'm inside you," I tell her, and her face colors even brighter red under her warm flush. "You are stretched wide to accommodate me."

"Braggart," she says in a teasing tone, and her hand trails down my chest thoughtfully. "We probably did that all wrong, by the way."

"We did?" I'm shocked that I've somehow displeased her. "Is there a human ritual that I have missed?"

She chuckles and her finger trails over one of my pectorals, then flicks my nipple. "Not exactly, unless you call foreplay a ritual." She shifts, and I feel every muscle in her body against my cock. I inhale sharply, because I'm ready to claim my mate again but she's talking, so I try to pay attention. "Most of the time," she continues, "women want to be wooed into sex."

Wooed into sex? I do not understand. She was screaming for

me. I can still taste the wet arousal of her on my tongue. I study her for a moment, considering. Ah—maybe this is the time for the courting word. "*Newwwp*," I tell her.

Her hand slams on my chest. "What do you mean, *newwwp*?" She looks affronted. "I can want some fucking foreplay! I don't think that's too much to ask."

"Wait. Is this not a courting word?"

She makes an outraged noise. "I asked you for foreplay and you said no?"

"I said newwwp," I correct. "This is not right? You said it to me and it was clear you liked my touch."

Liz gives me an incredulous look and pushes at my chest. "I have no idea what you are talking about, weirdo. Let me go—"

"Never," I state, and fist my hand in her hair, like she did to me. She stills in my grip, and I study her, the pulse racing in her beautiful throat, the hot anger—and lust—flaring in her eyes. "Explain to me this 'foreplay.'"

"You're fucking kidding, right?"

I roll the words around in my head, but the translations do not sound right. "My cock does not claim you as a jest, no."

"Oh Jesus, that's not what I meant. I . . ." She blows a breath out, frustrated. "Okay. Foreplay. That's like, titty squeezes and stuff. You gotta work a girl up for sex. Make sure she's good and wet and into it."

I frown down at her. "You were wet."

"I know! But—"

"I licked your wetness off of the insides of your thighs. Your cunt was so wet it was dripping—"

Her fingers press my lips together and she looks . . . embarrassed. "Don't say such dirty things."

Dirty? It was beautiful to see all that wetness that I caused. I would drink of her sweet nectar for hours, but she seems uncomfortable with the thought. Humans are strange. "Then tell me," I insist. "What is a titty squeeze? I do not know these words."

"Oh lord," she breathes. "What on earth did that translator teach you?" She pats the top of her chest. "You know, boobs. Breasts. They feel good when you touch them."

I immediately place a hand over one and give it a caress, then look at her face.

Liz giggles. "Not right now. Before sex, to warm me up. So I'm ready to go."

"I am ready to go," I point out to her. My cock is hard and still inside her, and I want to start thrusting again, but I am waiting for her very human signal that this is okay to her. That this is foreplay. So I give her breast another tentative squeeze. "Like so?"

Her brows draw together. "You mean . . . you want to have sex again?"

"Is that what this means?" I squeeze her breast again.

"No, that's you honking my tit."

"That is what you said you wanted!"

She rolls her eyes. "I talk in slang, babe."

"And now you say I'm a child?" Now I'm offended. "I—"

Her fingers go to my mouth and silence me again. "'Babe' is an affectionate term for a partner. Don't your people have words like that? What would you call me?"

"Liz?"

She smacks my chest. "Like a pet name. A nickname that one says out of affection."

I think for a moment. "Woman?"

She makes an exasperated sound. "You know what? Never mind. Just forget—"

But now I understand what she is asking. "My woman?" I murmur, tilting her head toward me and brushing my lips over the fine line of her jaw. "My Liz?"

I feel a little shiver ripple all through her body, and she quakes deep inside her cunt. "Oh God, you are hard again, aren't you? I can *feel* you." Her khui thrums and resonates louder, and I'm encouraged.

"What other things do humans do for foreplay?" I lick her skin at the spot where her lip meets the little divot below her tiny human nose. It's soft, so soft.

She sighs softly in my arms and her eyes close. "Kissing is a good one. Stroking. Soft touches. Caresses."

Ah. So I have been foreplaying her before. I just did not know the word. "I would foreplay you now, Liz. I want your cunt ready for my cock to fill once more."

"You're already inside me, so we've got that part down," she says, but she squirms a little against me, as if the reminder of my body buried inside hers is making her fidgety.

My hand is still twined in her hair, and I like that I have her pinned in place. I can tell she likes it, too. Her breath is starting to come in soft, rapid gasps, and when she opens her eyes to gaze at me, she has a sleepy, aroused look in them.

I will foreplay her now, then. She wants kisses? I can give her kisses. It is the mating of the mouth that humans like so much, and that Vektal spoke highly of. I enjoyed it before, too. Liz's mouth is as soft and smooth as her cunt. So I brush my lips over hers, and when her mouth parts for me, I slick my tongue against hers like stroking my cock deep inside her.

She gasps and moans in response.

I like this. No, I decide. I *crave* this. My mate is finally in my arms, letting me claim her. There is nothing better in the world. I have never experienced the like, and I intend on being greedy with her. My mouth takes hers over and over again, until she is gasping and trembling underneath me. I lick her full, pink bottom lip with my tongue and then gently bite down on it, because it is soft and sweet and reminds me of her lovely cunt. A soft little cry escapes her, and I feel her cunt tremble and clench around my cock, even as her pupils dilate and she stiffens under me.

I slick my tongue over her parted mouth again. "Did I fore-play you correctly?"

"I think I just came again," she sighs, a glazed look in her eyes.

"Do you wish for me to stop?"

"God, no." That hazy look focuses on my face, and I feel her roll her hips under me. "I feel incredible."

"It is the khui," I tell her, and press my hand between her breasts. "We have acceded to its wishes, and now it rewards us."

"Yay cootie." She lifts her chin, a subtle suggestion that I kiss her again. I am happy to do so, even as my hand moves to cup her breast. Her human chest is shivering with the force of the khui vibrating inside it, and her nipples are taut and erect. I graze my hand over them and she cries out again, her eyes closing.

Ah. More foreplays. "Shall I put my mouth here?"

The look she gives me is dazed, but hungry. "I'm down for that."

I pause. "Is that a . . . yes?"

"Boobs now," she says, pushing my head down toward her breasts. "Talk later."

I move lower as she demands, and my cock slides out of her wet warmth. She makes a small noise of dismay, but I will return there soon enough. As she says, boobs now. I capture her soft nipple in my mouth. She gasps and squirms under me, practically coming off the furs with her need. Ah. I like this. I flick my tongue over the tip, enjoying her cries.

Liz moans and her hands go to my hair, my remaining horn, and she clings to me, desperate. She likes this very much. My cock aches, wanting to be back inside her wet warmth. I'm unable to resist touching her, my hand sliding to her cunt and toying with the soft, wet folds there. She is slick between her legs, my spend and hers mingled together, and she moans when I push my fingers inside her again.

"That's not enough," she says.

I bite gently on the tip of her breast. "My fingers?"

"We can play 'Find the G-spot' later," she says, more nonsense human language. "I want you back inside me, Raahosh. I ache for you. Please."

My cock surges, but I'm not done playing with her yet. I'm still exploring my sweet, soft mate, no matter how much she protests. I gaze down at my fingers as they pump in and out of her cunt, and a dribble of my spend trails down her folds. Automatically, I catch it with my fingers and push it back inside her. I will take her so many times that we will make a child together. And then when her belly is rounded with our mating, we will return to my people and no one will be able to take her from me.

"What are you doing?" She shifts against me, restless.

"I am ensuring that my seed stays inside you."

"How very barbaric of you," she murmurs. Her legs part a bit wider and she sighs. "You know what would put even more of your seed inside me?"

"What?"

"If you fuck me again." Liz gives a little wiggle. "Cut out the middleman and go directly to the source."

Again, some of her words make no sense but it doesn't matter. She is demanding more sex, and that is all I need to know. My khui resonates hard, insisting I take her again. And how can I refuse when she asks so sweetly? I slide back up her body and kiss her mouth, and she whimpers and clings to me. Her hips rise again, and so I fit my cock at her entrance once more, dragging the head of it through her wetness.

"Oh, God, yes," she moans, and her hands fist in my hair again. "Give it to me."

I sink home and she shrieks with joy. My eyes nearly roll back in my head with pleasure. There is no sensation like the warm grip of my mate's cunt tight around my cock. And as I begin to push into her with rhythmic thrusts, one thought cycles through my mind, over and over, resonating as my khui does.

Liz is mine.

Liz is mine.

My mate.

My everything.

Liz

Sometime in the early morning hours, I wake up with my cheek pressed to Raahosh's chest, drooling on him a little. Oops. I sit up and wipe my mouth and then his bare skin, but he only shifts in the bed and pulls me against him once more. "Gotta pee," I tell him sleepily, and slide out of bed.

I waddle out to the lip of the cave to do my dirty business—waddle being the important word there. I've been fucked so hard and so often in the last night that I'm surprised my legs are even functioning.

Now I see why Georgie was totally cool with Vektal claiming her as his mate. If he's anything like Raahosh, he dicked the brains right out of her. I feel pretty brainless and giddy myself. I mean, I've had sex before, but sex with Raahosh? It's kinda SEX with capital letters and little hearts drawn around it. That shit was incredible. I feel sticky and battered all over, but I'm dopey with endorphins and pleased as punch.

I rub a little snow over my aching girl parts to clean up, and then smooth a few more handfuls over my sweat-sticky skin to clean it off. Then, yawning, I head back into the cave.

He's awake now, sitting up amidst the furs and watching me with a predatory look that makes my cootie start to hum again. I don't know that I can stand another round of fucking without melting into a boneless little puddle, so I primly sit near the fire, legs tightly locked together, and stir the coals with a stick.

"Come back to bed," he says, and pats the furs.

Yeah, I'm pretty sure he doesn't have sleeping in mind. "It's almost dawn," I say. "I have a lot to do today."

"It can wait."

"You know, you sure do have a lot of energy for a dude that had a gajillion broken bones just last week."

He lifts one of his arms, and for a moment, I almost think he's going to flex. But he only examines it and shrugs. "The khui helps us heal faster." He looks over at me again and then pats the furs. "Come back. I would fill you with my seed again."

My stupid cootie starts humming like an idiot, but I ignore it. "How about we, you know, chat about what comes next?"

He tilts his head and gives me a curious look. "Why?"

I sputter. "What do you mean, why? Because we're building a relationship here!"

Raahosh's eyes narrow at me in that way that tells me he thinks he's being patient, but he's really not. "I do not see that there is anything to discuss. You are my mate. You belong to me."

I sputter again. "So we're back to property now?" There goes my post-coital afterglow. I get to my feet and head for my clothes. "You know what? I don't want to talk to you right now."

"What are you doing?"

"Getting dressed. I need to check my traps."

He gets to his feet and snatches my clothing from my hand. "You cannot go hunting. Even now, you might be carrying my child. Our child."

Oh, no he did not just throw the *barefoot and pregnant in the kitchen* thing in my face. "You really want to see my head explode, don't you?"

He frowns. "I would never wish harm on you—"

"Aaaah!" I throw my hands up. "Fine. You want to be like this?" I jab a finger into his chest—which stings, because the damn thing is plated. "Nothing has changed between us other than a little rompy-pompy. We had sex, that's it. I did not become your magical property, and you did not magically become my man. We are the same as we ever were, which means we are two jerks who like to bicker with each other. My hunting skills have not been affected by your jizz. I know it's dangerous out there. Remember the part where I dragged your broken body for like three goddamn miles in the snow?"

His arms cross over his chest.

"Yeah, I thought so." I gesture at the cave mouth. "So now I'm going to go out and catch us breakfast. You can sit in here and, like, beat your chest like a caveman or something." I move to pick up my bow, and he catches it before I can sling it over my shoulder. I glare furiously at him.

When he speaks, Raahosh's voice is low and serious. "Before you arrived here in this world, I had nothing to live for. I hunted. I existed. I did not look forward to anything. But now you are here, and you might be carrying my child even now." His jaw flexes. "I know you are more than capable. The problem is not with you. It is with me. This world is dangerous, and I think of you, alone, out in the wild, and it is more than I can bear." He stares at me for so long and so hard that I think his jaw is going to snap from grinding his teeth. "If I lose you," he finally says gruffly, "I have nothing."

And because I'm a total marshmallow, I soften. I reach up

to pat his cheek, but he leans into my touch and it turns into a caress. "Raahosh, seriously. I know how to take care of myself."

"So do I. I was still downed by a band of metlaks."

He's got a good point. "So come with me. We can hunt together." I nod at him. "If you're feeling up to it."

"I have a better idea," he murmurs, and pulls the bow out of my hands. "We eat the smoked meat. You come back to bed and let me fill your soft cunt with my hard cock." His arms go around my waist and he drags me against him. The moment we touch, our cooties start to resonate. "And then we will go hunting tomorrow. Together."

It's hard to stay mad at a guy when he strokes your skin and makes you prickle all over with desire. I consider for a moment. "My traps?"

He glances out at the entrance to the cave. "It is snowing. Whatever is in them will stay frozen another day."

"Mmm." I pretend to consider. There's really no considering to be done. My cootie's going a mile a minute, and I can tell I'm already wet between my legs with need. I look up at him. "If we're going to be mates—"

"There is no *if*. We *are*," he insists.

"Then we need to be equal partners," I tell him. I brush my hand over his gorgeous, naked chest and then move up to his neck, caressing the back of it. "There's no ownership. You are mine as much as I'm yours. Understand?"

"I am yours," he agrees. "Completely and fully."

"Then I can be yours, too."

He leans down and kisses me gently on the lips. "My mate. My Liz. You are my everything."

Yep, definitely hard to stay mad at that.

We end up lazing about in bed for a few more hours, making love a few more times and napping. To his credit, he promises to be more understanding about the hunting. All the while, he caresses my abdomen when he thinks I'm not paying attention.

I've never particularly thought about being someone's mom. But it's clear that to Raahosh me and this baby are everything. And it makes me wonder what his life is like back at the caves. Vektal made it sound like everyone was all happy-go-lucky in igloos or some shit, but maybe it's lonelier than I think for someone like Raahosh, who has scars and sucks with people skills. The fact that he was a big ol' virgin tells me that with the few ladies in the tribe, they weren't exactly banging down his door for his dick.

No matter how magnificent his equipment is.

And it's weird, but I'm kind of glad he's all mine. There's no chick waiting for him back home. No ex-girlfriends I might have to confront. He's just . . . mine. It's like he's always been waiting for me.

So . . . I guess I won't go hunting alone if it really gets his panties in a wad.

But by the time we're hungry for dinner, I balk at the thought of more of the dry, tasteless smoked meat. "You can come with me," I cajole Raahosh. "We can check the traps and have something fresh and tasty to eat. Wouldn't that be nice?" I tap my stomach. "And fresh food is better if I'm truly pregnant."

He grunts a response and puts on his loincloth, so I suppose that means we're going out. It's odd, but I'm excited to get out in the fresh air and tromp through the snow. I like seeing what's wandered into my traps. And I'm really craving fresh, raw meat. Weird, I know.

We bank the fire, straighten up the cave, and then head out, dressed and armed for a trek. The weather's overcast and it looks like it could snow again. Big surprise there. It snows every damn day.

While Raahosh was recovering, I pulled two more of the ugly spear-fish things from the water and made two bows and a whole slew of arrows. I even managed a couple of makeshift quivers with some extra pelts. I'm a regular Daniel Boone around here.

It's strange—I remember hunting with my father when I was a girl and never thought anything of it. Now that I'm out on my own with Raahosh, I'm remembering things I've forgotten, and more than that . . . I'm enjoying myself. I never thought of myself as the outdoorsy type, but there's nothing more satisfying than letting a well-made arrow fly into a kill.

Well, okay, sex with Raahosh is more satisfying. Hunting is a close second.

Raahosh hovers a bit as we go tromping through the snow, until I slap his hands away when he tries to help me through a particularly deep patch of snow. His lips quirk with amusement when I shoot him a pissy look, and I realize he's baiting me.

Dick. He's so getting it tonight when we get back to the cave. As we check the traps, I mentally think of ways I can sexually torture my alien. Withholding's off the table—that would be punishing me as well as him. Maybe a nice, languid blow job and I won't let him come—

"Ho!" calls a voice from a distance, the sound faint on the blowing wind.

I look over at Raahosh in surprise. Was that English? Am I imagining things?

He stills, and then scans the horizon. Immediately, he grabs my arm and begins to hustle me back from where we came. "Hurry, Liz."

"Wait. What are we running from?" I ready my bow as we slog through the snow. "Is it more metlaks?"

"Raahosh!" a voice calls out, and then says some words I don't understand.

I gasp. "Are those your people?" I stop and turn, shielding my eyes from the overcast skies to see if I can make out who is there.

"Back to the cave," Raahosh growls, and he stumbles in the snow.

My heart skitters in my chest and I tug on his arm. Playing around in bed is a different sort of activity than slogging through heavy snow, and I worry he's overextending himself. Just last week, he had a broken leg. "Raahosh, wait. Don't hurt yourself—"

He grabs the fur of my heavy cloak and hauls me against him. It takes me a moment for me to realize that he's picking me up and carrying me away. He's going to try and outrun them?

"Raahosh, wait!"

"They will not take you from me, Liz," he says fiercely. "You are mine! My *mate*."

"They can't take me," I say soothingly, trying to pet his shoulder. I'm worried he's going to hurt himself. "Raahosh, please. You're scaring me."

That stops him in his desperate treading. He stops in the snow, and gently sets me down again. His hand touches my stomach, and then he cups my face in his hands. "You are my everything, Liz," he murmurs before he kisses me.

"I know," I say, confused.

"Raahosh! Human called Leezh!" Two voices, and new ones. "Do not run!"

We've been found.

Raahosh closes his eyes and holds me against him, gripping his knife. It worries me. I place my hand over his, a silent request not to attack.

And we wait.

PART FIVE

PART FIVE

Liz

Two men approach in the snow, spears in hand. They're not running, and the spears are used more as walking sticks, so I'm not too worried. Yet.

But Raahosh? Raahosh is beside himself.

"Human called Leezh," one of them yells again, his hand cupped to his mouth. "Wait there!"

I give Raahosh an uncertain look. There is defeat written all over his proud features, and that concerns me. I slide my hand into his to reassure him, and he squeezes it tightly, then pulls me against him in a possessive hug. "Who are they?" I ask him.

"Aehako and Haeden," Raahosh replies. There's a toneless quality to his voice that I don't like.

"Friends of yours?"

He grunts.

Ah. He's unhappy because they've come to take us back to the tribe and I'm not knocked up and starry-eyed with love.

Theoretically, anyhow.

I pat his back and then rub it. "You knew they'd come after

you at some point, right? I mean, from what it sounds like, you ran off with the cookie jar and all."

His hand strokes my braids. He doesn't move, but I can feel the tension growing as the others approach.

They slog through the waist-high snow as if it's no big deal. One is smiling as they approach, and he's got a friendly, open look to his face that's nice. His features are blunter than Raahosh's blade-like ones, but his expression of good cheer makes him that much more handsome. Unlike Vektal and Raahosh, his hair is short, buzzed close to his scalp. It makes his big, arching horns look that much more prominent. He's a slaty sort of blue all over, and while not as tall as Raahosh, he's got arms like friggin' tree trunks.

Earth trees, not the Not-Hoth trees.

The other alien with him looks decidedly less friendly. He's got the same charm-school glower that Raahosh does, but that's where the similarities end. He's a pale, milky blue, almost as muscled as the one at his side, and has a strong nose and square jaw that make him look pissy as hell. His hair is shaved on the sides and the long crest on top is braided and falls on his back.

They're both wearing simple leather tunics and pants, and armed to the teeth.

Not a friendly hello, then.

"Raahosh! We've been looking everywhere for you." The friendly one moves forward to clap Raahosh on the back, but Raahosh bares his teeth and glares at him, pulling me behind him. The newcomer looks surprised at this reaction. "You knew we'd be out. Vektal set us after you the moment we didn't resonate." He claps a hand to his heart and pretends to be grieved.

The other one has no expression whatsoever.

"Hi, I'm Liz," I say, stepping out from behind Raahosh and offering my hand.

They look at me like I'm crazy, and the unfriendly one pulls his spear back.

"No, I'm not reaching for your weapons. This is a human greeting." I shake my hand with the air. "You know, like an introduction."

Raahosh grabs me and pulls me back before they can examine my hand more closely. "She is my mate," he grits out. "We resonate for each other. There is nothing to discuss."

I smack a hand on Raahosh's arm, because now I'm getting annoyed. "If you're done being an utter Neanderthal, I can speak for myself, thank you."

The newcomers exchange a look. "I am called Aehako," says the friendly one. He gestures at his buddy. "This is Haeden." Aehako smiles down at me. "You are Leezh?"

"It's a short I, actually. Liz." I correct his pronunciation.

"It does not matter," Raahosh says, and tries to pull me back again. "They should refer to you as Raahosh's mate."

I frown at this. "Hold the fuck up. I don't get my own identity anymore?"

"You do," Aehako assures me. "He's simply being overprotective. Happens with every resonance." He looks nonplussed, but I see a sneer cross Haeden's face.

Haeden lifts his chin. "Just like your father, I see. Ignoring the rules as you see fit. Impulsive, headstrong, and foolish. You are your father's son."

It's clearly not a compliment. Raahosh bristles visibly. His mouth curls and I see a flash of his teeth. "I did not wish for my story to end like yours."

Haeden snarls and lunges for Raahosh, knocking him backward into the snow.

I scream as the men push me aside, Aehako pushing his way forward to break the two men apart. I stumble backward, falling on my ass into the snow. Raahosh snarls again, and then the next thing I know, he's pushed both of the men aside and is tenderly helping me to my feet. He pulls me against his chest once more and strokes my braids, and I can hear the hammer of his heart in his big chest.

"Simply being protective" is perhaps an understatement.

"I'm fine," I say, patting him on the arm. "I just don't understand what is going on."

"Get your things," Aehako says in a careful voice. He scans the skies. "We have a few hours before the suns go down, and we can get started back to the tribal cave. Rokan says there will be a storm coming in a few days, and you know he is never wrong."

I look to Raahosh.

He touches my chin, the look on his face thoughtful.

"Do not make this harder," Haeden warns.

Raahosh just strokes my jaw. "We'll go with you."

It takes about an hour to get back to the small, cozy cave that Raahosh and I have called home for the last while. Aehako's the only one that talks, carrying on a cheerful monologue. Raahosh is silent and Haeden is, too. I'm quiet because I'm watching all three of them, trying to determine my place.

Fact is, they're aliens. Their culture is different from mine, and what may seem innocent on the surface might end up being a big problem later. So I'm watchful, and I try to absorb everything.

To their credit, they speak English as we go, so I don't feel left out. Aehako expresses surprise at the sight of our cave, and claps Raahosh on the back for setting himself up such a cozy place "right under their noses." Raahosh doesn't look pleased, though. He's pretty good at keeping his emotions under wraps but I can sense his anger and frustration.

"What is this?" Aehako asks and holds up my bow.

"It's a weapon," I tell him, slinging it over my shoulder as we pack our things. I make sure I have it and the quiver full of bone arrows. "I use it for hunting."

"Hunting?" His brows draw together. "But you are female. You should not be hunting."

"Did I take a wrong turn and land on Planet Chauvinist?" I ask. "I can fucking hunt! What, you think wild animals are going to be so enamored of my lady parts that I'm going to lure them like some Pied Piper of Pussy? What—"

Raahosh puts a calming hand on my shoulder. "The women of my tribe do not hunt, remember? They are too few in number."

I snort. "We'll see about that shit. You're not exactly outnumbered three to one anymore." And I make a big show of adjusting my bow on my shoulder, glaring at Aehako and Haeden.

Aehako just looks amused.

We clean out our small cave of extra food and blankets and pack up our waterskins. I roll up the extra pelts, and when the cave is in order, I give it one last look around. I feel a twinge of sadness that we're leaving. I'm looking forward to seeing Georgie and Kira and my fellow humans again, but I have to admit, staying in this cave was kind of . . . nice. Cozy. Private.

And I kinda liked being here with Raahosh. The big jerk's growing on me. Just when I get settled, we're moving again. I'm craving someplace to call home.

But then Raahosh takes my hand, and the feeling of loss disappears. Instead of feeling uprooted, I just feel vaguely annoyed that our little idyll is interrupted just when things were getting super sexy.

Cockblocked by the aliens. Damn it.

We walk in the direction of the setting suns for a time. I'd say it's west except that's how it is on Earth, and this place is most definitely not Earth. When the skies turn pink and a washed-out orange, we head for a small copse and make camp. Aehako has been picking up dung chips as we walk, and has a bag full of them for fuel.

It's . . . probably a good thing I didn't shake his hand.

We bunk down for the night around a campfire, and Haeden immediately stalks off to the ridge nearby and says he's on first watch. Works for me. He's not exactly a ball of fun, and I've got Raahosh if I want to hang out with someone quietly seething.

As I settle in near the fire and wrap my fur cloak around me, Raahosh grabs his spear and leans down to kiss the top of my head. "I will find some fresh meat for you."

"Oh, but . . ." I watch him leave the small camp, and then it's just me and Aehako, who's feeding another dung chip into the fire. I frown at him. "You're not going to go chasing after him?"

"Why?" Aehako shrugs easily. "He will return. You are here."

Ah. So it's not Raahosh that's the hostage. It's me. Gotcha. He's right, though. As long as I'm here, Raahosh will return. Just the thought of that kind of gives me the warm fuzzes. Whatever else happens, Raahosh has my back. I'm determined to do the same for him.

But my feet hurt and it's nice to sit by the fire, even if it's cold outside and there's no shelter from the elements. I scoot a little closer to it and prop up my wet, booted feet so they can dry a bit. "Tell me how the others are doing. Are they all well?"

"Healthy as can be," Aehako reassures me, and a big smile splits his face. Despite the situation, I like the guy. I think it'd be impossible not to. "Your friends have brought much joy to our people," he says. "For a long time, we thought a mate was a dream, and it is now a dream possible for many."

His words make me wish Raahosh was here. I scan the trees, but my "mate"—I'm still coming to terms with the whole situation—is blowing off steam by slaughtering dinner. "That's nice."

"We are all squeezed into our caves like quilled beasts in a snowstorm, but no one is complaining."

"Mmm. Did anyone, you know, get a vibrating cootie?"

"Resonate?"

"Yeah, that's the word." I'm sure Raahosh has said it to me before, but he also says things like "mine-mine-mine-mine" and "your cunt is full of my seed," so I sorta have to pick my words carefully around this guy. "Did anyone else resonate?"

"Oh, yes." He stirs the fire. "Georgie you know of, of course. Pashov and Stacy resonated for each other right away, I think before her khui was even inside her. I am surprised you did not hear it." He chuckles.

"Mmm," I say again, because my memories of that night are of me saying "no" to the cootie and Raahosh stepping on me to hold me down and forcing me to absorb it. That was not the big guy's best moment. My betraying cootie purrs at the thought of Raahosh, though, and I rub my chest absently. "I don't remember Stacy all that well. Is she the weepy one?"

"She cries some, but less now that Pashov is there to dry her tears." He grins and sits back to relax. "The one that weeps the most is Ariana. She is Zolaya's mate. He is much beleaguered by her tears."

"Yeah, I imagine this is all pretty new to her." Were the only ones that resonated the girls from the tubes? "What about Josie? Or Kira? Or Tiff?"

He shakes his head. "No resonance yet for them."

"Oh."

"They are young," he says. "There are many years ahead of them. Plenty of time to resonate to the right man."

"Mm-hmm. And no mate for you?"

He sighs, and for the first time, his laughing smile falters a little. "No mate and family for me yet. Plenty of time for me as well." But he looks wistful. "Marlene and Zennek, too. And Nora and Dagesh."

Dagesh has a weird name—the way it is said, it's almost like the middle syllable is swallowed and chewed up again. It's definitely not a human sound. So I just say, "Good for them. I hope they are happy."

"Some are. Some are adjusting. But the entire tribe is pleased. Many new couples and dens created. Soon, there will be many kits running around." He stretches his legs and then flops on his side in the snow, then props up his chin with his hand. "So many new matings means new quarters for the new families."

"Oh?"

"No one wants to hear their khui resonate all night," he says with a wicked grin.

I feel myself blushing. I suspect that's not the only thing they hear all night. "Sounds like everyone's got a cozy setup."

"Mm. Cozy for the new couples. Haeden and I volunteered

to come after you two. It's too crowded for a lot of the men. All the hunters are spending much time out on treks. They say it is for the extra mouths to feed, but it is also because it is cramped quarters for those that do not have a family." He shrugs. "It's not a problem we thought we would have again."

"Again?"

Aehako nods and his cheery grin disappears. "Our tribe was larger before. We had many matings, many families. It was a good time for the sa-khui. But fifteen years ago there was a khui-sickness that swept through the caves. Many died." He picks at the snow in front of him. "There was not a den that was not affected by the khui-sickness. So many lost mothers, fathers, mates . . ."

He sits up abruptly and I see Haeden stalk past the edge of the trees. I open my mouth to speak and Aehako gives a small shake of his head, a meaningful look cast Haeden's way.

Ah. So Haeden's sensitive about that subject. Got it. "What about Raahosh's family?" I ask. It's the first time I've actually thought that Raahosh might have a family waiting for him back home. He hasn't mentioned one. Is it that he doesn't want to talk about them? Or is it that he lost them in the khui-sickness like I assume Haeden did?

Aehako glances around, then leans in. "Did he not tell you of his family?"

I shift forward, lowering my voice. We're gossiping, but this is gossip I need, so I don't care. "He hasn't said anything. Are they at the cave? Or dead?"

"Long dead," Aehako says in a low voice. "His situation was . . . an interesting one."

I move a little closer. "I like interesting." Plus, I really, really want to know. I want to understand what makes my Raahosh tick.

Weird that I'm starting to think of him as "my" Raahosh now.

"His mother, Daya, never liked his father. Vaashan was not a very patient man, and Daya was in love with someone else. But when the khui chooses, it chooses." He shrugs. "Raahosh was their child, and when he was five, his mother resonated for his father anew. That meant another child. She insisted she did not want his kit. Refused to have anything to do with him. She even went to the chief—at that time, it was Vektal's father." Aehako rubs his jaw and looks troubled. "The chief declared that she could have his child, because resonance cannot be avoided. But she did not have to live with him. This made Vaashan furious. He lost his temper and kidnapped her away from the tribe. He took her and Raahosh away and did not return. We looked for them for many years, but no one found them. It was as if they had disappeared. Then, after the khui-sickness had killed many, Vaashan returned with only Raahosh, and Raahosh covered in scars as you see him now. We asked him where Daya and his child were, but he said they were dead. Killed by metlaks. Vaashan's choice to take Daya away and force her to give in to the resonance? To become his mate even though she did not want to? It cost her life and that of their kit, and so the chief punished him with exile. Raahosh was left with the tribe so he could grow up in safety."

My heart aches at this story. It's an awful one, and it explains a little as to why he's so worried he's going to lose me. "Poor Raahosh."

Aehako nods thoughtfully. "He went looking for Vaashan some years later when he was old enough to hunt on his own. He never found him, but he said he did find some old leathers eaten by animals, and the old cave destroyed. Whatever was left of Vaashan is long gone."

Oh, Raahosh. I think of his mother and the baby, dead. His father's misery. How had that affected such a small child? No wonder he is so desperate to keep me, even if it means pissing off his tribe. It's the only way he can think to react after his parents' example.

It's such a sad story. I lost my mother when I was very young, but I had my father and I always, always felt loved until the day he died. To have such family strife and then lose both like that made my heart break for my alien. This was why he was so possessive, so resolute in his desire to keep me hidden away. Suddenly I want to comfort him and let him know that he's got me. That I'm his and he's mine. Cootie or not, I'm having feelings for the big guy and he's made life here on this strange planet interesting.

The conversation with Aehako dies and the alien returns to stirring the fire. I sit by it with my legs crossed, lost in thought, until Raahosh returns. He's got a kill in hand, and judging from the arrow sticking out of the quilled beast, he used the bow I made for him. He must have watched me use it and figured it out from there. Wow. The wide smile I give him in greeting is genuine, and I get up to greet him with kisses.

He's a little dazzled by my enthusiastic greeting, but puts his arm around me and nuzzles me close. And when he cuts open the kill, he makes sure I get the tastiest bits and feeds them to me, and won't give the others—or himself—a bite until I'm good and full.

And really, it's not the worst thing to be the center of someone's universe. I'm kinda digging it.

And I plan on showing him my appreciation.

Raahosh

Liz's good mood makes me wary. It's a pleasure to see, of course, but I can't help but wonder if my devious mate is up to something. She usually greets me with caustic words and grumpiness, but now that Aehako and Haeden are here? She is all smiles and reaches for me when I walk toward her.

I am not pleased to see the two men. They are good men, but the truth is that I would keep Liz to myself for at least a few more turns of the moons, so when we returned to my people, it would be clear that we are a family and we must be together.

Now, I am not sure what they will think. I have broken the laws of our tribe, and Liz's belly is still flat with no sign of our child. My only consolation is that she smiles at me and her hands reach for me when I am near. It is clear that we are mates, and I can see the envy in both Aehako and Haeden's eyes.

They did not resonate. For them, life goes on cold and mateless, but with the added agony of seeing so many others find their joy. For the first time, I am the envied one. It is an unusual feeling.

The evening is a quiet one. Aehako talks easily, but he's always been a cheerful one. His conversations about hunting, and life back at the caves hold Liz's interest, but her hand is locked in mine. Haeden is silent, but he watches every time Liz touches me or brushes her arm against mine.

As the hour grows late, Liz yawns and puts her cheek on my arm. "Can we go to bed now, baby?"

She is calling me the love word of her people. My heart swells and my khui begins a soft resonance in my chest. "Of course." I stand up and pull her to her feet.

Haeden stands as well. "She should stay here, near the fire with us."

Before I can snarl a protest, Liz snorts. "Uh, we're resonating, remember?" She taps her chest and I can hear her khui singing a song to mine. "I thought the goal was that you wanted him to impregnate me so you can have more blue babies running around, right?"

Haeden's jaw clenches. "We are protecting you."

"From his jizz?" A little smile curves Liz's pink mouth. "Bit late for that. Now, I'm gonna go sleep with my mate." She takes my hand and leads me a short distance away from the fire, near some bushes. With a yawn, she shrugs her cloak off and then gestures at the pack on my back. "Blankets, please."

Wordless, I obey. I make a bed full of furs for her, since I know my human can only take so much cold. Even now, she shivers amidst her yawns. When the bed is as perfect as I can get it, I take the cloak from her hands and bundle it around her shoulders. "You must stay warm."

"Oh, I'm going to stay warm," she says with a soft smile. "We're going to snuggle."

I look over at the fire a short distance away. Aehako and Haeden are watching us. I'm not sure if "snuggling" is a good idea. Already

I am resonating for my mate, and my cock is beginning to strain against my loincloth. "Perhaps I should sleep by the fire."

"Fuck that noise," she says sleepily. She gets down onto the furs, stretches out, and then pets the spot next to her. "Come on. I'll make it good for you."

Those are sex words. My body reacts even as I glance back at the fire again. She must not mean what she is saying. The humans are modest, from what Vektal has said. Shorshie didn't want his touch when others were around. It is just more human chatter.

"Brr," she says, and chatters her teeth. "So cold. I need my big alien to squeeze up against."

I cannot refuse such a call from my mate. With one last look at the two men by the fire, I get down in the bed next to Liz and she immediately burrows against me, her cold hands moving under my vest and pressing against my skin. I endure it stoically; I want her to be comfortable and warm. My arms go around her, holding her close, and I tuck her small head under my chin. My khui sings a song of protest, but I am content. With Liz in my arms, the world outside does not matter at the moment.

"Mmm," Liz says softly, her hand stroking my chest.

I caress her arm under the furs. "Liz?"

"Yes, baby?"

"What is jizz?"

She giggles, and my cock gets even harder. "It's your seed."

I feel strangely embarrassed that she has said such things to the other males. She jokes about being protected from my seed? "Your words are forward."

"I know, but they don't understand them so it's cool," she says, and I can hear the smile in her voice. Her hand slides down my stomach and then cups my cock. "There's no protecting a girl from this monster."

My breath hisses out and I pull her hand away. "Liz!" I sit up and look between the spiky leaves of the bushes to where the fire flickers. Sure enough, they are watching us, though I doubt they can see more than our feet.

I am sure they can hear Liz, though. My mate is not quiet.

"Lie down," she tells me, and presses a hand to my chest.

"They can hear you."

"So?" Her hand goes to my cock again and she drags her fingers over the length, then caresses my spur. "Let them hear what they're missing out on."

I swallow back a ragged groan. My khui is resonating wildly in my breast, and Liz seems determined to play. And I? I am a weak man because I am going to let her. I reach for Liz, but she slides under the blankets.

"Let me make you feel good," she whispers, and I feel her tugging at the ties to my loincloth. Then, the leather falls away and I feel her hot little hand around my cock.

I bite down on my hand to keep from moaning aloud. I don't want the others to know what pleasures I'm getting from my mate, for fear that she'll stop. Because I'm selfish and greedy, but I want more of this.

Her hand tightens around the base of my cock and I feel her when she giggles, then rubs the head against her lips. "God, you're so hard already. That's sexy, Raahosh." Liz's lips close over my cock head and I feel her tongue swirl over it.

I nearly spill my seed right then. Instead, I bite down harder on my hand, determined to be silent so this lasts longer. My body arches, and I want to press farther into her mouth, into that warm wet that reminds me of her cunt.

Her tongue laps at my cock. "So much pre-cum for me," she murmurs. Her hand grips and strokes at the root, and then her mouth seems to be everywhere: licking along my shaft, nibbling at the head, and then teasing and licking at my spur, which I never knew was sensitive until she played with it. I am beside myself with pleasure, and when she makes soft little noises of delight and her khui vibrates, it pleases me even more.

Then, her mouth clamps down on the head of my cock and starts sucking again. She takes me deeper, working my length down her tongue, until I can feel my cock butt up against the back of her throat.

And her khui begins to vibrate even harder. It's like she's encouraging it, because it's so loud that I can feel it making her skin shiver, and I feel the vibrations of it against her tongue, even as she grips me in her throat.

It is . . . like nothing I have ever felt before.

Even biting my hand cannot stifle my groan, and I come then, my seed spurting into her hot, wet mouth. She makes soft little noises of pleasure, and I feel her swallow even as she releases my cock, and she's drinking it.

Drinking my seed like I drink from her sweet cunt. I groan again, and my hands tug at her pants. I want to reciprocate.

But she stops me with a little pat on my chest and a smack of her lips. "It's okay, baby. I wasn't doing this because I wanted you to lick me." Her hand smooths down my chest. "I just wanted to make you feel good. For you to know I'm with you." A little giggle escapes her throat, the sound sweet and musical. "And for them to know I'm with you, too."

Clever Liz. She pleasures me with her mouth so the others can know she's with me willingly? My mate is devious . . . and wonderful. I pull her against me, feeling my khui resonate in time with hers.

"You are everything to me, Liz," I say softly. "My world. My heart."

"Is that a declaration of love?" she asks sleepily, her voice muffled by my chest.

I nod. My people normally do not declare love boldly, but I love Liz. She is mine and I am hers. "I love you, Liz."

Her soft sound of appreciation is all I get in response. I wonder—does she love me? Does it matter as long as she is my mate? For some reason . . . it does. Perhaps I'm not doing enough to please her.

My hand goes to the waist of her leggings and I push my fingers inside, seeking her cunt. She makes a sleepy sound of protest, and then her arms go around my neck and tighten as I find her third nipple—her clit, she calls it. Then, the breath hisses out of her throat.

"I guess I'm in the mood for some reciprocation after all," she says, and then gently bites at the base of my throat.

Her cunt is soaked with honey, and I drag my fingers through her juicy folds even as I knot my other hand in her hair and angle her mouth so I can kiss her and mate her tongue with mine. She whimpers again, the sound louder, and I muffle it with my lips. Surely the others can guess what we are doing, but Liz's cries of pleasure are mine alone.

I slide a finger deep inside her and begin to thrust, mimicking my cock. Her hips rise, and she murmurs against my throat. "My clit," she says over and over again, and I realize she wants me to touch it even as I pump into her with my hand. I angle my thumb over it and brush the nub of it while thrusting my finger into her, and she cries out loudly. This time, there is no muffling that. I hear a low comment by the fire, and then the sound of someone walking away—farther from the camp.

Good, I think savagely as I pleasure my mate. When she comes, she does it with little shivers and soft cries, her body tensing against mine, and a flood of honey between her legs. I dip my fingers into all that sweetness before I pull them from her leggings and then lick my hand clean of her taste.

"Filthy barbarian," she murmurs with a chuckle, and then sighs, contented. Within moments, she's asleep against me. Trusting. Happy.

I hold her close, savoring these moments in case they don't last.

Liz

The tribal "home" cave doesn't look too impressive from the out-side. In fact, the only way I know it's different from every other cliff we've passed is that Georgie flings herself out from the cave mouth, arms outstretched and squealing happily at the sight of me.

I'm surprised to see such an effusive greeting from her, but I extend my arms and allow her to jump all over me in a boister-ous welcome. A moment later, Josie's right there, flinging her arms around me next, until I'm being swarmed by my fellow captives. It's strange to see everyone with the glowing blue eyes, though I know I must have them, too. The glow in our eyes says we have a cootie, and everyone's healthy and happy looking. Weirdly enough, I feel tears pricking. It's like I'm coming home, especially when Kira comes in and embraces me in a long, silent hug. She and I have known each other the longest, and seeing her is like seeing a sister. I burst into tears at that and blubber for a moment, sniffling and happy to see all of them. I touch Kira's ear, where the shell-like translator is still attached. "Hanging on to your accessories," I tease, happy.

"It's not so easy to remove," she says with a soft smile on her solemn face, and then steps away to allow Tiffany in to hug me.

As Kira steps away, I see Aehako move toward her, opening his arms for a hug. "No greeting for me, sad eyes?"

Kira blushes and waves him off.

"How are you?" Georgie asks, pulling me by my arm and tugging me into the cave. "Are you all right? Have you guys been okay? Did Raahosh hurt you?"

I look back at Raahosh as I'm being carried away on a tide of happy human women. He's standing back with Aehako and Haeden, and the narrow-eyed look has returned to his face, but for a moment, I think he looks . . . lost. Miserable.

"Raahosh has been wonderful to me," I say loudly. I blow him a kiss from afar, and then let Georgie and Tiffany drag me inside the caves.

The "home" caves aren't what I'm expecting. I guess I was thinking it'd be something super primitive, much like the cave I shared with Raahosh, but the cave itself looks like the hollowed-out inside of a donut. If this isn't man-made, I'll eat my leather shirt. The doors to each individual cave are perfectly rounded, a leather curtain drawn over the entrance. The center of the cave is warm and almost humid, and there's a bright blue pool of water in the center that smells faintly of sulfur. A baby alien with tiny horns and bright blue skin splashes on the steps, clinging to what must be a female alien. She's tall and brawny and just as covered in bumpy plates as Raahosh and the men are, which looks almost overwhelming on her female face.

It's weird, because there are people everywhere, and I'm quickly overwhelmed by the sensation of crowding. There's more people playing near the water, and someone's weaving baskets in the distance. I hear the chatter of many voices, and everywhere I look, there are people. I see the freckled girl from the tubes leaning over a stewpot as someone tries to instruct her on how to cook. Over off to one side, the weepy one—Ariana—is cuddled in the lap of another alien. She doesn't look all that weepy to me.

"Wow, this is so . . ." I pause, unable to think of a snappy comeback for once.

"It's great, isn't it?" Georgie's arm goes around my waist. "They've really made room for us here. The hunters have been going out and spending a lot more time on the trails because there's so many more mouths to feed. And Kashrem's tanning all the hides he can because he needs the leather for us, and they've given us caves, and it's all so wonderful." Georgie gushes as she leads me inside.

It is nice of them, but all I see are people everywhere. A lot of people. It's a nice living space, but it's also noisy with laughter. I kind of miss my quiet cave with Raahosh. It is primitive, but cozy. It's not like there's exactly a shopping mall here anyhow. Fact is, my life changed completely and utterly the day that the Little Green Men kidnapped me from my apartment and stole me into outer space.

Georgie steers me through the caverns, smiling at people as they find an excuse to come out and stare. I guess Raahosh's kidnapping of me is pretty scandalous, though I'm getting annoyed with all the whispering. He did what he had to do and I don't regret it. I'm guessing we're going to be grist for the gossip mill for a while, though. It's such a small community that I'm sure everyone's going to be in our business.

I look for Raahosh, but he's not around. Vektal's ahead, talking to a pair of elderly aliens with long, white hair and frowns on their faces. Vektal looks over at Georgie and me, and nods.

"Come on," Georgie says, steering me into a side cave. "Let's get you checked out by the healer."

"I'm fine," I protest, but Georgie's stubborn. She won't take no for an answer, so I give up and let her lead me into one of the covered grottos.

There's a woman inside, one of the tall, strong-looking alien women. She has curling horns and long, flowing dark hair. Her belly is round and obviously pregnant, and her eyes glow brightly in her face. She says something in the alien tongue, her voice sweet.

I shake my head. "I don't speak Na'vi."

Georgie snickers and bats my arm. "Be nice, Liz. This is Maylak. She's the tribe's healer."

"Howdy," I say.

Maylak puts her hands out and smiles at me. "Leezh?"

"Close enough." I put my hands in hers. "But tell her, Georgie, that I feel fine. Raahosh took really good care of me. He's great."

Georgie's brows draw together as if she doesn't quite believe me. "He kidnapped you, Liz. You don't have to defend him."

"Dude, the Little Green Men kidnapped me, too, and you don't see me singing their praises." I give Maylak's hands another squeeze. "I'm telling you, Raahosh is fine. We're all mated and shit. So go on and tell the healer that I'm cool." I love Georgie for saving us, but I'm starting to get annoyed that no one seems to believe me when I say I'm fine with Raahosh. When she hesitates again, I say, "Do I look like I've been browbeaten into submission?"

She chuckles. "I think you would talk anyone to death that tried."

"Exactly!"

Georgie looks over at Maylak and speaks the fluid alien language. I watch their faces as they speak, but I'm unhappy that I don't know the words. Georgie knows them because she got an info dump from the spaceship crashed somewhere around here that Raahosh's people came from. Raahosh can speak English for the same reason, but I haven't had the info dump, so I'm out of the loop. And I'm not a fan of being out of the loop.

Maylak says something, then Georgie relates it. "She's going to speak to your khui and see how you are doing."

"Super. Tell it I said hello and he's a little bastard."

Georgie grins and gestures for Maylak to begin.

The alien closes her eyes and hums, and for a terrible, corny minute, I think she's going to start chanting "ommmm." But her eyes begin to glow even brighter, so bright that I can see the glow behind her eyelids, and my cootie starts to react. It's not singing or purring like it does when Raahosh comes close, but it's almost like it's . . . talking to her. I feel it twisting inside me, and then it almost dances.

It's creeping me out.

She continues to hold my hands, and I feel my cootie moving and vibrating in response. It's a different kind of vibration, higher and more rapid than when it's sexytime with Raahosh. I try to pull my hands from hers.

"It's all right, Liz. She's just checking stuff out inside you. I promise it's fine." Georgie puts her hand on my arm.

Maylak opens her eyes and my cootie stops vibrating. It slows to a faint hum and then ends, and the healer exhales slowly. Then, she smiles and releases my hands.

Weirdly enough, I feel better. I didn't feel bad before, but I feel . . . rejuvenated. Like I just had an hour-long massage on the inside.

Maylak begins to speak, and Georgie translates. "She says you have a bit of exhaustion. That it's normal for the humans because we're all still acclimating to the climate and having a khui, but for you to take it easy."

"I'm not surprised. I've been taking care of Raahosh since he fell and broke his leg." My eyes widen and I clutch at Georgie's hands. "Oh—tell her she needs to check out Raahosh. He hurt himself a while ago and took some time to recover. She needs to check him over to make sure he's okay."

Georgie looks at Maylak and speaks, and a small, unhappy frown crosses Maylak's face. She says something, and Georgie argues back with her.

"What are you guys saying?" I ask when they ignore me.

"It's complicated," Georgie says. "I'll tell you later."

Maylak continues to speak, and she gestures at my stomach. Georgie breaks out into a smile and looks at me.

"Let me guess," I say before she can translate. "I've got a bun in the oven."

Her eyes widen. "You knew?"

"Uh, I shake like I've got a vibrator tucked inside me every time Raahosh gets near," I say in a dry voice. "We might have banged a few times without protection."

"A few?" She chuckles.

"Okay, a few times a day. But seriously, that's what the cootie's about, right? So I'm not surprised. I don't know how I feel about it, but I'm not shocked."

She gives me a sympathetic look. "Not sure how you feel about it because it's Raahosh's?"

"No." Dang, why does everyone think I hate the guy? "Not sure how I feel about it because I'm not sure I wanted to be a mommy, and I'm kinda young. I'm only twenty-two. You're only twenty-two. We're all only twenty-two and now we're going to be having kids if the cooties have their way."

Georgie's hand goes to her stomach. "I'm pregnant, too."

I look over at the silent, waiting healer. "Is she sure? How do we know it's not just gas or something? Maybe the alien food makes our colons explode."

"First of all, gross? Second of all, she *knows*. She's the healer." Georgie looks at Maylak and says something, and Maylak gestures at her chest, speaking more fluid syllables. I really need to visit the alien ship and get the info dump, because I'm tired of people talking around me already. Georgie nods and then looks at me, translating. "She says she can feel the changes in your womb. Your khui knows it's there."

"Then why does the damn thing still vibrate all the time when I'm around Raahosh?"

Georgie's mouth curls in a slight smirk. "Because you're turned on? I imagine it likes sex endorphins as much as the rest of us."

Girl has a point. I exhale, staring at the cave walls. "So I'm pregnant."

"Me, too. You're not alone." She smiles. "Vektal is so excited."

I imagine the excitement on Raahosh's face when I tell him that there's a baby blue alien in my stomach. I touch my belly. He's going to be . . . happy but terrified. I remember the story of his parents. That won't be us. I promise Baby Blue that it won't. I look at Georgie. "Raahosh is pretty excited about the whole resonating thing, too. He really wants a family."

Her smile fades a little. "Did he hurt you?"

I shake my head. "He came on a little strong a few times, but I had things under control. When we finally got together, it was my call and not his." Well, it was the cootie's call, but I don't point that out. I sense that Georgie might not listen. She's utterly crazy about Vektal the way I am about Raahosh and I'm going to defend him, even if it puts us on opposing viewpoints.

Because for some reason, I'm feeling *mighty* defensive. Something about all of this feels wrong, and I can't put my finger on what it is.

What Georgie says next floors me, though. "Settle in for a long wait, though. It seems their ladies carry for three years or so."

The breath explodes from me. "What the fuck?" I'm appalled. Nine months of bloated belly and swollen ankles sounds bad. Three years of pregnancy sounds like sadistic torture.

She grimaces. "I know. Apparently, they stay pregnant a lot longer. Maylak says thirty-five moons or so, but it's hard to tell how long their moon phases are compared to ours, because no one exactly has a watch or a calendar, and this doesn't line up with Earth."

I moan in horror. "So we're going to be pregnant somewhere between nine months and three years? Shoot me now."

"If it makes you feel any better, you're handling the news a lot better than Ariana did."

"Let me guess—she cried."

"Bingo."

Maylak looks between us curiously, and so Georgie translates for her. As she does, another question comes to mind. "So who all is pregnant?"

"Let's see—Ariana, of course. Me. You. Marlene. Nora. Stacy. That's it so far."

"No resonance for Kira, huh?" I think of the way Aehako flirted with her outside the caves. "Or Josie? Tiff?"

"Nope. Maylak says sometimes the resonance happens later, but so many of us resonated at first sight that I don't know." Her voice lowers. "Some are disappointed."

Weirdly enough, I understand that. It's like their cooties decided they're not good enough for alien babies. And since the tribe seems so desperate for kids, that has to sting. "It'll happen. Or, you know, it won't. Maybe their cooties don't want to be moms."

Georgie laughs. "Maybe they're not ready yet."

"Any sign of the Little Green Men?" I rub the spot on my arm where the tracking device was implanted weeks ago and then cut out shortly thereafter.

She shakes her head. "Everything's been quiet . . ." It's left unspoken. *Except for you.*

To be fair, she's trying to protect me from a kidnapper. I can't hate on that. "I'm fine, Georgie. Really."

She bites her lip and then sighs. "Vektal is really pissed at Raahosh." The look she gives me is uneasy. "Did he tell you about the story of his parents?"

"I heard from Aehako. It's not quite the same thing."

"Maybe not in Raahosh's eyes, but to Vektal, it is. Their tribe has very strict laws about that sort of thing, Liz." She shakes her head. "Just be prepared for a shitstorm. That's all I'm saying."

"Commence the shittening," I tell her. "I'm ready."

Maylak finally deems me fine and dandy, and Georgie and I leave her cave behind. I don't miss the fact that they exchange a few heated comments between them in the alien language, or the worried look on Maylak's face as we leave. I'm not blind. There's an ominous feeling to our return, and I know it can't bode well.

In the center of the cave, Vektal sits on a few carved steps. He's casually lounging, but there's nothing casual about his demeanor. He looks tense. Pissy. Aehako and Haeden are talking to him, and Raahosh is nowhere to be found. Other men are standing around, and as Georgie and I return, all attention is fixed on us.

Vektal gets to his feet. He looks past me and I turn to see that

Maylak has emerged from her cave and is a few steps behind me. He says something in alienese and I catch my name. It's not hard to hear "Leezh" mixed in with the patter of their tongue.

This is getting irritating. Everyone's talking around me. I snap my fingers in Vektal's face. "Hello, I'm right here. Don't speak as if I'm not."

I hear Aehako muffle a laugh and Vektal turns a shocked look on me. "What are you doing?"

"Does it look like I'm snapping to the beat? I'm getting your attention." I'm also getting mighty tired of everyone talking around me. I want a say in my future, damn it. I've been pushed around too long, and I'm not going to be pushed around by another big blue alien with horns just because he says he's the chief. "I'm right here. You can talk to me about my favorite topic—me."

His brows draw together and he gives me a fierce frown. "I am confirming with the healer."

"That I'm pregnant? You could ask me. Yes, my ovaries have met their match, and it's alien sperm." I cross my arms. "Where's Raahosh? I want my mate."

"Liz," Georgie murmurs, trying to calm me.

"Unless you want to see a show of pregnancy hormones in full effect, I want Raahosh, and I want him right now," I say in a deadly voice and point at the ground. "I realize you think I'm being impossible but you have not seen impossible yet. I will be the biggest pain in the ass on this snow-covered planet if you don't get me my man, stat." I don't understand. Why are they keeping us separated? That weird sense I have of "something wrong" is getting worse.

"This is their home, Liz," Georgie says.

"I thought we were all supposed to be one big team now,

remember? That makes this my home, too, and I want my fricking man."

Georgie looks at Vektal. He throws his hands up in the air as if to say "you deal with her" and storms away. Georgie gives me an exasperated look, but I don't care. I need to see Raahosh and know that he's all right. And I want to tell him we have a baby. She pulls me aside, though, and leans in to whisper in my ear. "Raahosh broke the rules and he's in trouble, Liz."

"I know," I say, and then clasp my hands under my chin. "But I want to see him and tell him we're having a baby, okay?"

"Okay," she says softly. "I can stall things for a little while and talk to Vektal, but when they decide his punishment, there's nothing I can do, all right?"

I shrug. What are they going to do? He's a tribe member and a soon to be dad. If he gets more hunting duty, I'll just go with him. If they give him a fine of some kind, I don't think he'd care. And from what I've seen, lashes or physical punishment would be a bit extreme. Whatever it is, it can't be that bad.

And whatever it is, we'll face it together.

After all, I feel as if I've survived a few "worst-case scenarios" so far. Kidnapped by aliens to be sold as cattle? Crash-land on an ice planet? Starve while stewing in your own filth for a few weeks?

I got this "worst-case scenario" shit nailed. Everything after that is a cakewalk.

Georgie says a few words and two warriors head out of the caves. We wait in silence, and then a few minutes later, Raahosh stalks in, flanked by the warriors. He looks pissy as hell, his fists clenched and his body vibrating anger. His weapons are gone, and there's a small bruise on his jaw.

Maybe all of this is getting to me, because at the sight of him, I burst into girly tears.

His expression immediately changes to the possessive one and he pushes through the crowd in the cave to get to me. I hear murmuring, but I don't care. My cootie has started vibrating, singing a song to his. He sweeps me up against him and presses me against his chest, his big arms holding me close. I can hear his cootie vibrating in time with mine, and I give a small little sigh of happiness.

I'm in his arms. Everything's okay.

"Liz?" He brushes his hand over my cheek. "What is wrong?"

I scrub a hand over my eyes like a child. "I'm just tired. I want to go lie down somewhere quiet and talk."

His hand strokes my hair. "Of course."

Kira comes up to us, and I'm surprised to see Aehako at her side again. She watches me, her sad eyes intent as Raahosh holds me close. I can't tell if there's envy on her face or worry. Both? "They've had to change a lot of the sleeping quarters around," she says. "I don't know if there's a quiet place to be had."

Aehako nods and crosses his big arms. "Raahosh's things have been moved with the other hunters. There are five sharing that cave. Zolaya and his mate are in your old cave."

Raahosh snarls. "Then where—"

"Let's just go outside," I tell him, gripping his arms. I'm already tired of this cave packed full of people, with the humidity and the staring. "I'd rather be out there with you."

"You can't," Aehako says. "I'm sorry. Vektal wants you watched for now."

Me, because they know Raahosh won't go anywhere without me. I blow out a breath of frustration. "Then where can we go?"

"You can come to the bachelorette cave," Kira offers. "That's where the human ladies who didn't resonate are staying."

I nod and hold on to Raahosh tighter. "You guys won't mind if my big blue friend shows up?"

"Not at all," she says, and a smile crosses her solemn face.

Aehako adds, "It's not as if they are not entertaining other big blue friends—"

Again, she bats at his arm and I see a blush creep up her face, but they're both hiding smiles. There's a story there, and probably a juicy one, but I'm too tired and mentally worn out to ask about it right now. I just want to curl up with Raahosh for a while.

"You can have my bed," Kira says. "It's about as private as you get around here." She nods and gestures for us to follow her. We do, and Kira leads us to one of the back caves. Two familiar human faces look up as we approach, but Kira waves them off. "Liz needs to rest. There'll be time to chat later."

The "bachelorette" cave is fairly roomy, the ceiling smooth and tall. If I had to guess, the room's about twenty feet long and maybe half as wide. There's a couple of beds along the floor, a fire-pit in the center that Tiffany's feeding fuel into, and a curtained area off to one side. Kira brings us there and gently pulls aside the leather curtain, revealing a niche in the wall that holds her fur-strewn bed.

"I was going to share my bunk with Nora, but then she resonated . . ." Kira shrugged. "I'll bunk with another one of the girls tonight. You rest. If you get hungry, let me know and I can bring you guys something."

"Thanks, Kira." I crawl into the hidey-hole of furs and blankets and sigh happily when I lie down. My feet ache from all the walking, and when Raahosh draws the curtain again, it's private. I can almost imagine we're alone again.

Almost. There's still the hum of voices nearby, all speaking a strange language.

My big delicious alien lies down beside me and pulls me gently into his arms. His fingers brush over my cheek and his worried gaze sweeps over my face. "Are you well, Liz?"

I nod. "Just . . . stressed. They don't seem like they are happy to see you again."

"In their eyes, I have done a bad thing." He shakes his head and then lightly kisses my mouth. "Yet I would not change it for anything."

I kiss him desperately, twining my fingers in his hair. I love the hot, hard feel of his body against mine, and I'm starting to love the way my cootie vibrates whenever his is near. "I just worry about you," I tell him when I pull my mouth from his.

A flicker of surprise crosses his face. "Me?"

"Yeah, I don't know if you've noticed, but your people are kinda being dicks," I say softly. "But don't worry. I have your back."

"My back?" His brows draw together.

"It means I've got you. Whatever happens, you can depend on my support."

His lips part, and for a moment, he looks utterly speechless. Then, he crushes me against him again. "You are everything to me, Liz. You are my world."

"I love you, too, big guy," I tell him. And then I perk up, because I have some news, however early it might be. "Hey, guess who is going to be a father?"

Raahosh's eyes light up with happiness, and his hand reverently touches my stomach. "Truly?"

"Confirmed by the healer," I agree. "Junior will be born sometime between nine months from now and, uh, thirty-six months or something." I'm trying not think about that.

"Junior?"

"I guess we could Brangelina our names. Raahiz? Lizhosh?"

"Those sound . . . terrible." His fingers trace over my flat belly.

"You're not wrong." I'm smiling. "I'll give it some thought. Maybe shorter. Like Raaz or Losh."

"Our child," he murmurs, and places his head on my belly. "Our kit. We will be a family."

I drag my fingers through his hair, petting him. "I like the thought of that. A family."

Raahosh's family.

No one bothers us for the rest of the evening, and I eventually drift off to sleep. I'm too exhausted and unsettled to do more than just hold Raahosh close and snuggle with him, and so we cuddle through the night. In the morning, though, the small, peaceful bubble we have disappears.

"Liz?" Georgie says through the curtain. "We need you and Raahosh to come out, please."

I yawn and move to pull back the curtain. Before I can, though, Raahosh pulls me against him. He cups my face and gives me a solemn look.

"Know that you are my life, Liz," he says in a soft voice. His khui resonates with mine, and he gives me a gentle kiss on the mouth.

"I know," I tell him. Then, I pull back the curtain.

Vektal stands there, a frown on his face. Several of the other tribe men are behind him, and they look unhappy. Georgie is at Vektal's side and wrings her hands, her gaze worried.

"Raahosh," Vektal says in a proud voice. "At my mate's request, I have given you the night to say your goodbyes to your woman. But—"

"Goodbyes?" I sputter. "What?"

"But," Vektal continues in a strong voice. "Tribe law has been broken. You were forbidden to take the woman, Leezh. You did so and knew the cost." He lifts his chin and his face looks weary for a moment, and sadness flickers in his eyes. "The elders and I have conferred and your sentence is exile."

"Exile?" I parrot, unable to believe what I'm hearing. "For borrowing me for a while?"

"For accosting you and endangering your life," Vektal says. "For that, he is cast out of the tribe."

Raahosh's expression is shuttered, his eyes narrow, icy slits of blue. He gets to his feet and moves to my side. His arms clench tightly around me. "This is not right. She resonated to me."

"And I warned you," Vektal counters. "And you deliberately disobeyed my orders. These humans are unknown. What if she had rejected her khui? What if she had needed the healer? You endangered her by keeping her hidden. You forced her hand."

"The khui decides," Raahosh says flatly. "We do not. Liz is mine."

I'm a little concerned that Raahosh has fallen into the MINE-MINE-MINE trap again, but he's upset and I don't blame him. This is getting out of control, fast.

"You are exiled," Vektal repeats. "Pack your things and leave the caves."

I look at Raahosh, shocked, then turn back to Vektal. "But I'm pregnant! With his baby!"

"You are staying," the leader says, and crosses his arms. "You and your kit will be safe here in the caves."

"You cannot separate us!" Raahosh snarls. He holds me closer, and this time I cling to him. I don't want to leave him.

"She will be taken care of here. You know this." Vektal's voice is colder than anything I have ever heard. "I am sorry, my brother, but as leader, this is something I cannot ignore." With a sad look, he steps back and three big men step forward.

One is Aehako, and the look he gives Raahosh is unhappy. "Come," he says. "Do not make this harder than it already is."

"No," Raahosh says, and he presses his mouth to my hair. "I will not leave my mate!"

Georgie's hands tug at me. "Come on, Liz."

"But—no!" I don't want to leave him! I don't want any of this to happen!

Suddenly, there are people pouring into the small nook. Hands grab me and I scream as I'm tugged out of Raahosh's arms. He bellows like a wounded animal and begins to fight, and I see arms and legs flying—not all his—as he struggles to get back to me. They hold him down and separate us, and I watch, tears blurring my eyes, as they drag my struggling mate out of the cave.

"Liz!" He bellows. "LIZ!"

"Raahosh!" I scream back. I want to go with him. I shrug off the helpful people holding my arms and try to follow, only to have Georgie grab me around the shoulders. I try to push her away but she gives me a fierce look.

"Stop, Liz. You're making it worse."

"You can't exile him," I protest. I feel more stupid tears coming on. "You just can't."

"He's broken the laws," Georgie says in a soft voice. "They

don't have many, but that's the big one. Endangering a woman is like a death sentence around here."

"But—exile? What about his family? I thought that was the point of all this!" I smack a hand against my chest, where my cootie is silent. "You wanted me to have an alien mate and now you're taking him away!"

"LIZ!" Raahosh's pained bellow echoes in the caverns, but it's receding. They're taking him away.

This can't be happening. It can't.

How can I find a mate only to lose him?

PART SIX

PART SIX

Liz

I stare out at the snowy landscape from the entrance of the tribal caves. In the distance, high up on a ridge, there's a lone figure sitting in the snow, facing the caves. His shoulders are slumped in defeat, and if I squint hard, I can make out just one single horn.

My poor Raahosh.

They won't let him come any closer to the caves. Exile is exile, I am told, and he's not welcome anymore because he can't stick to the rules. I'm not allowed to go out and see him, either. My cootie sings a sad, lonely song when I see him, and I blink back frustrated tears.

"This is wrong," I say to Kira, who stands next to me. Someone's always at my side, or lurking around. I'm never alone here, and it's driving me nuts. We've only been back for a day and all chaos has set in. I stare at Raahosh's lonely figure up on the rise and my throat clenches around a knot. "His heart was in the right place."

"No, it wasn't." Her voice is gentle, but firm. Kira's always quietly strong. She doesn't have the determined grit of Georgie, or my irreverent commentary, or Josie's sunny smiles. Kira's the solemn, all-business one. "His heart wasn't in the right place and you know it."

"Okay, so he's a dick," I say irritably. "What do you want from me? He's *my* dick, though, and I want to keep him."

"Come on." Her voice is soothing as she steers me gently away from the cave mouth. "You're just torturing yourself with this, and it's not good for you."

"What about what's good for him?" I fight against the knot in my throat again. "Why does no one care what happens to him?"

"People are angry." Kira puts an arm around my waist and leads me back to the "bachelorette" cave. "They need some time for tempers to cool."

"I don't care if their tempers cool as long as their minds change," I grumble, but let her lead me back toward the others.

The bachelorette cave almost feels like the alien ship's hold, back when we were captured by the Little Green Men. Megan's there, and Josie, and Kira. Tiffany's out helping Maylak with her little one—the two have already become close friends, according to Kira, despite the language barrier. The only difference is that now instead of Georgie here, we have Harlow, the only tube girl that didn't resonate to someone.

Well, okay, it's not the only difference. We're warm and fed and no one's trying to sell us as cattle, and we don't have to poop in an overflowing bucket. There's heated water and soap for when we want to bathe. The people are friendly. We've been welcomed.

I should be pleased as punch.

Instead, I'm still stewing over Raahosh's treatment. I don't understand how a people that were so gung-ho about us mating are ready to just separate us that quickly. Don't they care that he loves me and I love him and we made a baby together? Isn't that all part of their master plan? But here we are once more, and I'm fighting to hold back my misery. Georgie may be happy as can be, and maybe whiny Ariana has stopped crying all the damn time, but if they think they're done with tears around here, they haven't seen anything yet.

Kira steers me toward the fire pit at the center of the cave and sits me down on a carved rock seat that is lined with furs and pillows. "Why don't I get you some hot tea?"

Josie touches my knee as I sit, and her small, round face is sympathetic. "You doing okay, Lizzie?"

Am I doing okay? I suppose that's the million-dollar question. I'm not sure I've been okay for a long time. I'd say maybe I haven't been okay for the last month, ever since the Little Green Men kidnapped me while I was sleeping and stuck me in a dirty hold with a bunch of strangers. But maybe I wasn't okay even before then, because I was lonely and unhappy, with a father that I missed every day since his death and a job that sucked my soul out.

So yeah. I'm not okay. Now that I have found someone that I love and care about and want to be happy with? Someone that I can see myself spending time with? And he's exiled and I'm here alone with his baby in my stomach? I don't think I'm okay, no.

But I'm also pretty sure that Josie's hopeful expression will crumple if I say otherwise, and it's not fair to the other girls to rage in their faces. They didn't make the decision. So I just pat her hand. "Ducky. Just ducky."

"You're a terrible liar," Megan says in a soft voice.

I give her a thin smile. So I am.

"You can help me with this," Kira says, and puts a soft pelt in my hands. "I'm making a hooded poncho. We have the khui but it's still not quite warm enough for us if we leave the caves, so we're making winter gear for all the human girls."

"I'm glad it's the cold season now," Harlow comments, and I see she has sewing in her lap, too.

Sewing. Someone kill me now.

"Actually, this is the warm season," I point out as I pick up the sewing and stare at it with something like horror. Turning my skirt into pants was necessity. Sewing for fun is just . . . ugh.

Silence falls in the cave.

Kira blinks and sits nearby with her own sewing, the big shell of the translator in her ear sticking out painfully. "I thought they said that this was the bitter season."

"Oh yeah," I say, stabbing my bone needle through the leather. "It is. But then comes the brutal season. They're a whole bunch of Eeyores, this group."

"You mean it's going to get colder?" Harlow doesn't sound happy. "I can't believe that this is considered warm to them."

"Did you not see the summer gear they all wear? Vektal's prancing around in a vest, for fuck's sake." They're silent, and I see they're all digesting this information.

"How did you find out?" Josie asks.

"Raahosh told me." I can't help but twist the knife a little. "Gee. I wonder what other things they're not telling you guys? I thought we were supposed to be equals but maybe the goal is to keep us all barefoot and pregnant and sewing."

More silence. I see Josie put down her sewing, upset.

"I think I need to take a walk," Megan says, and gets up and leaves the cave.

Seed of dissent? Firmly planted. I bite back my smile and sew cheerfully. If I'm going to be fucking miserable, I'm going to take them all with me.

The others scatter, the cheerful mood gone, and pretty soon it's just me and Kira sitting by the fire, sewing.

"What are you doing?" Kira asks.

I hold up the poncho. "Sewing like a good little woman."

"No, seriously, Liz. Are you trying to stir up shit?" Her weirdly blue-glowing gaze pierces me.

"So what if I am?"

She puts her sewing in her lap and her mouth flattens into a hard line. "Have you thought about this? Really and truly thought about this?"

"Look, all I can think about right now is my guy, and the fact that a bunch of jerks won't let me be with him! They wanted me to take a mate. I did. They wanted him to knock me up, then the moment he does, he gets exiled. So you'll forgive me if I'm not feeling charitable toward the ice Na'vi right now on Frosty Planet Avatar."

She exhales loudly. "Did it ever stop to occur to you that we're all dependent on their goodwill? They know how to survive here. We don't. They can hunt here and know the planet. We don't. Before they took us in, we didn't know how to build a fire or even feed ourselves. Look around you, Liz. There's no grocery store or snow-cone shack here. There's no Walmart for warm clothing and there's no central heat. So I don't want you pissing these people off, understand? Because if we have to end up back in the snow again on our own, there's a lot worse that could happen to us than doing a little sewing!" She gets to her feet and leaves, tossing her silky brown hair behind her.

In a network of overcrowded caves, I have somehow managed to piss off everyone enough that they've left me alone for the first time in a day and a half. A weird, miserable little half laugh bubbles from my throat, and it turns into tears soon enough. I sniff and wipe at my cheeks, hating that I'm crying.

I think I'd rather be out in the wild with Raahosh than in here, alone and missing him.

And it's only been a day. How am I expected to just carry on as if my heart isn't broken?

My cootie is silent. It agrees with me. This is no way to live.

I stab my needle into the fur again and sit in the humans' cave by myself.

I end up sleeping in Kira's bed again that night, except instead of Raahosh holding me close, it's Kira wrapped in blankets on the other side of me. I end up weeping quietly for most of the night, miserable. How is Raahosh able to stand this? He's out in the cold snow, alone. He can find a cave and take care of himself, but my mind is full of his lonely vigil up on the rise, staring down at the cave, hoping for a glimpse of me.

I sleep terribly that night despite all the comforts of the tribal caves. My mind is full of nightmares, and when I wake up, I'm queasy. I barely make it out of the bachelorette cave before I'm stumbling to the cave entrance, looking for somewhere to barf. There's a bathroom system in the caves but the entrance is a lot closer. I make it out into the snow a few moments before I puke, and then retch miserably for a few minutes before sitting up and wiping my mouth.

Kira's there a moment later and offers me something that looks like a foot-long pink eyelash. "Eat this."

"What the fuck is it?" I clutch my aching stomach.

She points at the pink, wispy trees. "A leaf, I think. They make a tea out of it, too, but Maylak says it's good for the stomach when it's upset."

"How do you know?"

A wry smile curves her mouth. "Because I got it from Georgie? I'm surprised you didn't meet her out here."

"Ugh. Is it catching? I thought the cootie was supposed to

take care of this shit." I shove the flimsy leaf in my mouth and chew. It tastes bitter and unpleasant, but then again, so does all the stuff that just came flying up my throat.

"You have a case of the babies. I don't think it's catching." Kira holds a waterskin out to me next and I rinse my mouth. "Unless you know something I don't."

I shake my head and spit the water out, then kick a bit of snow over my sick. "I thought it was too early for morning sickness."

"Yeah, but we're also human, and it's hard to say how things are going to affect us cross-species, remember? We don't even know when the babies will be due."

I grimace and pick leaf out of my teeth. "Don't remind me, okay?"

"If it makes you feel any better, Ariana and Marlene haven't shown any symptoms of morning sickness." She offers a hand to help me up.

"You know, actually that does not make me feel better. Not only did they get to sleep in the tubes, but they get the easy pregnancies, too? I hate those bitches." I let her help me to my feet and brush wet snow off of my leathers.

A horrified laugh escapes her. "Shhh, Liz." She giggles, then looks around to see if anyone heard us. "You're terrible."

"So I hear." We head back toward the entrance of the cave and I'm surprised to see Aehako lurking nearby, his arms crossed. He walks away when he sees us come back in and I frown. "Man, that guy is everywhere lately."

"Mmm." Kira avoids making eye contact with me.

A suspicious thought crosses my mind and I look over at my companion. "Is he stalking you or is he following me?"

One corner of her mouth lifts up in a rueful expression. "Little from column A, little from column B?"

I give her another curious glance. "And you just happened to be at hand?"

Her cheeks pink and she looks away. A small sigh escapes her. "You know it doesn't matter, right?"

"What do you mean?" She starts walking toward Georgie and Vektal's cave and I follow her, because I want to hear more about this.

"I mean Maylak says there's nothing wrong with our khui. And all of the women eventually resonate."

"So?"

"So . . . let's say I fall for a guy and then I resonate for someone else?" The expression on her face is sad. "There's no point in getting romantically involved with anyone if it's not going to go anywhere or I have to discard them the moment my body decides otherwise."

"Ah." I guess it hasn't occurred to Kira to fuck a guy for funsies. Maybe she's not that kind of girl. Actually, looking back, she's definitely not that kind of girl from what I can tell. Kira's so serious. Maybe it's a good thing Aehako's flirting with her. He's always smiling. She could use that in her life.

Someone deserves to be happy in this clusterfuck, at least.

Georgie meets us with a yawn and then sniffs her braid. "I smell. You guys wanna join me in the bath?"

I glance back at the bathing pool that's in the center of the cavern. It's a common gathering place for a lot of the people here, and for once, it's empty. There is a pair of women scraping skins nearby and chatting but things are pretty quiet. A bath sounds nice.

Except for one thing. "I don't have a swimsuit."

Georgie gives me a wry look. "They have different standards of modesty here. No one cares if you're naked."

"Uh, I care."

"Really? I heard you got frisky with Raahosh while Haeden and Aehako were a few feet away."

"Well, someone has a big mouth around here," I tease her back. She's not wrong, though. "Fine. Gimme some soap. I'll go nakey-bathing with you."

She grabs some soap cakes and hands me one. It smells like berries and a memory shoots through me. Raahosh uses these same berries for his soaps. I clutch it tightly and wonder if he's still lurking around this morning. I didn't see him outside earlier.

Georgie and I strip down to our skin and get into the pool in the center of the cavern. In the water, I can smell sulfur and the water is warm like a bath. I moan with pleasure. It's like having a hot tub in the middle of the house. Okay, maybe this cave isn't so bad, then.

"Good stuff, huh?" Georgie says, dunking her head and then coming back up for air. She looks over at Kira, who sits on the lip of the pool, hikes up her leather skirt, and slides her legs in. "You should tell her to join us."

"Yeah, Kira," I say, lathering up my soap cake. "What's up? You don't want to get in?"

Her cheeks are hot. "I'm fine." She swings her legs in the water but makes no move to dunk herself.

Georgie gives me a knowing look and lifts her chin, indicating something behind me. I look over, and sure enough, there's Aehako again, pretending to look busy off to the side. "That man needs a hobby," I tell them.

"Vektal asked him to watch over you for a bit," Georgie says in a whisper.

"I figured as much." I soap my arms and then start on my torso. "So, should I give him a show?" I pretend to wash my breasts in an obscene fashion under the water.

"Stop it, Liz," Kira says, but she's blushing.

"You're right. If I want his attention, I should wash your breasts," I tease.

She huffs and jumps to her feet, then storms away. I watch her go and then look over to Aehako, who is also watching her.

"She's a little sensitive," Georgie says, moving to sit on one of the underwater ledges.

"Aren't we all," I comment, thinking of my own man. Georgie has Vektal's ear. While part of me wants to hold her underwater until she gets him to cave, the other part of me knows that I'll get further on the Return-Raahosh-to-the-Fold quest if she doesn't hate my guts. I sit on another one of the ledges and set my soap on the lip of the bathing pool. "This sure is a weird cave."

"Right?" Georgie says, agreeing. "I asked Vektal about it but he says his ancestors carved it. I kind of wonder if they had some equipment back on their ship that we don't have now." She shrugs. "At any rate, I'm grateful for it. Especially the bath."

"A bath without the face eaters is nice," I agree. That sets off another round of memories of Raahosh and our first makeout by the river. Dammit. I miss him so much. It's like an ache in my chest that won't go away. Blinking back tears, I notice the women scraping the skins nearby have their heads together and they're talking and giggling while looking over at me.

"I thought you said they don't care if we're naked?" I ask Georgie.

"They don't," she says, and avoids meeting my gaze.

A curl of unease unfurls in my stomach. "What?"

She bites her lip. "Raahosh has been showing up every few hours with a kill."

"A kill?" I repeat dumbly.

Georgie nods and wrings out her wet curls. "Kills to feed his mate. He says you like the quilled beasts best. He's brought four so far over the last few hours, and they have to keep chasing him away."

Warmth suffuses my body, more than even the hot-tub-like pool can give. He's still trying to care for me. What a total sweetheart. Tears prick my eyes again. "I love him, Georgie."

"I know, Liz. We just have to give things time." She shrugs her shoulders helplessly. "Vektal can't cave on this, not with so many other men eyeing the girls. He worries about them, too. Six girls haven't resonated, and he is concerned that if he eases up on Raahosh, he's going to put them in danger. Some of these men have never had a mate. They're full of longing for a family. What's to stop one of them from kidnapping a girl and holding her captive for months—or a few years—to try and force her to resonate for him?"

"Would that work?" I'm shocked.

She shrugs again. "How do we know it won't? We're all young and healthy so it stands to reason that if they haven't resonated yet, they will soon enough."

The situation's a lot more complicated than I thought. I feel a little sorry for Vektal, who's clearly trying to look at all angles of the situation . . . and then I get pissed that I'm feeling sorry for the guy that's keeping me and my mate apart. "It's different," I point out to Georgie. "Raahosh was resonating to me when he stole me. It's not the same."

She gives a half nod. "Which I tried arguing to keep him here. Vektal's super torn up, you know. Raahosh is one of his closest friends. Exiling him was so hard on Vektal. Even now he's out there trying to talk to him, to make him understand." She grimaces. "Your mate is . . . not that understanding."

"All he sees is that you're separating him from me." Surely they can't expect him to be happy about that.

Georgie nods. "It's hard for me because I want to side with you . . . but Vektal's my mate. I have to trust him to know how to run his tribe or else I'm sabotaging him, too."

I sigh. "God, this is all so complicated."

"I know. I'm trying to smooth things out where I can, you know." Her hands make little circles in the water.

"Oh?" I don't know that I like the sound of that.

Georgie hesitates, then blows out a long breath. "Don't get mad, okay? Just know that I already defused the situation."

I stare at her, my entire body tense. "Well, now you'd better fucking spill the beans or I really will get mad."

She makes a pained little face and then wrings her curly hair again. "So . . . Vektal wants to get things settled and calmed as soon as possible so everyone can go back to their normal lives. And there's a few males that are widowers with grown children—"

"No," I growl immediately. I know where this is heading and absolutely fucking not. "No, no, and hell no!"

"He thought they would be willing to take on a mate and a child," she says quickly. "But I told him humans don't work like that and it would be really, really bad."

"I can't believe him," I explode at her. "Are you fucking serious? Raahosh has been exiled a day and he's trying to marry me off to someone else!"

Georgie waves a hand, trying to get me to lower my voice. "He's not thinking like a man with a mate would," she explains, "but as the chief of his people. I pointed out to him how he'd feel if the same thing happened to me and that shut things down fast."

I wrap my arms around myself under the water and try to hold back my trembling. This is ridiculous.

I have to find a way to fix this, and soon.

The tribal caves are pure torture.

For one, I'm surrounded by happy couples, several of whom are newly mated and doting on each other. It's hard to watch Vektal caress Georgie's arm while she works on braiding a net. It's hard to see Ariana all giggly over her mate. It's even hard to see Maylak handing off her small child to her husband, because I'm struck with such envy.

Nights are even worse, of course. The caves are mostly quiet, but they're not super large, so you can usually hear someone—or several someones—having sex. Occasionally one of the girls in the bachelorette cave will giggle when we hear Georgie's voice rising in a soft cry that she's not so good at muffling. Mostly it makes me jealous and sad, though. Some of the unattached girls sneak out of the bachelorette cave at night. I don't blame them.

In fact, seeing them sneak around gives me ideas.

I wait until things are super quiet and it's late at night. Then, I slide out of my own pallet of furs (since they've "thoughtfully" given me a permanent one now) and tiptoe toward the main room of the cave.

And of course, that jerk Aehako is sleeping at the mouth of the bachelorette cave. He gives me a sleepy look and sits up as I try to tiptoe past. "Where are you going?"

"Pee break," I tell him.

"There is a room for such things," he comments, getting to his feet.

"Now where are you going?" I ask as I try to step past him.

"I am following you, of course."

"Gah. Can you not?"

He sighs and looks around, then pulls me into the main cave. I follow him, curious, and we step into a quiet alcove. Then, he stoops down to whisper. "Are you trying to escape?"

"Escape implies I'm being held captive, doesn't it?" I cross my arms over my chest. "You tell me. Am I trying to escape?"

"You're very stubborn, aren't you?" He crosses his arms over his chest in imitation of mine.

"Buddy, you have no idea."

He looks confused. "If I had an idea, I would not be asking."

I wave a hand. "Sarcasm. Ask Kira about it. Look, I just want to see Raahosh, okay? I miss him." My voice breaks a little. "I want to know if he's okay." Actually, I know he's not okay, but I want to see him anyhow.

I expect Aehako to put his foot down and demand that I go back to my bunk, but he glances around the cavern instead. He leans in again. "If I let you go out and talk to him, I must ask you to do something."

"What's that?" I try not to let my eagerness show.

For once, he's not laughing or smiling. His face is drawn with tension. "You must tell him that he needs to leave here. He cannot stay." When I gape, he continues. "It's killing him. He's hunting endlessly and not sleeping. He feels his only purpose is to provide for you, so he is destroying himself to do so. He has no sense of worth at the moment. You must convince him to leave and start a new life."

My heart aches. What must Raahosh be going through? I feel guilty that I'm in here, with company, bathing in the pool while he's out there, miserable and alone. I force myself to nod. "Of course."

I'm full of lies. I have no intention on telling him to go away. But if that's what it takes for Aehako to be convinced, I'll say whatever I need to.

He studies me for a long moment and then nods. "Come, then."

I have to bite back my excitement. My cootie immediately starts throbbing in my chest at the thought of Raahosh, and I press a hand over my breast to quiet it.

Raahosh

I rip an arrow out of my kill, rage the only thing driving me to keep going. Rage, and the need to provide for my mate.

They may keep her from me, but they cannot keep me from doing my duty to her.

I return the arrow to my quiver and pick up my kill. It's a fat quilled beast, and should make a good meal for Liz. I picture her soft, pink lips curling up in a reluctant smile as she is fed, but lets me know she's not happy about it. That she can feed herself, thank you. That she is as strong and capable a hunter as me.

I rub my chest, where it aches at the thought of her lovely face. My khui is silent. It feels the loss of her as keenly as I do.

It's late, the moons high in the sky and spilling their light onto the snow. My bones ache with exhaustion and I can't remember the last time I ate, but it doesn't matter. Feeding Liz is the only thing that keeps me going. I have faint memories of my father's despair at my mother's death—his anguish and his inability to leave his bed for long periods of time to care for me or the sickly baby brother who was destined to die without proper care.

Then, I did not understand his suffering. I do now. I am living it all over again.

Snowflakes whip into my eyes and the night breeze picks up. I immediately tense. The cold doesn't bother me, but I worry about my Liz. Humans are so fragile. What if she is not kept warm by the others? What if they don't look after her as I do? Panic clutches at my chest and I immediately grab my most recent kill and stalk toward the tribal cave. I will deposit Liz's latest meal and then go hunting for the creature with the warmest fur I can find. Perhaps a shaggy dvisti. The females about to bear young have thick, woolly coats that would make a fine cloak for my mate—

Two figures appear in the snow. I see nothing but glowing eyes, and my hand clenches around my bow. One pair of eyes is about my height, but the other is much smaller and would barely reach my pectoral. The only things that size are . . .

Humans, I realize.

Liz!

I drop my kill and push forward through the snow, my khui immediately beginning to sing. Before I can even see her face, I can hear her khui, resonating to mine. It speeds my steps.

"Raahosh?" Her beloved voice calls out softly, and a moment later, her small body is in my arms. I crush her to my chest, my hand cradling her head as I rain kisses down upon her brow.

My Liz. My love. My everything.

Her arms go around me and she shudders. "Oh God, Raahosh. Your skin is like ice, baby. What are you doing out here at this time of night? You should be near a fire—"

"Shh," I tell her. Nothing else matters but that she is here, and she is in my arms. Off to one side, I see it is Aehako with her, and my jealousy surges for a moment. He lingers about my mate, even though she belongs to me. I don't like it, but she is safe at least.

Her small hands brush over my chest and then down my stomach and she gasps. "I can feel your ribs, Raahosh. Have you been eating?"

Have I? I don't know. My thoughts have been bleak and not entirely my own since they took her from me. I shrug. "It's not important. Are you well? Is our kit?" I touch her everywhere, stroking my hands down her arms and then across her belly.

"The baby's fine, I have the morning barfs, and I'm going to be pregnant for three stinking years," she says. "Can you believe that?"

"Yes?"

She pats my arm. "Sarcasm, baby." Her hands slide under my tunic and I feel her fingers against my skin. She's cold, but her khui is thrumming a song with mine and my cock reacts. I ignore it, because Aehako is still nearby, leaning against a rock and pretending he doesn't hear us.

I pull one of her hands into mine and lace our fingers together, then kiss her knuckles. It doesn't matter to me that she has four knuckles instead of three. She could have eight on each hand and she would be the most beautiful of all creatures. "Why are you here so late at night? Why is Aehako with you?"

"He's guarding me," Liz says, and turns her face up for a kiss.

I bend down to brush my mouth over hers, unable to resist. Then her words sink in and my body goes cold with fear. "Guarding you? Are you unsafe there? What—"

"Guarding me because they think I'm going to run away and join you."

"Fools."

"Smart," she says. "I'd do it in a heartbeat. I want to be with you. I want our family to be together."

Her words send an ache of longing through my body. I touch her pale, smooth cheek with infinite tenderness. "You must remain with everyone else, Liz. I have seen what it is like when one is exiled. It's dangerous to be alone."

"I wouldn't be alone. I'd be with you. We can hunt together and have each other's backs."

I smooth my thumb over her lip. "And what about when our kit arrives? What then?"

"We'll figure something out!" Her fingers tighten against mine. "I'm not letting them abandon you like your father did. You're my mate and we're going to be together."

I shake my head. "Vektal has decided."

She turns her face up to mine and the smile that curves her lips is one I recognize. It's Liz when she has a plan and doesn't care if you like it or not. "Then I'll just have to change his mind, won't I?" She wiggles her eyebrows at me. "I'm not going to rest until you're back at my side, where you belong."

"Do not put yourself in danger—"

"I won't be," she reassures me. "I have a get-out-of-jail-free card, remember?" And she pats her stomach.

None of those words make sense to me. "Jailfree?"

"Just trust me, baby." She raises our linked fingers to her lips and kisses my knuckles like I kissed hers. "But give me a few days, all right? You have to take care of yourself for my sake. You have to sleep, and eat. I want my mate to live."

I nod slowly, because living hasn't really been on my mind. My only thought was to take care of Liz for as long as possible, until my energy was spent. But if she wants me to take more care with myself, I will. I slip my fingers from hers and brush them over her cheek again, where I feel the tears freezing to her face. "I will do anything you ask, my mate."

"All I want you to do is trust me and take care of yourself," she says. "I'll handle the rest." And when she turns her face up for another kiss, I cannot resist.

Liz

It takes two days for the first present to show up at my doorstep.

It's a present from one of the widowers. At first it enrages me, but then I decide it can be a tool.

I offer the small pouch of herbal teas to an elder woman named Sevvah at the pool that morning. She's a nice lady, and the unofficial "mom" of the caves. She's Aehako's mother, and affectionate with him and her other sons, Rokan and a young boy named Sessah. She always fusses over the pregnant girls despite the language barrier, probably because she wishes one of her sons had resonated. Sadly, she has three boys and all three are still at home with her. But I like her.

Georgie frowns as I offer the teas to Sevvah. The elder woman says something, smiling, and there's not much that shows that Sevvah is older than the rest of us except for a few lines at the corners of her glowing eyes, and a pale streak of white in her long braid. "She says she can't take it, Liz. That it's a courting present from Vaza."

"But I have a mate," I say sweetly, and offer it to Sevvah

again, with emphasis. I force it into her hands and then walk away before she can refuse.

Georgie gets up and follows me, a frown on her face. She's pissy because, well, I'm being a dick and causing trouble. I question everything, from why the humans who mated have the smallest caves (which sets Ariana off into another crying fit), why the aliens lied to us about the seasons, and anything else I can think of. I have French Marlene convinced that she's having a litter since her mate Zennek is close in age to his two brothers and they're just lying to her about not being triplets. Oh, and Tiffany ended up fooling around with a guy but that went badly when she was surprised by the existence of his "spur," which led to me, wide-eyed and declaring that they were withholding all kinds of information from the humans. Couple that with me not being super pleasant and now every time Vektal sees me, his eyes narrow and Georgie seems to wear a constantly exasperated look on her face.

Okay, so I might have taken things a bit too far when no one got me materials for new arrows and I spent the day declaring that "the man" was keeping me down.

But really, it's all part of my plan. I'm going to be such an asshole until I get what I want, and what I want is Raahosh back.

He's still hanging around outside, and there's a fresh quilled beast for my breakfast every morning. Overall, though, the hunting has slowed and I hope he's taking my advice and looking after himself.

"What are you up to, Liz?" Georgie asks, still following me as I wind my way through the caverns and head back to the bachelorette cave.

"Who, me?" My voice is sweet. Truth is, she's right to be suspicious. I'm always up to something.

"Yes, you. You're going to give Vektal an aneurysm if this attitude of yours keeps up."

"Then both of us will be without our mates," I say as I glance over my shoulder.

"Very funny," she says, her black expression telling me that she doesn't find it funny at all. "You just gave away a courting present and hurt Vaza's feelings. Now Sevvah feels awkward because she feels like she is interfering."

"Then you keep it," I say to Georgie. "Lord knows I don't want it. I have a mate, remember? No one seems to be remembering that part."

"Yes, but he's exiled," Georgie says, moving forward and grabbing my arm. "Is that your goal, too? To be such a jerk that you get exiled also?"

"Oh come on," I say with a roll of my eyes. "Haeden's a jerk and he's not exiled. We both know that the only way you get exiled is to pull a stunt like Raahosh did . . ."

And then my plan blossoms into my brain.

I stare at Georgie, wide-eyed, as she continues to talk, lecturing me about how we need to learn the rules of the sa-khui people and how to be good tribesmates and blah-blah. I'm not listening, because my mind is racing, instead.

Of course. Why didn't I see this before?

I hug Georgie and cut her rant off mid-stream. "You're the best, you know that?"

She blinks at me, surprised. "I am?" Her eyes narrow and for a moment she looks as suspicious of me as Vektal. "You're not going to tell Stacy that they're feeding her rats again, are you?"

"*Moi?*" I put a hand to my breast in mock surprise. "And I didn't tell her that they were rats. Just that they were *like* rats and they were doing it to see what humans would eat."

"Uh-huh," Georgie says. "You realize she makes other people take a bite out of everything first now?"

Okay, so it wasn't one of my finer moments. But in a sabotage campaign, a girl has to do some desperate things if she wants to get her mate back. And getting Raahosh back is my one and only goal.

It takes me a few hours to find the right time to implement my plan. I'm restless and wander through the caves, annoying everyone I run into until Kira takes pity on me. She hands me a woven basket. "Here. You can come with me to get more soapberries. We're running low with all the new people in the caves."

"You sure I can leave?" I give a pointed look over at Aehako, my ever-present guard. He stands a few feet away, whittling something out of bone with his knife. It looks a bit like a figure of a girl, but one side of her head has a blob on it that might be too obviously Kira. Interesting. The man's making no bones about his interest in her, but Kira seems to be keeping him distant.

Not my problem at the moment.

She flushes and moves to Aehako's side. "I'm taking Liz to go get soapberries. We'll be in sight of the cave at all times. We won't go far."

He sheaths his knife, gets to his feet and stretches languidly, then rubs his stomach. "I'll come with you." I notice Kira's gaze follows his hand.

My gaze follows his knife.

She makes a frustrated sound but Aehako won't be deterred. We humans bundle up in cloaks and heavy boots, and then head out, baskets in hand. Aehako trails behind us a few steps, unobtrusive but always present. The day's a bright one, with the twin suns high in the sky. They peek out behind the ever-present gray cloud cover and nearly give me snow-blindness with all the white around us. White hills of snow, white cliffs, white endless plains, white white white.

I see no Raahosh. It's for the best if I'm implementing my plan, but I'm still hungry for a glimpse of his tall, lean body and scarred face.

I don't feel whole without him.

Thinking about my exiled mate gives me the courage to implement my plan. It might backfire on me, but I'm running low on options and this is the best thing I can do to prove how serious I am about having him back. So as we go up the ridge, I pretend to stumble in the snow and fake having trouble getting up. I fling my basket to the side and watch with satisfaction as it rolls down a nearby snowbank. "Dang it."

Kira turns around and looks over at me with concern. "You okay?"

"Fine. Just twisted my ankle a little." When she moves toward me to help me up, I point off to the side. "I'm good. Can you get my basket?"

She nods and trots over to get it, and I stay down, pretending to rub my ankle. Out of the corner of my eye, I see Aehako jog forward (no mean feat given all the snow), and then he bends down at my side.

"Help me up?" I say, offering him my left hand.

When he takes it, I immediately grab the knife sheathed at his waist with my right hand.

He reaches for it, but not fast enough. I have the knife, and then I point it at his groin. "Don't move," I say.

The alien's big brows go up, and he looks more amused than afraid. "What are you going to do with that?"

"I'm taking you hostage," I say and get to my feet. I move to his back and press the tip of the blade where a kidney is on a human. No clue where it is on a sa-khui but the intent remains the same.

"Hostage?" he repeats.

"Yup. If that's what it takes to get someone exiled from this group, you're my hostage. Hands in the air, buddy."

Aehako laughs but does as I say, and when Kira comes up the hillside, she has both baskets and a fierce frown on her face.

"What are you doing, Liz?"

"Hostage situation," I say cheerfully. "I need you to go back to the caves and tell everyone my conditions of release."

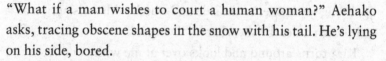

"What if a man wishes to court a human woman?" Aehako asks, tracing obscene shapes in the snow with his tail. He's lying on his side, bored.

"Kiss her silly." I'm sitting cross-legged next to him and we're both scanning the horizon. After Kira left, Aehako took his knife back but agreed to stay "captive" for my sake. So we'd sat and started talking.

And like any guy, Aehako wanted to know about humans. Which was how we got on the topic of courting and sex. "She doesn't want kisses."

No? Crazy Kira. "Then you give her gifts."

He considers this. "What kind of gifts? Something I make with my hands?"

Since I'm still in shit-stirring mode, I think of the thing that might embarrass Kira the most. "Human men give the woman they want to mate a very special gift."

"Oh?" He sits up taller.

I nod authoritatively. "A replica of his penis made out of

leather or wood, or bone. So she can try him out and see if she likes what he brings to the table." You're welcome, Kira.

Instead of looking shocked, Aehako ponders this. "I do have a nice cock."

"I'm sure." I'm pretty sure I don't want to see, either.

"And a large spur. Very large. Do I include that as well?" He looks over at me. "In my replica?"

"Hmm. That's a good question. Humans don't have spurs."

This shocks him. "No spur? Why not?"

"Dude, like I know? I didn't take 'comparative anatomy' in college, and I'm pretty sure we can't compare the spur to anything else. What purpose does it serve?"

He thinks for a minute and then shrugs. "What purpose do balls serve?"

Is he for real? "They create semen."

Aehako looks surprised. "Truly? But how—" He pauses and then points off into the horizon. "They're coming."

"Finally," I say, getting to my feet. I'm kinda glad we're getting off of the whole "sex ed" topic because I only know human anatomy. Kira can finish this conversation with him. "I should probably take the knife back if we're going to do this captive thing right."

He gets it out and hands it to me, handle first. "Try not to cut me." He pauses. "Unless you think Kira will like to play nursemaid."

"I sincerely doubt that," I say, moving behind him and putting the knife in place as the others trail up the ridge. It's a fairly large group, and I see Kira, along with Vektal, Georgie, and a few other male aliens.

And Vektal has a furious look on his face. I keep my chin lifted and stare him in the eye. I won't let anyone boss me around anymore. It's my life, and Raahosh is my mate. They can't keep him from me anymore, and vice versa.

"You are quite the burr in my tail, Liz," Vektal says as he approaches. "Is your goal to anger me so greatly that I cast you out? Because it won't happen. You are a woman and a child-bearer."

"I'm kidnapping someone," I say, and gesture with the knife at Aehako's back. "That's the punishment for kidnapping, right? Exile? So exile me."

The chief of the aliens narrows his eyes at me. He crosses his arms. "Your situation is different."

"Oh, are we throwing situation into the mix? What about if I was resonating to Aehako and I kidnapped him? Would you still let me stay in the caves because I have a vagina?"

He frowns and looks over at Georgie. "Va-shy . . . ?"

She pinches the bridge of her nose. "Girl parts. She's refer-ring to her girl parts. Liz, what the hell is your problem?"

"I want my mate back!" I bellow. "That's my fucking prob-lem! If he can't come back to the caves, then send me with him!"

"You would leave the comfort of the tribe behind?" Vektal asks, and he's not pissed anymore. He just seems weary. Like I've exhausted him. Good.

"It's not my tribe." For some reason, I suddenly feel as tired as Vektal seems. Tired, and just sad. "You guys forget that about six weeks ago, I had an entirely different life. Then I'm captured by aliens and no one asks me anything. They don't say, 'Hey, Liz, how do you feel about being sold as meat? Or a slave? You cool with that?'" Georgie rolls her eyes but I continue. "Then we land here, and again, I'm captured by aliens. And again, I'm told what my fate is going to be, except this time it's wife and baby maker. No one asks if Liz wants kids. No one asks if Georgie does. No one asks us anything." My voice trembles a little. I hate that I'm still emotional over all this shit. "But we go along with it. And I meet Raahosh, and at first I can't fucking stand the guy, right? But then as time goes on, I realize that he's just trying to take care of me the best way he knows how. And when I stop being so irritated with him, I realize that I like him. He's smart and caring and determined. And then I fall in love with him. And then, boom, you take him away from me again." I swallow hard around the knot in my throat. "He's home to me now. So, yeah, I would leave everything behind for him. He's mine and I'm his. You'd do it for Georgie. I'm doing it for him."

Vektal sighs again, but there's a hint of a smile and a shimmer of tears in Georgie's eyes. She understands, even if her mate doesn't. He looks over at her and his expression softens. He pulls his mate against him and tucks her under his arm, perhaps imagining himself in Raahosh's place. "There must be rules," Vektal says again. "There must be punishment."

"Make him live with Liz," jokes Aehako. "That's enough punishment for anyone."

I don't even protest that one.

Vektal rubs his chin. "I shall think on what you say, Liz. And I shall discuss Raahosh with the elders. It is ultimately my decision, but . . . I shall think on this."

"I have things to say, too," Georgie murmurs, and puts a hand on his arm.

His expression softens as he looks down at his mate and nods. "We will talk as well." He turns to the man standing in front of me. "Aehako, get the hunters and find Raahosh and bring him back. We will talk."

Aehako lifts his chin and nods in my direction. "I'm being held captive."

"Whoops. Sorry." I hand him back his knife. "You're free to go and stuff."

He grabs me and pulls me against him and ruffles my hair like a big brother. "This was a good idea," he murmurs in my ear before he releases me.

Then, Georgie steps forward and takes my arm. "Come on. We're not taking our eyes off you for another minute." She peers past me to her mate. "And hide your knives, Vektal."

I'm waiting impatiently in the caverns for what feels like hours. Days, even. Since I've proven that I can't be trusted, two men are posted at the entrance to the bachelorette caves, both mated males who won't be swayed by any of the human charms, I suppose. Tiffany has managed to make a pair of knitting needles out of bones, so I take the extras and make arrows. Even though I'm not allowed to hunt (which is bullshit), I can at least do what I'm good at, and that's make weapons.

It's either that or go stir-crazy waiting.

I'm not allowed knives, of course, so I can't do much more than select good arrows and then rub the head against a rough rock, sharpening it like a pencil.

Vektal's been in his cave all day, and I've been told a few people have gone in and out. Georgie's been gone, too.

So have Aehako and his group. Not that I'm worried or anything. But . . . what if they can't find Raahosh? What if he's so tired and hungry that he's been careless and hurt himself? My mind is full of worry. I don't know what I'll do if I lose him.

There's a commotion at the front of the caves, and I hear the sound of voices rising. I immediately fling down my arrows and run to the front of the bachelorette cave in the hopes of seeing a familiar head with one horn and a broken stump where the other used to be. "Raahosh?"

"Stay back," says one of the aliens guarding the cave. His name is Dagesh. Nora's mate, I think, and he watches me like I'm a snake. I guess he worries my obnoxiousness is going to be catching.

Either that or he's heard that I was mean to Stacy and is worried I'll pounce on his mate next. Oh well. Sometimes you have to break a few eggs and all that.

But then a large figure appears in the doorway and pushes the men aside, and I can't help the girlish squeal of delight that escapes me when Raahosh sweeps me into his arms.

"You're here," I cry, and wrap my arms and legs around him like a monkey. He grabs me and holds me tight against him, and then we're kissing wildly, my hips settling against his as I cling to him. My cootie hums a happy song and I can feel his in his chest . . . and I can also feel the woody he's sporting in his breechcloth.

Damn, I missed this man.

"You are crazy, my mate," Raahosh says in a low voice even as he presses his mouth to mine over and over again, unable to stop kissing me.

"Hey, it got results, didn't it? You're here." And now that my arms are around him, I'm never letting go again.

He holds me close and our chests resonate in a mixed song. To think that I fought this just a few weeks ago. I feel complete with him. I might not have known what good taste my cootie has, but thank goodness for it.

"Come," Dagesh says and he glances toward the main cavern. "Vektal will talk with you both about your punishments."

Oh dear. I hear the plural in that statement, and it worries me. But I nod . . . and continue clinging to Raahosh. They're going to have to pry me off of him if they intend on separating us again.

My mate only chuckles and his hands go to my ass, cupping it and carrying me into the main cavern with him.

A few ripples of laughter meet our entrance. I don't care. Let them laugh. I press my cheek to Raahosh's warm chest, hearing his cootie resonate to mine. *Please be fair*, I say silently to Vektal. *Please let Georgie have given you the world's greatest prostate tickle and convinced you that Raahosh and I need to be together.*

There's a crowd in the main cavern, and the air feels redolent with sulfur and humidity. We pass by a few people and then Raahosh reluctantly sets me down. I hold my breath, tension vibrating through me. I'm terrified of what's going to happen. If we get a "no" at this point, I don't think we'll ever be able to convince Vektal that we should be together.

People are everywhere in the main cavern, a few lounging in the pool but more clustered at cave entrances and seated off to the side. There, sitting on the steps that I've come to think of as his "chief hangout," is Vektal. He's seated between Georgie's legs, his big arms resting on her knees. His pose is casual, though the look on his face is solemn. Georgie's face is equally emotionless, though when she meets my eyes, she winks.

And I stop holding my breath.

Everything's going to be okay.

"Raahosh, son of Vaashan, you have broken the laws of this tribe." Vektal gets to his feet and clasps his hands behind his back, pacing.

I stiffen and my hand goes to Raahosh's. He clutches it tightly. This doesn't sound promising.

"Normally the endangerment of another's life would be exile. However, the humans are not familiar with our ways, nor are we familiar with theirs."

"Agreed," mutters Aehako.

Vektal continues with a stern look over at the hunter, then turns back to us. "The resonance can affect both parties in ways unexpected, and this is what has been decided in this case. Both of you were mindless to your khui, and thus that must be factored in as well."

My death grip eases on Raahosh's hand, just a little.

"You and your mate will be exiled to the hunter caves. For the next two and a half years—or until your kit arrives—you must remain out on the hunt for seven days to every one. You must bring enough meat to feed the tribe and fill the ice storerooms for two of the brutal seasons. Our numbers have grown, but our number of hunters has not, and this will be more important than ever." He levels a firm gaze at us. "You will have no family cave until your punishment has been removed. Should you endanger the lives of another tribesmate at any time, exile will once more become permanent."

Raahosh exhales through his nostrils. He nods slowly. "Thank you, my chief."

"So what does this mean?" I ask, trying not to sound excited.

"It means you will be out hunting more than you will be here in the caves," Vektal says.

"Really? Both of us hunting?"

Vektal nods. "You say you wish to hunt? We shall treat you like a hunter. We will do the same for any other woman that wishes to contribute. Georgie and I have discussed many things this afternoon. Just because it is the sa-khui way does not mean that it is necessarily the human way, and we cannot force you to be sa-khui women."

Georgie has a pleased smile on her face.

"We will work hard to feed the tribe," Raahosh says in a hushed voice. "Thank you again, my friend."

Vektal nods, and the stern chief expression leaves his face. He moves forward and clasps Raahosh in a hug that surprises my mate. "Welcome back, my friend," he murmurs. Then, he smacks Raahosh on the back with a staggering bro-hit and both are grinning. "You have tonight to prepare. Tomorrow you and your mate begin your work!"

"So we're good?" I ask. I hold my breath again, just in case I'm misinterpreting this. I get my man. I get to hunt. I get out of these crowded caves and we get to be us again. I mean, it'll be a lot of work, but I like hunting.

"We are good," Vektal says.

This is . . . awesome. I squeal and jump into Raahosh's arms again.

⌒

"All right," Georgie says as we survey the storage area in the back of one of the new dens. This is Ariana's cave that she shares with Zolaya, and it used to be storage. Unfortunately for poor Ariana, there's still a lot of storage around the walls of the cave. "Let's get you prepped for hunting so you can be on your way in the morning."

At our side, Kira makes a soft sound. "I'll be sad to see you go, Liz. I liked having you back."

"I'll be back again soon enough," I tell her. Truth is, I'm excited. I'm ready to be out with Raahosh again, in the snow and sun, hunting and loving and exploring and . . . well, just enjoying life. I survey the piles of furs, the baskets of dried leathers, bones, and anything else that might be deemed useful. My mind isn't on hunting at all. It's on Raahosh. I just feel so . . . happy. My mate is talking with Vektal in the chief's den, and I'm getting geared up.

Tonight, we sleep in the hunter cave along with all the other hunters.

In the morning? We take off.

This feels like Christmas.

And I suspect I have Georgie to thank for all of this. She had to have softened up Vektal for me. So instead of grabbing gear, I turn to my fellow human and fling my arms around her in a hug.

She laughs and pats my back. "What was that for?"

"That was a thank-you for fixing things."

"I didn't do anything special," she demurs. "You forget, Raahosh is his friend, too. I just reminded him of how different our societies are."

Uh-huh. Well, if she doesn't want to admit to some persuasive lovin', I'm not going to force her to. I give her one last happy squeeze, then hug Kira, whose sad face is smiling for a change. I feel suspiciously weepy. Happy, but weepy. I turn to the pile of storage. "What do you think I need?"

"One of everything warm?" Georgie pulls out a basket of old leathers and starts to dig through it. "Where do you think you guys will go first? Any ideas? Vektal says that there's tons of hunter caves scattered for miles around. They have a system, and since the hunters stay out in the field a lot, they're all set up like mini-houses with firewood and blankets and stuff."

I consider for a moment. "If it's up to me, I want to go to the old ship—the one that their people came from. I'd like the language dump, I think." I'm tired of everyone talking around me. I want to be part of things.

"I like that idea," Kira says. "I might see if I can head there myself at some point."

"Oh?" I turn to her. "What about the earpiece?"

She touches it with a grimace. "I hate it. I want it gone. Plus, I worry that they'll come back for it if they find it still active."

Kira has a point. I know she can't remove it—they'd surgically attached it to her ear. I didn't realize how much it bothers her, though.

We continue to chat as we prepare a pack for me full of essentials—a sewing kit, some extra cord, dried soaps, warm boots, and leather cloaks, and then there's nothing left to do but say goodbye to my friends.

Kira's expression is sad. "I wish I had some sort of newlywed advice to give," Kira says. "I feel like it'd be appropriate."

Georgie's expression turns . . . well, a bit like a cat who's licking the cream. "I've got some advice for you."

"Oh?" I ask.

"You wanna blow his mind? Two words for you." She ticks them off on her fingers. "Doggy. Style."

My eyes widen. "But the spur will go . . ." When she nods slowly, Kira gapes. "Ohhhh," I breathe. "You are a filthy, filthy girl, Georgie."

"A filthy girl with a happy mate," she says.

Can't argue with that.

The rest of the day runs away from me. There's preparation to be done, weapons to be checked over and repaired before we go back into the field, clothing to be mended, people to hug, and Maylak is determined to send us with every kind of healing herb she has—along with an explanation—in case we need anything.

Hunters, Georgie explains to me as she translates, are used to going without, but because Raahosh and I will be a team (and I'm pregnant), everyone wants to make sure we're well prepared.

Before I know it, dinner is over and then Raahosh comes to collect me from my friends, who have been fitting me for new tunics. Apparently, there's a lot of sewing going on in the bachelorette caves, and I now have two new tunics and two pairs of pants to go with sturdy fur-lined boots.

"Come," Raahosh says, tugging me away gently. "We are leaving early in the morning."

With one last round of hugs, I say goodbye for now and head off with my mate. It's not like we're leaving forever—we're actually just leaving for a week before we return again. But it's a change, and we humans have had so much change recently that I don't blame the other girls when they get teary eyed at the thought of me going.

I'm not sad, though. I can't wait to spend the time with my mate. I can't wait to be alone with him and lick all of his skin until he's pulling my hair.

Totally weird, but I'm into the hair pulling.

Unfortunately, my horniness is thwarted by the hunter cave. We're staying here tonight—and every night that we're back with the group. I thought it would be . . . gosh, I don't know. Empty? Private? Something?

It's literally a row of pallets with zero privacy. The cave is small and light on possessions and most of the unmated young males live here. Raahosh introduces me to them: Ereven, Taushen, Cashol, and my best buddy Haeden, who scowls at the sight of me. Then, Raahosh and I set our packs down and curl up in the last bed, which has been left for us since Zolaya recently moved out with Ariana.

This is part of our punishment, I know. Basically, we're in public sleeping quarters until the exile is up. And it . . . sucks. Because I have been days and days without my Raahosh, and I want nothing more than to sex him into next week.

And we have zero privacy.

He lies down next to me and pulls the blankets tight around us, then drapes an arm protectively around me. My cootie starts purring, and I hear Raahosh's pick up the song and continue it. One of the men snorts, gets up, and leaves the cave.

Well, at least one is gone. That only leaves three others besides us. I sigh.

I'm lying on my side, facing him, because I just want to gaze at him all night. I trace each of his scars with my fingers and let my hands skim along his horns, until he finally catches my palm and kisses the center of it. "Stop, or I will take you here in front of the others," he murmurs, and his hips push against mine.

I can feel his erection, hard and insistent against my body. And I want him.

Fucking cave full of fucking hunter dudes.

I thrum harder, and my hand moves to his chest. I love touching him. I'm almost to the point where I don't care if he takes me in front of the others or not. As long as he takes me, and takes me good.

But then one of the men sighs and rolls over in his bed, and I get an idea.

"Oh, Raahosh," I moan loudly. "Do that thing with your tail again."

My mate's eyes widen in shock and I have to bite back my laugh. Somewhere off to the side, another man mutters something in alien, and then leaves the cave, followed by another. There's just one other than us left, and I bet I can scare him off, too.

"Just like that," I cry out, even though Raahosh is staring at me with horror. "Do me like that with your nasty tail!"

Raahosh's hand clamps over my mouth to silence me, but it works. Another person gets up from his bed and I look over Raahosh's shoulder to see Haeden shoot me a glare before leaving the cave.

Then it's just the two of us.

"You are full of mischief lately," Raahosh murmurs, and pulls me against him to nibble on my neck. "Now they are going to ask me what it is I do with my tail every time they see me."

"You have a good imagination," I tease him. "Use it."

"I don't need imagination." His voice takes on a growly note. "I have hands." He pushes me onto my back and goes to my pants, jerking them down around my hips. I eagerly undo the laces, desperate to have him with me, to be naked with him. The moment they fall loose, I kick them down my legs and then toss them aside. Next goes my tunic, and under the furs, Raahosh is removing his own breechcloth as quickly as possible. My cootie's singing up a storm.

He puts a hand on my breast and rubs his thumb over my nipple, and I moan. "My Liz," he breathes. "My mate."

And then something flicks up and down over my pussy. I gasp and look down. His tail.

"You said to use my imagination," he murmurs, and slides his hand down to my folds. His fingers part them and his tail glides up and down through my slickness. "Is that all you want me to use?"

"God, no." I reach down and cup his cock while he uses his tail to tease my clit. "I want you to use this most of all."

He groans and moves over me, his heavy weight a welcome sensation. Fuck foreplay—I want him in me fast and hard and now.

As he pushes my legs open and kisses me, I remember what Georgie said about blowing his mind. I put a hand on his chest to stop him. "Hey, baby. I have an idea."

Raahosh rears back and gives me a puzzled look. "What is it?"

"I want you to do me from behind."

He tilts his head so comically I almost giggle. "But your tail—"

"Doesn't exist," I point out, and trace one finger around his nipple. "Humans do this sort of thing all the time. You can just flip me over and push into me and—"

No sooner do I say the words than his big hands are turning me over and then my ass is in the air. I giggle even as I get on my hands and knees. Not gonna be hard to drag Raahosh to the dark side, I see.

His hand smooths over my ass and I give a soft sigh of pleasure and close my eyes. "That feels good."

"You are so . . . bare." The big hand moves over my butt, and his fingers trail down the cleft. "It's . . . ."

"Sinful?" I offer, feeling rather wicked myself.

"Beautiful."

Aww. I start to make a comment about his sweet choice of words, but then his fingers glide between my legs and stroke into me from behind. My entire body jolts and I gasp. Jesus, that feels entirely too good.

"Are you wet enough to take me?" he asks, and his fingers stroke in and out. I'm so wet that I can hear his fingers moving, and I nod in response. An excited gasp builds when he pushes the head of his cock against my entrance, and I lean forward, bracing myself.

"Please," I tell him. "Now." I feel like I've waited forever for my lover.

He pushes into me and I cry out because it feels so amazing.

Inch by delicious inch, he works his cock into me, and I wiggle and push back against him, determined to speed things along. Just when I think I can take no more of him and feel stretched to my limits, something nudges against my ass and prods.

Oh *God*.

That has to be his spur.

And there aren't words for how good it feels. My fingers dig into the furs and I cry out again.

Raahosh hushes me, but then he pulls back and thrusts again, and I'm unable to keep my cries to myself. With every stroke of his cock into me, the spur presses and penetrates into my ass, just enough to drive me insane with lust. It's not long before I come, and I come hard, crying out his name. Every muscle in my body locks down around him, and his fingers dig into my hips. He thrusts wildly into me, and then he's coming, too.

With a happy little sigh, I reach backward and hold on to him as he rolls our locked bodies onto our sides. He presses kisses onto my neck and shoulder, and I wiggle against him, because I feel weirdly aroused that his cock (and spur) are sunk into me. I'm tired, my knees are weak and I'm breathing hard . . . but I'm also ready for round two.

"I think you must learn to be quieter if we're going to be in this cave, my mate," Raahosh tells me. "Your shouting likely woke up all the kits on the other side of the caves."

"Fuck 'em," I say, dopey with pleasure. "They want us to be quieter, they'll get us a cave of our own." Because that doggy style . . . whoa. Mind: blown.

"We must finish our exile first." Raahosh nips at my shoulder. "Are you sure you wish to do this, Liz?"

Bleary with endorphins, I run a hand through his hair as he caresses my breasts. "Doggy style? I dug it. A lot."

"No. Leaving with me. Sharing my exile."

What a silly question. "One hundred percent. There's nothing for me here if you're not here."

"It'll be hard work. We have many more mouths to feed with the expansion of the tribe. We will hunt nonstop until it gets too cold to leave the caves."

"Then we'll hunt nonstop," I tell him. "I like hunting."

His hand moves to my belly and traces over it. I'm still flat— and probably will be for quite some time if this three-year pregnancy thing is legit. "It will be easier for you to stay here."

I shake my head. "Do you not understand, Raahosh? You're my life. You're my reason for living. When those aliens took us away from everything, I felt . . . lost. I'm not lost when I'm with you. I'm happy." I touch his cheek. "I'm complete."

"My mate," he murmurs. "My Liz. My everything."

"All yours," I tell him. And it's the truth. As long as I'm with Raahosh, the world can snow all it wants, the tribe can pile all the work they want on us, and we can sleep in the hunter caves.

As long as I'm with him, I'm happy.

BONUS EPILOGUE

GAMES

Liz

Raahosh is in a shit-ass mood this morning.

I glance over at him as we walk away from the home caves, but it's clear he doesn't want to talk. Not that that's ever stopped me before. But I'm trying to be fucking sensitive. I know this is hard for him. Even though we're together now, the fact that those dicks he calls his tribe "exiled" him for one teeny tiny kidnapping still sits wrong with me.

I mean, sure, set an example for the tribe, blah-blah-blah, but fuck all that. He's my man, and when he's sad, I'm angry at everyone who made him sad.

I reach over and brush his hand with mine as we walk down the snowy trails. He's carrying both of our packs, and his bow is slung over his shoulder, his spear in his hand. I'm carrying only my bow, because he insisted on handling everything else, like a true chest-beating caveman. But it leaves my hands free, and so I nudge his pinkie with mine when he doesn't respond to my first hand-touch.

Raahosh looks at me, and no smile curves his mouth.

"Let me guess," I say. "You're already having regrets that you're stuck with me, because you know I'm a better hunter and you hate being shown up."

I expect his mouth to twist up into a smile, but he only reaches out and brushes his fingers over my cheek. "I am grateful we are together. That is all."

Man. I can't even get a hint of a smile out of him today.

I'm tempted to race ahead and pull my pants down, just to see if mooning him gets a reaction of some kind. Any kind. I don't mind Raahosh's anger or his pissiness. I love his laughter and his teasing.

It fucking guts me to see him sad.

Since we're together now, though, it's my job to break him out of this funk. If I have to be Clown Liz to make him smile, I will. If I have to be the horniest human who's ever walked the face of this planet (and let's be honest: I might already be that woman), I will. We're going to be the happiest goddamn exiles anyone on this ice planet has ever seen.

But if he needs a little time to brood, I'll let him brood. I brush my pinkie against his again, and the look he gives me is downright irked. Grr. "I just want to hold your hand, all right? I like touching you. Sue me."

He grips my hand tightly in his, as if he needs something to hold on to, and my heart hurts all over again. I can't imagine how hard it was for him each time he left alone, and it just makes me angrier at all the others. Don't they realize how fucking lonely he's always been? And then to be tossed out by his best friend . . . Well, it's not endearing any of them to me.

We walk in silence, and the weather's nice enough, as if the world is giving us a break on something at least.

"I am sorry," Raahosh says after a time. "I am not good company."

I squeeze his hand. "That's the cool thing about being mated. You can be an absolute dick, and I'll still love you. I'm going to have days where I'm not all sunshine, either, believe it or not." I glance over at him, grinning. "I might even be slightly unpleasant to be around myself."

He grunts, the only response I get to my teasing. Well. Maybe he'll perk up once we're farther away. "So what's the hunting plan?"

"We will go into the mountains," Raahosh tells me. "The caches there are the most difficult to fill because they are the farthest away. It seems as good a place to hunt as any, but we will have to be careful for metlaks."

It's on the tip of my tongue to tell him we should leave the hard stuff for someone else, but I suspect he wants the challenge—and the distance between us and the tribe. Plus, the thought of a long, hard hunt is kinda thrilling. "I'm game."

My big alien glances over at me. "It will be a difficult journey. Are you sure you do not wish to stay behind . . . ?"

My brain fills with a thousand cusswords to shout at him, but I manage a tight smile. "I thought we went over this. I don't care where we go as long as I'm with you. You think I'd be content sitting around the fire with a thumb up my ass, waiting for you to return home? No, thank you. I can hunt at your side. I can help fill the caches. And everywhere you go I'm going to go. That's how this works." I want to snarl that if he tries to leave me behind, I'm going to gut him like a fish, but I'm attempting to be Nice Liz and not Psycho Liz.

"I know you are capable. No other female is as capable as

you." He pauses, and then the somber look returns to his scarred face. "I just want you to be sure—"

"I'm sure if you leave me behind, I'm going to burn shit to the ground."

That doesn't get the laugh I was hoping for. Raahosh frowns in my direction.

"It's a figure of speech. I'm still angry at how they treat you. You're my man. I don't want anyone making you think that you're a bad guy. You're amazing, and every minute we're together, I'm happy. This hunt is going to be fun. You'll see."

He manages a hint of a smile for me, and it feels like sunshine pouring down.

I'm going to get more smiles from this man if it's the last thing I do.

Raahosh

Last night I was beyond excited that my mate would be joining me in exile. Not because we were banished together but because I would not be alone. We would hunt together and spend the nights by the fire together. Truly, it is the best outcome I could have hoped for.

But by the light of morning, I began to wonder if I am being reckless. My Liz is not nearly as strong as the weakest sa-khui female. She is a capable hunter, but she does not know this world like I do. It is cruel and unforgiving, and the predators are many. The weather will be hard for her. The walking will be hard for her. And . . . she carries our kit. This morning, before we left the main cave, she vomited the moment she woke up. She did not eat breakfast, only drank some water before we set out. She also swears this is normal, but I have my doubts.

Perhaps I should have left her behind. Perhaps it is selfish of me to take her with me.

But Liz is the most stubborn person—female or male—I have ever met. I know if I tried to leave her behind, she would follow and curse at me the entire time. She would be hurt, and the thought of hurting Liz tears me apart inside. So I clutch her close and we walk. I know my mood is unpleasant. I always hunt alone, and it is difficult for me to try to "entertain" another. When I was younger, I hunted with Vektal, but now that we're adults, it makes sense for us to hunt separately to bring in more food. Having company is . . . new.

When the twin suns head toward the horizon, I start scanning the hills for the nearest hunter cave. There is one over the next rise, but Liz is slowing down, her strength flagging after a day of travel. She nibbled on jerky as we walked, but she has not eaten as much as I would like. I should carry her the rest of the way, but I am not sure how well that will go over with her.

My mate can be . . . prickly.

"Let's play a game," Liz says suddenly, glancing up at me.

"A game?"

She nods, studying the snows. "We could play 'I Spy.' I could tell you the color of an object around us, and you can try to guess it."

I gesture at the snowy hills, snowy cliffs, and snow-covered mountains nearby. "It is all white upon white. This will not be a good game."

The sound she makes is exasperated. "It's just a suggestion. We can play something else if you like."

"I do not like." I point at the distant cliff. "We will stop there tonight. I should carry you."

"*Excuse* me?" Her gloved hand jerks out of mine, and she gives me a defiant glare.

I knew she would get offended. I pause in my walking and study her flushed cheeks. Her yellow mane is escaping her braid, tendrils drifting around her sweaty, reddened face. Her eyes blaze blue as she stares back at me, and for some reason, that makes me smile. So angry, my mate. So fierce. I love that ferocity of hers. "You are tired, and you are slowing us down. I should carry you."

Her eyes narrow, and I think she's going to fight me on it. My tail flicks, and it's strange how arousing I find the thought. I like her challenges. It is one of the things I cherish most about my mate—that she is unwilling to give up . . . ever.

"I'll let you carry me . . . if we play a game."

I bite back a groan of irritation. "Fine. Name your game, and we will play it as I carry you."

"Let's play . . . name the baby." And she flings herself into my arms with a grin.

I catch her with a grunt, because Liz is solid for all that she is small. "You are already eating for two, I see."

"I'm gonna ignore that," she says cheerily, and wraps her arms around my neck, pressing her face close to mine. "Carry me away, my cranky prince, and let's figure out a name for our kid."

An odd game, but at least she is letting me carry her. "We do not know if it will be male or female."

"Then we'll come up with names for both." Liz reaches up and brushes a lock of my mane away from my face, the move tender despite our bickering, and my heart aches with how much I need this female. I hold her a little closer, feeling protective. "Shall we start with boy names?" she asks. When I give her a brief nod, she tilts her head, considering. "Let's roll down the Brangie route for a while."

"What is Brangie? Is that an ancestor?"

"Fuck me, I wish," she mutters. "Only the two most beautiful people in the world. They're people back on Earth, and instead of referring to them as Brad and Angelina, everyone just shortened it to Brangelina. It's become a thing to combine names."

In that, we are not so different. "We do something similar. Many parents create the kit's name by combining sounds from the mother's and the father's names."

"Sweet. So for a boy, what do you think about Raahiz? Half your name and half mine?"

"I think I hate it."

She laughs, and the sound makes my heart squeeze. It takes everything I have not to bury my face in her mane and just hold her tightly, like an emotional fool. This is a silly game, but I am glad she is here. So glad.

"Okay, so not Raahiz. Losh? Rizzosh?" She wrinkles her nose. "Sounds like Snoop Dogg is naming our children."

"Another ancestor?" I ask, though I am teasing.

She snicker-snorts. "Razzosh? Rizzo? Raahozo? My full name is Elizabeth, but that just might make it worse. Lizzaraa sounds like a villain from an eighties cartoon show."

I do not know the things she references, but I am content to listen and carry her over the rise as she tries out name after name. She does not like any of them, declaring them all equally terrible, and by the time we arrive at the hunter cave, she is weary of the game. Perhaps she will grow weary of traveling with me, too, and will demand to return in the morning.

The thought makes my heart drop.

Liz

Raahosh is still moody when we get to the cave, and as I rattle off a million bad combinations of our names, none of them manage to wrest a smile out of him. That's all right. I love a challenge. I'll get him to be happy on this trip. My bag of tricks is not nearly empty. I have ways to get him under my spell.

The cave is cold, though, so once Raahosh makes sure that nothing's crawled inside, we spend the next while building a fire and putting on something hot to drink. I'm nosy, so after I set up our bedding, I poke around in the cave to see what we can use. Most of it is the normal nonsense—quickly treated hides, some bones for weapon repairs, dried fish and jerky, and a few furs. There are a couple pouches of a sloshy liquid hanging from a rocky ledge in the back, and I open one and get a whiff. It smells fruity and sweet. "What's this?"

Raahosh takes it from me, gives it a sniff, and then immediately hands it back. "Sah-sah. It is a fermented drink. My people enjoy it at celebrations."

Booze. And here I am, pregnant. Figures. Maybe I can get

Raahosh drunk. Maybe he'll have some fun then. I shake it at him enticingly. "I think you should have some. And by some, I mean all."

He glances over at me and then hunches by the fire, feeding another fuel chip to it. "No."

"I think you should get drunk since I can't."

Raahosh shakes his head. "It will give me a morning headache, and we will be leaving at dawn."

Man, this dude is allergic to fun. "So we stay another night? Who cares? It's not like they're expecting us back anytime soon."

"I would prefer to keep my senses alert." He gestures that I should come sit by the fire. "Warm up. You are cold."

I need to break him from this mood. Raahosh is already acting like I'm a million years pregnant instead of a few weeks. I sit by the fire and lift one of my feet, shoving it into his face. "Take my boot off?"

Instead of arguing with me . . . he simply does it. Well, that's no fun. He peels the last of the damp leathers off my toes and then leans in, exhaling his warm breath on my skin before he presses my foot against his stomach. I squirm at that, but he only gives me a sharp look. "I am warming it for you."

Well, now. A whole new game just occurred to me, due to that sexy puff of breath. "Thank you," I tell him sweetly. "You don't have to warm my feet for me, though. I can manage."

"I am your mate. I enjoy warming you."

"That's good. I've got something else that needs a little warming. It's really, really cold and needs some attention."

Raahosh looks alarmed, as if he's somehow failed me by letting me trudge through the snow and get cold. "Where? Show me."

Show him? Don't mind if I do. I wriggle free from his grasp and shimmy out of my leggings, then rub a hand up and down over my mound. "Right here. This needs warming. And I think we should use your face."

His eyes narrow as he realizes I've tricked him.

I keep smiling, though, and run a finger through my folds as I do. "So cold. It needs something warm against it pronto."

The irritation on his face flashes to something else, and I know I've won. Raahosh's expression turns challenging, and he lies on his back on the cave floor, his head on the furs I've spread out to make our bed. He indicates I should join him. "Come and press it against my face, then. I will warm it for you."

I squirm with arousal. Face-sitting. Hot damn. He's taking me up on my dare. Part of me is annoyed that I'm losing the upper hand, but the other part of me is excited as hell, because . . . face-sitting. Sex with Raahosh is always good. He's the most attentive man I've ever been with, and he eats pussy like a goddamn beast.

"Come," he demands, waving an impatient hand at me. His eyes are full of heat, and I can see his cock straining against his loincloth, hard at just the thought of eating me out. "You wished to play. Let us play. We will see how long I can lick your cunt before you come."

Hearing that makes me shiver. I strip off my sweaty tunic and toss it down onto the cave floor. "You totally have an advantage with those tongue ridges and the fact that I'm super horny from being pregnant."

"Would you prefer I not use the ridges on my tongue?" he asks, all politeness.

"Let's not get carried away here. You do whatever you think will make me get off the fastest, and I'll do my best to defy you."

"You are good at defiance," he practically purrs at me, and my pussy clenches in response. Oh, good God, this man is a sexy beast.

Well, who am I to resist all this deliciousness? I toss my hair like I'm a queen and saunter over to his side as if I'm doing him a favor. The moment I kneel next to him, he's reaching for me, and I barely have time to slide a leg over his shoulder before his mouth is on me. A choked noise escapes me, and I fall forward, using his horn as a handle to support myself. Oh fuck, he's good at this. His tongue strokes over my folds, slippery and hot, and those ridges drag along the most sensitive parts of my skin. One big hand grips my thigh, holding me in place, and Raahosh makes a sound of utter contentment as he laps at my cunt.

"Fuuuuck. Fuck fuck fuck," I chant as I rock against his mouth. He moves back and forth between lavishing attention on my clit and teasing his tongue at the entrance to my core. His nose bumps against my clit, and it makes my hips jerk in response.

"Still cold?" he asks between licks.

"Getting warmer," I whimper, clutching his horn as I rock over his face. His fingers dig into my leg, and his tongue pierces deep, making my thighs tighten. I rock harder, forgetting all about my vow to last as long as possible. This feels too good, and I'm greedy when it comes to him. I work my pussy against his mouth like the shameless woman I am. When he adds a finger, sinking deep inside me as he tongues circles around my clit, I explode, soaking his face with my release and collapsing over him.

Even then, Raahosh doesn't let go of me. He just keeps lapping at my pussy, dragging out the aftershocks until I pull on his hair. "My mate," he murmurs, and his voice has the low vibration in it that tells me his khui is thrumming with contentment. "Did I foreplay you well?"

I moan, rolling off him to collapse onto the furs at his side. "That was so good." I'm panting, utterly spent. "Your tongue kills me."

That elicits a rusty chuckle. "What about the rest of me?"

"It can stay, too." Hey, I made him laugh. Clearly sex is the way to loosen up his mood. I'm down with that. I roll over and curl up against his side. "How are you doing, babe?"

Raahosh presses a kiss to the top of my head. "I am good."

Even though he's hard and aching? Even though he's been in a shit mood all day? I want to call him on it, but I also don't want to start a fight when I'm feeling loose and content. So I decide to carefully edge into the topic. Resting my chin on his chest as if nothing is wrong, I ask, "Is having me with you on this hunting trip bothering you?"

I can feel him tense up against me. "Why would you think that?"

"I just want to make sure we're good. You seem a little distracted today."

He holds me closer. "Having you with me is a joy. I just wonder if it is a selfish one."

"Why would it be selfish?" I prop myself up to look him in the face. His mouth is swollen from pleasuring me, his lips a deep blue shade that makes me clench inside with lust.

His hand trails down my spine. "Because it is safer for you back with the tribe. The healer is there, and you vomited this morning. What if you are sick when we are out hunting?"

It's something I've considered, but I'd rather be with him than play it safe. "Then you shove a bunch of healing herbs in my mouth and let the khui get to work. I took care of you when you hurt your leg, remember? You weren't treating me like glass then."

"You were not pregnant with our kit and vomiting then," he points out.

I stick my tongue out at him.

"I am serious. You are human. This is not your world. I worry that it will be too much for you."

I roll my eyes at that. "It's not your world, either, buddy. You got stranded here, too. Remember the ancestors' cave? And you adapted. As for the throwing up, it's called morning sickness, and it happens to a lot of human women when they're pregnant. It should fade in a few months. Until then, I just have to pay attention to what I eat in the morning and avoid the things that make my stomach turn." I shrug. "I'm not going to lie in bed and wait for it to go away. If your people are pregnant for three years, I could be pregnant for almost that long, and I'm not about to sit around—"

"—with thumbs in your ass. I know. You have said as much."

I bite back my laughter. "Precisely. I'm here with you, and I could not be happier. Well, I take it back. I might be happier if you cracked a smile." And because I'm at his side, I run my fingers over his ribs, tickling. Surely he's ticklish, right?

Raahosh only blinks at me, puzzled. "What are you doing?"

"Motherfucker, you're not ticklish at all?" I tickle his sides harder, trying to elicit a reaction. "That's so unfair!"

"Is that supposed to do something?"

"Yes," I grump, frustrated. "Your sides are supposed to be—"

He tickles me, his hands moving over my sides.

I shriek as if I'm dying and squirm away. *"No!"*

Raahosh laughs at that, the cruel man, and pins me down on the furs. "A new weapon to use against my mate?" His fingers skate over my sides, tickling madly, and I scream with laughter even as I wriggle, trying desperately to get free. "Are you ticklish, Liz?"

"Noooo!" I cry, but I'm laughing so hard it hurts. "No, no, no! Stop, stop!"

He doesn't stop, though. He just keeps tickling me until I'm a wrecked mess, and after a while, the ticklishness turns into arousal and I start moaning. He groans, and instead of moving his hands over my sides, he cups my breasts and teases the nipples. "Does tickling lead to this?"

I just keep moaning, wrung out and exhausted.

"I know," he murmurs, and a sly gleam is in his eyes. He watches me avidly. "We shall play a game."

Oh fuck, why is that so hot? My pussy clenches. "What kind of game?"

Raahosh sits up and moves to the only seat in the cave, a fossilized log that was dragged next to the firepit by some enterprising soul who sought to make this place a little more comfortable. His cock sticks up obscenely into the air, so stiff and erect that I can see the tip is the same deep shade as his lips and coated with pre-cum. A hot lick of arousal flutters through me at that realization. "I have something that is cold," he tells me, gesturing at his cock. "You can come and warm it for me."

Tricky motherfucker. He's turning all my games against me, and I've never been so aroused in my life.

I get to my feet slowly, my knees feeling far too wobbly, and cross the small cave to stand next to my mate. He's beautiful to look at, my Raahosh. I don't care about the scars that cover one side of his face, or the broken, twisted mess of his horns. His eyes are bright and lovely with that ornery spark I adore so much, and when he watches me, it's with sheer reverence. He reaches out to pull me against him, then holds me close, burying his face in my breasts, and I drag my fingers through his thick hair.

"Turn around," he says.

"I thought you wanted me . . ." I gesture at his cock.

He nods. "You can warm it by sitting on it."

I moan again, because if I sit on him with my back to his front, it's going to push his spur into my back hole and amp up the naughtiness by a thousand. Of course, now that he's mentioned it, I want it more than I've ever wanted anything, and I let him pull me back into his lap. He settles me over him and helps me straddle him backward. His cock breaches my body, big and thick and so perfect I want to cry with how good he feels. Inch by inch, I slide down his hard, ridged length, and when his spur pushes into my backside, I know I've taken almost all of him.

I'm panting by the time I'm fully seated on him, and his hand rests on my belly. And then . . . he doesn't move.

"Raahosh?" I squirm.

"Hush," he says, pressing a kiss to my shoulder. "You are warming my cock for me."

Raahosh

If my mate wants to play games, we will play games.

I hold her tight against me, fascinated by this new pose. Her suggestion of me warming her cunt with my face made a new idea form in my head, and so she is here, squirming atop my cock as if she is desperate to get away. The moans she makes and the way she quivers, though, tell me that she does not actually want to go anywhere—she likes this.

I like it, too.

Holding completely still while Liz writhes atop me is . . . difficult. But part of my enjoyment comes from watching her responses. Watching her pant and shift her weight as she tries to hold steady. It makes me want to remain like this for as long as possible, just to hold out and increase the pleasure.

"Raahosh," Liz whimpers. "Move already."

"Move?" I pretend to consider this. Her cunt is tight around my cock, and my spur is buried in her back entrance. Like this, I can feel every quiver she makes, every twitch of her body. It feels incredible . . . but the best part is her response. "I thought you wanted to play a game, my mate."

"You're a fucking asshole." She pants, then whimpers again as her cunt tightens around me.

That makes me grin. "But I thought you liked foreplays. And you were the one that suggested a game."

She moans and clenches tight again. "Not . . . fair . . ."

My angry, wonderful mate. I run my hands over her body, holding her on my lap. My cock twitches inside her, and it takes effort not to rock her atop me. Holding her still is making her wild, and when she turns her head to look at me, her expression is one of frustration. So furious when she does not get her way. "You think I am not fair?" I tease, because there is nothing better than teasing Liz. "I will show you fair."

"Please," she moans.

I move my hands to her sides and wriggle them, tickling her as she tried to do to me. It felt like nothing to my toughened skin, but Liz's reaction is sharp. She jerks, spasming, and I realize as she cries out and squeezes my cock that she is coming. I growl with surprised pleasure, moving her over me as she comes and comes and comes. Her body's reaction prompts mine, and as she squeezes, I let my own release surge, pumping into my mate as she shivers.

I nuzzle the back of her neck, clutching her against me as I struggle to pull myself together. Mating with Liz is always so good. I do not expect it to be boring, but sometimes I wonder when it will become routine—when I will stop feeling my heart race and my khui sing just at her nearness. It has not happened yet, but I worry Liz will get sick of me long before I get sick of her.

She shivers against me again and then rubs her arms. "Can

we move to the furs? Some of us can't run around in the snow in a loincloth."

I press a final kiss to her skin. "You go to the furs. I will get something to clean us."

We separate, and I am absurdly pleased when Liz staggers dramatically over to the furs, as if I have pleasured all of the strength out of her body. I hurry to the fire to warm water in a pouch, adding a hot stone from the coals to speed it along. When it is sufficient, I dampen scraps of fur and clean my cock, then move to my mate and clean between her thighs.

Liz just watches me, her expression thoughtful. "Feel better?"

"I did not feel bad before."

She makes a noise of disbelief. "You were super cranky. Don't tell me you weren't. I know you better."

I shrug. "It is hard to walk away each time, knowing that my people are angry at me. That I have failed them. It eats at me more than I thought it would."

"Mmm." Liz rolls onto her side, patting the furs to indicate I should join her. I do so, sliding in next to her and pulling my mate close. Her skin always feels colder than my own, and I try not to grimace (much) when she tucks her cold feet against my warmer skin. "Would you change anything? If you could go back and change things, would you?"

Change things? Not steal Liz away to be my mate the moment she got her khui? Not have that time alone with her? I snort. "I would not change anything, no."

"Then don't stress about the consequences." She moves closer to me, adjusting her head so her mane is not trapped underneath my arm, and tucks herself against my side. "We're together. That's all I wanted. Now we can hunt and fuck and do as we please . . . and occasionally bring the others food. If they're nice to us, that is." Her hand skims down my stomach. "You might not know this about me, but I can hold a grudge."

I laugh at that. Not know that about her? "My mate, everyone knows this about you."

She chuckles, grinning. "I'm not good at hiding my emotions, what can I say?"

She is not. But I am not, either. In that, we are very alike. I run my fingers through her soft, soft mane and wish I could stop worrying that Liz will be unhappy. It is the shadow of my father and his mate, I think. I was young when they died, but I remember how bitter the fights were and how much my mother hated my father. Part of me expects to see Liz turn on me, show her disdain just like my mother did to my father. It is that memory that prompts my next words. "If you wish to go back, I will understand."

Liz sighs. Heavily. "Raahosh, I did not spend my time pissing off the entire tribe and kidnapping Aehako just to spend one night with you. When are you going to figure out that when I say I'm your ride or die, I mean it?"

"Ride or die?"

"It means I'm with you to the bitter end. No matter what happens, it's gonna be Liz and Raahosh, Raahosh and Liz . . . and eventually Ra-shizzle, or whatever the hell we name our poor kid." She picks up my hand and plunks it onto her flat belly. "You, me, and the kid. If I have no one else, I will not give a single solitary crap. Understand?"

"I understand." I hold her tightly, pleased. "I will strive not to be so . . . silent."

"That wasn't silence," Liz tells me. "That was you being ultra-moody. It's just . . . we're together, and I'm awesome. So you should be thrilled."

She is correct. She is awesome, and I *am* indeed thrilled we are together. "You are right. I will no longer be moody. I will be happy and talk into your ear constantly . . . just like the small one." I think of the female with the broken leg, the one who talks nonstop and drives Haeden insane with her chatter.

"Like Josie? Oh, hell no. Them's fighting words." Liz sits up and grabs my wrists—as if she could hold me down—and mock-glares at me. "I like you as you are. You don't have to be chatty all the time. I just want you to be *with* me. That's all."

I understand what she means—when I am at her side, I need to live in the moment, not worry about other things. I nod and then break free. Reversing our hold, I grab her wrists and give her a challenging look. "I think I should be on top if we are going to mate again."

"Who said we're gonna mate again?" Liz retorts.

"Me." I release her hands and reach out to tease one nipple. "Or are you too tired?"

She sucks in a breath and then narrows her eyes at me. "'Rock Paper Scissors' to see who's on top."

"What?" I frown at her. "What is this?"

"Another game." She demonstrates for me, showing me the hand signals and which one beats which. As a kit, I played similar games with Vektal, though nothing with *see-sores* or *pay-por*. "You ready?" she asks me, holding up her fist. "Count of three."

When she counts to three, I flatten my hand even as hers remains in a fist.

"Son of a bitch!" Liz swears, angry at losing.

I smirk at her. She does not care who is on top, truly, but she hates to lose. "I am starting to enjoy these games."

"Oh yeah? Best two out of three," she challenges, and slides a leg over my hips, settling her weight on my cock as it hardens. She rocks atop me as we throw hands again, and by the time I finally win, my mate's cunt is wet with fresh arousal, and I no longer care who is on top or what game we play.

I have Liz. I have won already.

ICE PLANET HONEYMOON

RAAHOSH & LIZ

Liz

"We're totally going to do a honeymoon, too," I tell Georgie as I add a fresh pouch of herbal tea to my carrying pack. "I love that idea."

"You are?" Georgie seems surprised at my declaration.

"Sure, why not?" I consider the bag of tea in my hands. I'm raiding the storage room before Raahosh and I go out for our second round of "exile." We came back to drop off some meat we'd hunted and some extra furs, and Raahosh is talking with Vektal while I rummage through the storage room. I told my guy I was just going to get some soap, but since I'm here, I'm helping myself to a little bit of everything.

I mean, if they bitch about the tea, I'll pick some leaves and replace them. But I'm part of this tribe, too, and if the tea's for anyone, that means it's for me as well as everyone sitting on their asses by the fire.

If Georgie has a problem with my grabbiness, she doesn't say anything. She just gives me a curious look. "I'm surprised you're in such a good mood about having to leave again."

"Why?" I take the soap she hands me and sniff it, then wrinkle my nose. "We got anything that doesn't smell like a salad? My pregnancy nose doesn't like leafy smells."

She picks through another bundle and holds a pink-colored bar out to me and it smells like the soapberry pulp that's been used to make it. Better. "I don't know, I just thought you'd be more upset . . . about everything. And at me."

"I admit I might have said a few choice words about everyone in the tribe once or twice." Or twenty. "But then I woke up and realized that I'm with my guy, I'm doing what I love, and I don't have to listen to Josie natter on by the fire about how many kids she wants to have if she ever resonates."

"She's excited," Georgie says gently. "And lonely."

"And talky." I lift a hand and mime a chattering puppet. "But no, I'm over the anger. I don't want to spend the next three years—or however long it takes for this baby to bake in my belly—full of anger. Which is why a honeymoon should be awesome. We'll get some bonding time in, some sexytime, and we'll connect so deep as a couple that bitches won't be able to pry us apart ever. It'll be great . . . even if you guys are wrong for exiling us."

She chuckles at my jab. "There it is."

I beam at her. "You knew I had to try. So, tell me what fun shit you two did on your honeymoon. Did you see anything cool? Do anything cool? Try anything kinky?"

Her face tenses, and I'm surprised at her expression. She looks . . . guilty? Which is weird. "Just your usual honeymoon stuff."

"That's a boring answer. Give me ideas," I prompt. "I want to steal them to use on Raahosh."

"We were boring." She shrugs, putting back the soap I rejected and then straightening the stack. "I wish I could tell you we did a million crazy things, but we didn't. It was just the two of us, alone, and . . . it was nice." Her smile turns sweet. "It was nice to just be Vektal and Georgie and not chief and chief's mate."

"Mm-hmm. That's fine, keep your secrets. Your kinks will eventually be common knowledge."

"Bullshit they will."

I arch my brows at her. "Were we or were we not discussing how much Nora likes to be spanked not ten minutes ago? I mean, hello."

Her face flushes red even as I slide another pouch of something into my pack. "It's because they're so loud. We're quiet."

"But you *are* kinky," I tease, and her face goes even redder. "It's cool, I won't tell anyone but Raahosh." I close my bag and drum my hands on it. "Sooo, give me ideas. Honeymoon stuff. Come on."

"You could go somewhere pretty?" Georgie spreads her hands helplessly. "Enjoy the scenery?"

Enjoy the fucking scenery? It's a honeymoon, not a sightseeing tour. "You suck at this, you know that?"

She sticks her tongue out at me. "Okay then, how about giving each other sexy baths? Do a strip tease for him? Give him some tail play?"

Ooo, perhaps Georgie's not as vanilla as I thought. I tap the side of my head. "I like the way you think."

"Steal away." She glances around at the storage cave. "Do you need anything else?"

"Nah." I pat my bag, which is now bulging with supplies. I can't take too much, since we're supposed to be helping re-stock the caves and not cleaning them out, but I also want to send a bit of a "fuck you" to everyone that exiled my man. So I've taken more than I should, and I don't even care.

Georgie gets to her feet, brushing off her leathers. "I think I hear the men anyhow."

I heft my pack onto my shoulder and head out of the supply cave with her, a calm smile on my face. It's all for show. Raahosh knows that even though I say I'm fine with exile, I'm also ridiculously protective of him in my own way, and that means letting everyone in the tribe know what dicks they are for exiling him when all he wanted was to be with me.

I mean, I was the one he kidnapped. If I'm fine with it, shouldn't they be? But whatever. It just means me and Raahosh get a lot of quality alone time together.

There are two big alien men standing at the large, triangular mouth of the cave, and my Raahosh is easy to recognize. It's not just the one busted horn and the scars that cover one side of his face that give him a permanent scowl. It's the way he carries himself, like he's got a stick up his ass. His back is ramrod straight and his shoulders tight and set like he wants to fight anyone and everyone.

It's so fucking hot. I love that irritated little swish of his tail, the stiff way he holds himself, all of it.

He turns as we approach and his gaze locks onto me with that possessive, overbearing way he has. Like he wants to snatch me up and shield me from anyone who dares look in my direction. Like he wants to devour me whole just so no one else can have me. Like he wants to throw me down on the cave floor and nut all over me just so everyone knows I'm claimed.

Maybe it shouldn't be so thrilling, but I fucking love that look in his eyes. Like I'm his everything. Like he'd become unhinged if anyone tried to separate us ever again.

Even now, I approach and he holds his hand out to take my satchel. I offer it to him and he glances at it, noting how heavy it is, and then tosses it over his shoulder as if it weighs nothing. His tail goes around my thigh, curling possessively, and his mouth flattens even as he pulls me closer to him. He's not good at showing affection, my Raahosh, but I don't mind. I know how to read him. He's frowning because he's worried someone made me upset, or that I'm wanting to stay here without him.

I just ignore his surliness and put my arm around his waist. "I'm ready to go whenever you are, babe."

He grunts and looks at Vektal, who stands nearby. He nods and lifts a hand in farewell, then heads back inside the cave. I kinda want to slap Vektal around for being so stubborn. I want to shake him and scream in his ear about how he's hurting his best friend, but I know it's all because he has to be the unbiased chief. Raahosh doesn't hold it against him.

It's me that's the grudgy bitch. I'll be angry for him.

But not today. Today, it's sunnyish and we're heading out for our honeymoon. I stand obediently while Raahosh checks my leathers over like I'm a child that doesn't know how to dress herself. He tightens straps on my boots, tucks my leathers closer to my body, and then tugs my cape down over my face. "You get red in the wind," is all he says, voice gruff.

So protective. If he knew how horny it made me, he'd get all shy and weird, so I try not to let him know just how much it cranks me up when he's fussy like this. "Are you ready for our honeymoon?"

He straightens and offers his hand to me, his spear gripped in his other. I put my gloved fingers against his and squeeze, even as we head out of the cave and out to the muddy trail that winds away from the main dwelling of the sa-khui. When we're far enough away that no one will overhear us, my grumpy mate says, "I do not see how this is different from any other hunting trip we will take together."

"The difference is that this one is our *honeymoon*," I say, emphasizing the word as if that explains everything. "It's about romance and sex and learning about each other and more sex and bonding."

"And this is what you talked to Shorshie about."

"Some girl stuff," I agree. "I wanted romance ideas." I'm admittedly not the most romantic woman in the world, so I figured Georgie might be better at this sort of thing than me. I like her suggestions, too. Sexy bathing? Sexy stripping? Sexy tail play? All of that sounds fun.

Raahosh just grunts, stepping ahead of me and then lifting me over a muddy iced-over puddle in the middle of the trail. "It should not be all mating."

"Have you suddenly decided you're not a fan of mating, then?" I tease. "Because I seem to remember some things you were yelling out when my mouth was on your cock—"

"If we want to bond, we should learn about each other through talking and sharing." He won't look at me, and the stick is back in his ass.

"I would think you can learn a lot about a person by putting your tongue on their cock but maybe that's just me."

He says nothing. I peek at his face while trying not to be obvious about it and he's definitely flushed at the base of his horns. My Raahosh is shy, and it makes me want to fucking pounce on him.

Actually, pretty much everything makes me want to pounce on him.

"You could give me lessons," Raahosh says, distracting me

from my dirty thoughts. "The bow. You are very skilled and I would like to learn more. You can teach me if this is our honeymoon."

Oh. A hot rush of pleasure moves through me. He admires my archery? He wants to learn from me? This man knows just what to say to make me happy. I squeeze his bigger hand. "I would love to show you some tricks. And you can teach me some hunting stuff, too."

He thinks for a moment. "You already know how to do more than most of the humans. You know how to make a fire, how to lay a trap, how to track . . ." Raahosh continues to think. "You could learn to be quiet."

I blink. The *fuck* did he just say?

It's like he knows he messed up. He looks over at me and sees my expression, and his changes. "Not like that," he amends with a scowl. "Though you could learn that, too. I meant I could teach you how to be quieter when you are on the trail. Your feet are noisy."

I pat his arm. "It's our honeymoon and I'm going to pretend like you didn't just insult me because I love you and I know you love me. I'm sure you'll think of something awesome to teach me and we'll learn from each other." I grin up at him. "And also have lots of incredibly filthy sex because it's our honeymoon and that's what you do."

His horns flush again.

Raahosh

I do not know how I came to be so lucky in my khui's choice of mates. When I first saw the humans, I thought they were skinny and pale, and Liz was the loudest and stubbornest of all of them. I knew she was mine the moment I resonated, but I did not realize what that meant until I was exiled and Liz stood up for me. She tried to take on the entire tribe and make them miserable so they knew they were wrong in exiling me. Even now, she fills her pack with things we do not need just so she can silently protest.

Liz is loud, yes. And pale. And skinny.

But she is strong, and graceful, and lovely. She is free with her kisses, looks at me with lust in her gaze, and is utterly loyal to me and me alone.

I never thought I would experience the joy of a mate in my life. I am ugly and scarred and quiet. But every day with Liz is a gift, and every time I look at her, I am filled with such a deep ache of pleasure and longing both. She has captured my withered heart into her slim hands and I want to spend the rest of my days making her realize how precious she is to me. How much I "love" her, even though the human word is strange on my tongue, it means a lot to Liz.

I knew she wished this "honeymoon." She spoke of it yesterday after we arrived in the cave, and spoke of it again last night in our furs.

A trip, but one for love and bonding between a newly mated pair.

I am good at hunting. I am good at tracking. Good with a spear and with making weapons. I am passable with nets and fast on my feet . . . but I do not know how to give a mate "romance." I do not know how to do "more" for her to show her my pleasure.

I do not even know where to begin.

Liz holds my hand as we walk, chatting about Shorshie and the healer and the chief's kit, which Shorshie will not be having for many, many moons yet. I should be listening to her, but instead, I think of the conversation I had with Zennek this morning, while my mate was asleep.

I sat by the fire, stitching thicker soles onto Liz's boots so the snows would not make her feet so cold. It was very early, but it was hard for me to sleep. We bedded down with the rest of the hunters, and while Liz is unbothered by this, I cannot sleep next to all of them and just hold her. Not when she presses her body to mine and makes delicious little sighs as she moves closer.

It is too distracting.

So I worked on her boots instead, and Zennek came to the fire and crouched by me. He seemed . . . happy. Content. His neck is covered in deep blue welts, though, and I cannot help but point that out. "Did something bite you?"

He is confused, and when I gesture at his neck, his smile changes to a slow one of satisfaction. "My mate."

Ah yes. The fierce Mar-lenn. Of all the females, I have heard she is the boldest, and she seems quite eager to lead Zennek around by his cock. He would know what to do on a honeymoon, I realize. Zennek is quiet like me, but where I am quiet because I am awkward and ugly and a loner, Zennek is just silent in nature. That has not changed since he took a mate, I noticed. Mar-lenn is just as content as he is to stand apart from the group. They need no one but each other.

I envy that serenity.

Even so, Zennek is a good one to ask. "My mate wants me to give her romance on our next hunting trip," I say, feeling foolish. I shove my awl through the leather of Liz's boot, hoping Zennek does not see how awkward I feel. "I am open to ideas."

His mouth curls with amusement. "You are asking me how you should woo your mate?"

"I know how to woo her," I snap. "I am asking for new ideas. Things to surprise her. Things that humans like that I have not thought of."

Zennek looks thoughtful even as I stab the boot in my hands. "I see. You ask me because Mar-lenn is not shy about such things." When I nod, he rubs his jaw, thinking hard. "The easiest thing to do is pleasure a female, but you know that."

"I do." I take a calmer stitch. "I had no mate before Liz. I . . . want her to be happy." *And I am ugly and an outcast and I do not know if I can keep her satisfied.* I keep those terrible thoughts to myself.

He considers this. "Mar-lenn likes words," he says after a time.

"Words?"

Zennek nods. "Strong words. Bold words. I tell her what I am going to do to her and how, and I say these as I touch her. It makes her excited."

Interesting. Do I speak to my Liz when we mate? I try to picture myself telling her "I am going to put my cock inside you now" and cannot imagine how that will arouse a female. But Zennek's mate looks well pleased. I eye him, curious, because of all our tribe, Zennek is the quietest.

Yet if his mate wants words, she must be happy to give those welts to him.

I think about those welts on his neck as I walk with Liz's hand in mine. Words. Bold words as I touch her. I might need to practice this.

So as we walk, I think about what words I will say to Liz and how.

This is harder than it sounds.

We walk for most of the afternoon. Liz is stronger than a lot of the females, but her legs are shorter than mine and I clip my strides to keep pace with her. We do not get as far as I would on my own, but when we near a hunter cave, I steer her toward it. "We will stop here for the night."

"Finally," she says dramatically. "I'm exhausted."

I cup her face in my hands, noticing that her eyelids are heavy. She smiles up at me, leaning into my touch. "You did not tell me you were tired," I say, my voice accusing.

"I didn't want to slow us down." She yawns.

"Liz," I say, frustrated. "We are in no hurry. We will be exiled for a long time. There is no rush to go anywhere. I do not want you to walk until you are so tired that your eyes cannot stay open." I stroke her soft cheek. All my thoughts of tonight and mating with her as I describe it in great detail are gone. She is tired and needs her feet rubbed and to be tucked into warm furs by the fire. "Come," I say, and lean in to press a kiss to the tip of her cold red nose. "I will make a fire and warm you up."

She just gives me a tired smile, her eyes soft. "Idiots think it's some sort of punishment to send us away together. Big dummies. Little do they know I love being with you like this."

My heart squeezes painfully. My perfect mate. I want to clutch her to my chest and fight the world to keep her safe. I caress her cheek again and then go first into the cave to make sure that it is unoccupied. When all is well, Liz enters and then gasps.

"This cave is so big! And warm!" She frowns, confused. "Why is it warm?"

I kneel beside the firepit. "There is a hot pool in the back of the cave. If you want to bathe, we can."

"Oh my God, a hot bath? Can we make this our new home?" Her eyes light up with enthusiasm.

I snort. "The roof of the cave is low and the floor uneven to walk upon. You would get tired of it after a few days, but it will serve well enough for tonight."

"Party pooper," she teases, saying human words that make no sense but still carry affection. "Fine, we'll enjoy the bath tonight and then move on in the morning, then?"

I nod and finish making the fire, then put on a pouch of clean snow and sprinkle herbs in for hot tea. Liz unrolls the bedding and makes a nest of furs for us while I am busy, but her movements are slow and lethargic, and when the bed is unrolled, she flops down onto her back and closes her eyes.

I move over to her and begin to take her boots off. "You should sleep."

"Fuck that," she says sleepily. "I want a bath first."

"Then come and bathe." I pull her boots off and then help her to her feet, stripping her tunic and leggings off of her slender human body. She is small and lean everywhere except her teats, which are quite large and jiggly for one her size. The sight of them always makes my breathing quicken and my cock harden. She has nipples like a sa-khui female, but hers are soft even when taut and such a pale pink that they astound me.

I want to lick these.

The words spring to my mind but I push them back. Liz wants a bath and then she needs to sleep. I will not push my mate—my pregnant mate—into mating, even if it is all I thought about all day long. My needs can wait.

The ceiling of the cave lowers as we approach the back and the air thickens with moisture. The pool itself is not much larger than a few handspans across, but steamy and clear, and Liz lets out a moan of sheer pleasure at the sight of it. Her hand squeezes mine. "I got soap in my bag, babe. We can wash our hair and everything."

I grunt and take her hand. "You bathe. I will get your soap."

"You'll join me when you come back?" she asks hopefully.

As if I could stay away. I help her into the water, and then go to retrieve her soap. When I return, I slide carefully into the pool next to her, and then pull her into my lap. The water is not deep, and I have to fold my legs to sink down to my shoulders, but there is just enough room for me to hold my mate against me.

She relaxes against my body, closing her eyes and sighing with bliss. "This is now my new favorite cave."

I smile at that. There is a large heated pool for bathing at the main tribal cave, but it is also crowded . . . and we are exiled anyhow. "Then I am glad we are here."

"I'm happy to be wherever you are," Liz says softly, tucking her head against my neck. "So far? Not hating exile."

Me, either. Having her with me makes this all bearable. When I first heard my fate, I thought I would end up as my father, miserable and alone . . . but Liz has surprised me. She has fought for me every step of the way and now she wishes to be at my side constantly. Truly, I am the luckiest of males to have such a fierce, beautiful mate.

I wet the soap and lift her arm, then rub the cake of it down her soft skin, bathing her. "You must tell me when you grow tired, though. We are in no hurry and I will not have you wearing yourself out."

"I won't slow you down," she promises me with another sleepy yawn, lifting her other arm so I can wash it. Her eyelids are so heavy that it looks as if she struggles to stay awake. "That was part of the deal, you know? I go with you, but I have to keep up."

I grunt. I made no such deal. I just wanted my mate at my side. And she wanted a honeymoon but now she is too tired for anything but sleeping. Even now, she makes no effort to bathe herself, letting me take care of her. Not that I mind. I run the soap over her front, gently rubbing her teats and belly and she makes a soft noise of pleasure in her throat that sends a jolt through my cock.

Not tonight, I tell it. No honeymoon this eve. My mate is too tired.

"Sit up," I say gently, and she leans forward. I run a few handfuls of water over her mane and then soap it, burying my fingers in the soft yellow strands. She moans, and I stiffen but do not stop what I am doing. *Tired*, I remind myself. *She is tired. She always makes noises when she is tired.*

"Where are we going?" Liz asks, drowsy.

I continue to work the soap through her tangled mane, making sure to get all of it clean. I know she likes her mane to smell nice, so I do my best for her. "To bed."

"No, I mean in general. We're going hunting, yes? Where to? Anywhere in particular?" She turns to look at me over her shoulder.

"Ah." I think for a moment, then rub her scalp. "We are going very far into the mountains, like last time. We will work on filling some of the farther-flung caches again, since we must be out and others would rather stay home with their mates."

"Lazy bastards." A tired smile curls her mouth. She does not sound upset, though, just amused.

I grunt. "Perhaps. Let us rinse your mane and get you to the furs. You need to rest."

"You act like I'm so fragile."

I lean in and rub my mouth against her ear. "To me, you are." She shivers.

Once my Liz is clean, I help her back out of the water. I would carry her to the furs but the ceiling is so low in this cave that I cannot stand properly. I keep my hands on her hips, even so, and she shuffles toward the furs, yawning. "I hate that I'm so tired for the first night of our honeymoon."

I can hear the disappointment in her voice. "Why?"

"I don't know. I wanted to make this special." She rubs a drying-fur on her wet mane to dry it and then tosses it aside. Once she slides her legs under the blankets, she lies down and then looks up at me. "I wanted to make you think 'hot damn' when I touched you."

I quickly dry the dripping water off of my body, noticing that she watches me as I do. I slide into the furs next to her, and put a hand to her waist, pulling her close. I lie on my side so she is tucked half under me, and our gazes meet. "Every day is special with you, my Liz. Every day is 'hot damn.'"

She smiles, her arms going lazily around my neck. "Do you even know what hot damn means?"

"It means I have the most beautiful, gorgeous mate in the entire cave. It means that she is insatiable. It means that even though she has an ugly male for a mate, she makes him feel as if he is a chief in the furs." I nip lightly at her chin, her cheek, her nose, her brow, her ear.

"A chief in the furs," she giggles. "What exactly does a chief in the furs do?"

"Whatever he wants," I mock-growl and move lower, pressing my mouth down her smooth skin, past her prominent teats and down the slim length of her belly.

A sleepy moan escapes her throat and her hands brush over my mane. "I like where this is going."

"Do you?" I lick her navel, then lower, and lower still. I lick the tuft of fur between her thighs, and when she drags her legs apart, I move between them and settle in. This is my favorite place to be, I have decided. I love to bury my mouth between my mate's thighs and lick her until she coats my tongue with her arousal, until her cunt is clenching and needy, and she claws at my mane as if she will come apart. I put my hands on her hips and take a long, slow taste, savoring her.

"Oh," she moans, and for once, sharp words do not fall from her lips. She is soft and open, as soft and open as her cunt before my tongue. "Oh, baby, you're so good at that."

I growl with pleasure, teasing the third nipple that peeks out from between her folds. I love when she gets breathless, when her hips buck against my mouth as if she can encourage my tongue even more. I love her whimpers of distress when I lift my mouth, and I love the way my khui hums and sings low in my chest, pleased that I am claiming my mate.

Liz is breathless with need, squirming under me and digging her heels into the furs—and my back—as she gets closer to her climax. "Inside me," she pants. "Want you inside me, Raahosh."

I can refuse her nothing. I move over her, claiming her mouth in a hot kiss. Her legs go around my hips and I fit my cock at the entrance to her core and then push deep. She moans into my mouth, and I start a slow, steady pace, thrusting into her with languid, teasing movements. I take her slow and gentle, kissing her soft mouth with every thrust even if it means I must hunch my back to make our bodies line up.

She comes quickly, her cunt clenching hard around me, and a little gasp escapes her even as her body tightens, squeezing me. When I release inside her, it is with a growl, and we slowly come down, our bodies twined together.

For a long moment, we do nothing but breathe, content to lie in a tangle of limbs. "So far, I like this honeymoon," I tell my mate in a low voice.

Liz snores, already asleep.

I bite back a smirk of amusement and press a kiss to my mate's brow. Humans. So fragile and easily tired, even when they say they are not.

The next day as we hike through one of the snowy valleys, my thoughts are full of Liz and her honeymoon ideas. Last night she was too tired for play, but tonight I vow that we will make camp early. Perhaps tonight I will tell her about my cock as I put it inside her. I want this honeymoon thing to be good for her. I want her to be pleased she is my mate.

"I think I see someone up ahead," Liz says, shielding her eyes.

"Eh?" Startled—and a little annoyed I was too distracted to notice first—I look up and spot a familiar shape. It is indeed a hunter, heading back to the main tribal cave. He has heavy packs on his shoulders and I study the horns, trying to decipher who it is.

Then I bite back a groan of dismay as I realize it is Vaza.

Vaza is one of the elders in the tribe, a widower whose mate died long ago. Normally Vaza is easygoing, but since the human females arrived, he has been irritating in his eagerness to show what a good provider he is. He wants a human female for himself, and I know he is lonely.

It still irritates me.

It irritates me even more because now we are going to have to talk to him and he is going to stare too hard at my Liz.

I eye his distant form, wondering if it is too late for us to hide when Vaza raises a hand in the air and waves. "Ho!"

Liz looks over at me, and there is far too much amusement in her gaze. "Hey buddy," she calls cheerily, and then pokes my side. "Smile."

"Why? It is Vaza."

She snorts. "Be nice."

"I am always nice," I grit out as he jogs toward us.

Vaza beams a smile at us as he approaches, then claps his hands together as if so very pleased to see us. "What a joy to see the two of you out here."

"Right?" Liz murmurs. "So surprising. How are you, Vaza?"

"Very hearty!" He claps a hand on his stomach, then slaps his arm as if to show off his muscles. "I am bringing back much fresh meat for our fragile new females."

"Oh boy," Liz says, and I can hear the slight souring in her tone. "Aren't you just the biggest chauvinist."

"A what?"

"A hero," she amends sweetly. "You must not know that word yet."

He grins and taps his tongue. "It is because the human language is so ridiculous."

"So *very*."

I bite the inside of my cheek, because I recognize Liz's accommodating tone. It is a very dangerous tone indeed and Vaza does not realize it.

"We head out to the far reaches," I say, and put my arm around Liz's shoulders, squeezing. If I must be polite, she must be, too.

"Freshly mated and off to the far reaches!" Vaza rubs his hands and looks so pleased you would think he was the one who was "freshly mated." "You will be very alone out there. Of course, that might be exactly what you wish." And he gives me a knowing look.

"Gosh, you know what? I think I'm going to go see what's up ahead on that rise," Liz says, sliding out of my grasp.

"You should stay close," Vaza adds with a frown. "Humans are fragile—"

"And this one's about to puke." She smiles tightly at both of us. "Baby stuff, you know."

She walks away and makes a face behind his back and a throat-cutting motion. I know what that means—end the conversation.

Vaza just gives me a knowing look. "Fragile."

"Yes, well, we cannot stay to talk for long," I begin lamely.

"Because you wish to spend an early evening with your mate?" He grins, utterly pleased. "I understand this. It is a wonderful feeling, a fresh resonance and an eager mate." He leans in close. "Do you need . . . advice?"

"Advice?"

"On how to please a mate? I have much experience in the furs. I can share what I know." He taps his chest. "This elder has seen much in his day."

Oh. I hesitate, because I am not sure if Vaza is the one I wish to ask for such things. Yet, he is here, and he is offering, and more than anything, I want to make my Liz wild with need. "I want to surprise her," I admit, thinking of the bow lessons she has promised to give me. "To do something special, just for her."

"Ahhh." He rubs his hands again and looks thrilled. "I know how to do that."

"You do?"

"Yes. You surprise them in the furs. Do things they do not expect." He leans in close, grinning. "A finger in the hole, a bit of tail play, that sort of thing."

"Finger in the hole?" I echo. "Which hole?"

"The last one."

I stare at him in surprise. "They like that?"

Vaza shrugs. "I do."

Is this an entirely different area I have not even considered, then? I think of my Liz and how she put her mouth all over my cock in ways that stunned me. Before she did that, it did not occur to me that females would do such things to their males. It stands to reason that perhaps she would like a finger in her back hole. "I will think on this."

He claps my shoulder. "Trust me. Your mate will be beside herself with excitement."

Perhaps so. I grunt acknowledgment, but even as I mull Vaza's advice, I feel . . . terrible. Are there entire areas of my mate I have not pleasured simply because it did not occur to me?

Am I . . . lacking as a partner?

The thought is hard to stomach.

Liz

The cave we stop at that evening is in a lovely little valley with a sea of sashrem trees nearby and a burbling hot stream not too far away. It's perfect. The cave is large and full of supplies, and while it doesn't have the hot tub that the other one did, it's comfortable.

"We could stay here for a few days," I tell Raahosh excitedly. "Maybe start your bow lessons?"

He grunts and picks up a few fallen tree branches to use as firewood, not commenting. He's been like this all afternoon, and at first I just thought it was him and his usual taciturn self, but whenever I ask him questions, I get monosyllabic responses or no response at all, and that's wearing thin.

I put my hands on my hips and study him as he picks up another branch and shakes the snow off. "Did something crawl up your ass?"

Raahosh looks surprised and turns as if looking at the back of his pants. His tail flicks over his backside. "No . . . ?"

"I meant that you're in a bad mood. Is something wrong?"

"Nothing."

His answer makes me grit my teeth in frustration. Aren't we too early in our relationship for this passive-aggressive bullshit? It's not like Raahosh. If he's unhappy with something, he's quick to let me know it. He wouldn't just stew on it to force me to pry it out of him. Therefore . . . it must be something that's truly bothering him that he doesn't want to share. "I can tell it's *something*." I move forward and lightly stroke his arm. "We're mates, aren't we? You need to talk to me. Tell me what's on your mind."

Raahosh doesn't look me in the eye. He doesn't pull away, either, and after a long moment, he admits, "I am . . . thinking of pleasuring you." The base of his horns flushes a deep blue.

He's thinking about sex? Aww. Why does that make my insides all gooey and warm? "Nothing wrong with that," I tease, leaning forward and lightly nipping at his bare bicep with my teeth. "I think about it a lot, too. So when do we stop for the evening so we can turn our thoughts into deeds?"

The look he gives me is full of a mixture of emotions—relief that I'm not teasing him, need, and amusement. "Whenever you like."

"I vote the next cave we run across is our evening stop. I don't care how early it is. We need our strength for our honeymoon." And I give him the least subtle wink ever.

Raahosh snorts, sounding more like himself. He puts a big hand on my shoulder, his thumb rubbing over my layers of clothing as if he can touch the skin underneath. "There is a cave not too far from here. Not over the next ridge, but the one after that."

So maybe an hour of walking? I can deal with that. I stick my hand out, hoping he'll take it in his, and I'm pleased when he does. "Let's just hope Vaza doesn't turn around and decide to hang out with us."

"If he does, he will find my boot on his backside," Raahosh growls.

Damn, that is sexy. I love it when he gets all possessive.

~~~

We're both quiet as we make our way to the cave. I am dying to know exactly what Raahosh was thinking about sex-wise, but he still gets incredibly shy and awkward around me, the big virgin (well, no longer), so I have to be careful not to make him feel uncomfortable. It's a rather silent walk, but his cootie hums and purrs low, telling me that he's thinking about sex, which makes me think about sex, too, and my cootie revs up. Strangely enough, the lack of conversation between us is almost erotic, as if we're holding everything back so we can explode our hormones all over the cave once we get there.

By the time we arrive, I'm practically squirming with need, as if the journey itself was a strange form of foreplay. I wait as Raahosh inspects the cave to ensure no "visitors" have arrived, then he calls my name. When I enter, he's making a fire in the firepit, crumbling one of the poo cakes that are used for fuel.

"I'll take care of making the bed," I tell him. "You finish that and then wash your hands."

He grunts acknowledgment, and then we both get to work.

I finish before he does, of course, so I poke around, digging through the baskets of supplies as if they interest me, and trying not to watch him too closely. Of course, that's an impossible task because I want to follow every one of his movements, right down to the graceful way that he washes his hands with water from one of our skins and then soaps them up, then rinses them at the front of the cave. I never thought hands were sexy, but the way he slides his fingers over his palms in that briskly efficient way?

It's better than porn by a long shot.

Raahosh turns around and he must notice the look in my eyes, because he stalks toward me, all predator, and I get to my feet, full of need and yearning. He pulls me against him, his hands going to my hair, and then he tilts my head back and gives me the sexiest, deepest kiss ever. His mouth moves over mine, hot and claiming, and I moan with need even as he tears my outer layers off of me.

"Naked," he says between breathless kisses. "Need you naked."

Oh God, I absolutely want to be naked. I let him work the laces on my tunic even as I touch him all over, teasing my hands up and down his hard stomach and flat pectorals. I graze over the plated spots with my fingers, learning them as he tugs at my clothing, and when he grunts, I obediently lift my arms so he can pull my leathers over my head.

Then I'm wearing nothing but a breastband, leggings, and boots, and I drop to the floor to take care of the footwear. He groans, still looming over me as his tail skims up my spine, as if he *has* to touch me now, and I love that light caress. I finally kick my boots off and then reach for his, undoing the cords that crisscross up and down his muscular legs. Even here he's fine as fuck. Who would have thought that man-calves were hot? But I want to lick them as I pull his leathers off. "God, I am so horny."

"Hurry up so I can make you come," he growls.

Like I need any encouragement? I slide my hand up his thigh, heading for his loincloth, and he bats my hand away in the sexiest fucking move and then moves low, pushing me back onto the furs with a hand on my shoulder. He practically rips my pants off and pushes my thighs apart—as if they needed urging—and then dives between my legs.

I make a choked sound of pleasure as his hot, textured tongue finds my clit and he begins to lap at it, looking for the rhythm that will make me shiver and come. He teases my folds, moving up and down and licking me everywhere before returning to my clit and nuzzling. His hands grip my thighs tight, and I can feel his tail sliding around one of my ankles, tightening, and even that turns me on.

"Raahosh," I moan, burying my fingers in his thick hair. "Let me—"

"No," he growls against my skin, and swipes his tongue over my clit almost angrily. "I have waited all day for this. This is mine."

I shudder. Like I can argue with that? I squirm as his tongue grows more determined, more invasive, and the heat in my body ramps up. I want him to stop. I want him to keep going forever. I want him to lick me fast, then slow. I want all of him. And when he thrusts a finger deep inside my core, I arch and press against his mouth like I'm dying.

Sometimes I think I must be easy to please. That because I've never had a ton of great experiences with oral pre-Raahosh, that's the reason why I explode like the Fourth of July the moment he gets to work. Or maybe it's the ridged tongue. Maybe it's his eagerness and the clear pleasure he gets out of licking all of my most secret parts. Whatever it is, it never fails to make me spontaneously combust into a climax so hard that my entire body quakes with the response and I can feel my pussy clenching around his finger, as if desperately trying to trap him inside me. All the while, my amazing mate licks and sucks and teases as if it's his life goal to get me off. He continues to work my clit even after I climax, sweeping his ridged tongue around the sides of the sensitive bud and forcing me toward yet another orgasm. His finger pumps into me again, and then teases at the entrance to my core, toying with my juices.

"Oh, Raahosh," I say, loud and breathless and full of need. I love how he uses his mouth. Another moan builds in my throat. I love—

My moan turns into a screech of shock as he takes his finger—that glorious, wonderful finger—and pushes it into my butt.

The party train stops and the orgasm I was chasing dies a quick death. I clamp my legs shut with a yelp, accidentally slamming them around his ears. He groans and quickly moves backward even as I skitter away on the blankets, shocked.

"What the fuck was that?" I cry out, shocked. I mean, I'm not totally averse to butt play, but warn a girl first. It's one of those things I have to be coaxed into doing, and I'm sure not a fan of a surprise unlubed finger in my no-no places. "You never go backdoor without permission first!"

He rubs a hand over his ear, scowling. His eyes are so bright they look furious and he stares at me for a long moment, panting. He's still flushed from going down on me, his horns deep blue at the base, and when he sits up, I can see his cock is hard as a rock, gleaming with wetness on the tip. His shoulders are stiff with anger, though, and his mouth flattens as he stares at me.

I stare back, because what the fuck.

I wait for him to say something, but he remains quiet. Our staredown continues a moment longer, and then Raahosh gets to his feet and storms away to the back of the cave, where all the supplies are kept.

He's mad. That much is obvious. I recognize that angry twitch in his tail and the ramrod-straight way he holds his shoulders. Good, I'm mad, too. I know we're still new to being mated, but damn, warn a girl before you go into her butthole. I rub my backside, still shocked at what just happened. That totally isn't like Raahosh to try something like that.

Man, he is acting *so weird* lately.

I'm actually a little worried. He's acting strange and it's like something's bothering him, and that concerns me. I get to my feet and head after him when he doesn't come back right away. When I get into the next chamber, it's dark without the fire going but I can see that Raahosh is kneeling on the floor, unrolling several of the furs. "What are you doing?"

He doesn't look over at me. "Unrolling furs so I can sleep in here."

Sleep in here? Without me?

I sputter. "We're not going to talk about this? You're just going to get pissy and retreat in here without bothering to tell me why you thought shoving your knuckle into my ass was a good call?"

I didn't think it was possible, but his shoulders get even stiffer. His tail slaps the ground angrily. He doesn't look at me, just continues to unroll the furs with jerky, angry motions.

"Well?" I prompt. "You might not want to talk, but this isn't like you, and it worries me, so I'm going to just guess. Stop me if I hit on the right topic." I cross my arms and study his back. "You . . . stuck a finger up my butt because you got lost, right?"

Raahosh says nothing, simply ignores me.

"You . . . thought if you reached hard enough, you could pull a tail out of there and we'd match?"

His tail flicks, even though he's doing his damnedest to ignore me.

"You're on your hunter version of your period, which means you're hella moody. Or your midichlorian count is low and now you'll never be a Jedi," I add, throwing in a Star Wars joke for good measure.

He clenches his jaw and looks over his shoulder at me. "Stop. Just . . . leave it be."

I move forward and grab his horn—the one that's not twisted

into a stump that lies unevenly against his head. I give it a yank. "I'm not going to stop, you big dummy, because I love you and I want to know what's eating you. We're going to talk about this."

I keep tugging on his horn, tilting his head back so he's forced to look at me, and he just closes his eyes. After a long, stubborn moment, he sighs and brushes my hand away. "I . . . wanted to pleasure you." His voice is gruff, tight.

That makes my heart squeeze, and I put a hand on his shoulder. "You do pleasure me. Every time we're in bed together."

Raahosh shakes his head, dismissing my words. "It has to be more. *I* must be more. You need a good mate, a worthy one. I know I am not kind, or easy to live with. I know I am not attractive. And now I am in exile. I do not want you to feel as if your khui has chosen poorly. I must do more to please you and keep you satisfied."

Oh.

My poor, sweet alien.

My heart aches for him. I drop to my knees behind him and wrap my arms around his chest, setting my cheek against his broad back and letting my breasts press against his skin. "How can you think that?" I ask softly, stroking my hands up and down his skin.

He says nothing for a long moment, sagging against my touch. Then, finally, he admits, "My father . . ."

"Say no more," I murmur. I realize what this is about. The cootie makes sure we make a baby together, but not everyone's thrilled at a mating. I remember Raahosh's stories of how his mother hated his father and how miserable they both were. He probably thinks he has to be some amazing god in bed—like he's not already?—in order to keep me satisfied. I guess that's why he's getting all weird on me.

He worries he's not enough.

Just that sweetness makes me so happy. No man has ever

worked so hard to make sure that I'm content in a relationship. It means so much to him that I'm his mate, that I'm at his side. For the first time, he's envied by others because he has a human mate. He's envied for his relationship, for his future, and even though he's exiled, I know most of the other single men in the tribe would happily trade places with him if it meant getting a woman of their own.

But my poor Raahosh just thinks he's going to lose me.

Maybe I should be frustrated with him, but I'm just filled with so much love for the big alien man. I stroke my hand up and down his chest, loving how he leans into my touch. His head tilts back and I carefully angle my face so he doesn't stab me with his horn, and then lean in and kiss the side of his neck. I love his groan of response and the way his body shudders.

"I love you," I whisper to him. "I love all of you. I love looking at you. I love your scars and your unique horns. I love your scowl. I love that stiff way you hold yourself. I even love when you thump your tail all angry and pissy."

"Lies," he says, the word thick on his lips. His tail thumps hard again, and I realize I'm straddling it, and it's trapped between my thighs. I don't move, though. I just let him realize I have him, and I continue to kiss and pet his beautiful blue-gray skin.

"Truth," I say back. "Why would I lie? I love your scars." I lift one hand and trace along one of the more prominent ones. "They tell a story. Not a bad one, just a story about who you are and what you've overcome. They make you different from the others. And I don't know if you noticed, but I like different." I lean in and lightly bite at his earlobe.

His breath catches when my teeth graze over his ear. I let my hands slide lower, playing along his hard abdomen and teasing at the ridges there. I'm so fascinated with petting and stroking him that I almost miss his softly murmured words. "I was not sure if I could keep a human happy. I have never had a mate of any kind . . . or a family. I asked others how I can please you."

Okay, well, some freak told him that a surprise exploration of my backside must have been the ticket. I suppose it's karma getting me back for me telling Aehako that he needed to make Kira a dildo as a courting present. Even so, I'm still touched that Raahosh has been soliciting advice. It explains some of the furtive conversations he's had that he didn't want to tell me about, and why he's been so lost in his thoughts. "You've really been asking everyone in the tribe how to please me?"

"Some offer it without asking," he admits, caressing my hand as I scratch my nails lightly over his hard pectorals. "You feel good pressed against me."

I smile, nibbling his ear again. "That's because I love to touch you. I want to make you feel as good as you make me feel . . ." I lock my arm around his neck and lean in to his ear. "Now hold still while I stick my finger up your butt."

He stiffens. That tail thrashes between my thighs again.

I giggle. "I'm not going to do that. I'm just teasing you. And for the future? I would be down with butt play as long as I know to expect it and all body parts are properly oiled up. Got it?"

Raahosh nods.

"And maybe don't listen to whoever told you to do that." I nip at his ear again. "If you want to try new things in bed, maybe run them past me first. I'll tell you if they're a good idea or not."

"Very well." He pauses for a moment, enjoying my touch, then admits, "Are you displeased with how I pleasure you?"

"Never." I lick the cords of his throat and I love how he jerks against me ever so slightly. "I was just thinking to myself how amazing you were. I mean it when I say you make me crazy and I'd never want another, ever."

He doesn't smile, but he takes my hand in his larger one and laces his fingers through mine, covering his heart. I can feel the low, satisfied hum of his khui, the song different now that we've fulfilled resonance.

"So, what else did others recommend you try in bed?" I ask, curious.

"Mm. Tail play?"

I wish I could see his forehead to see if he's blushing or not. "Tail play, huh? That could be exciting." I think of the tail already trapped between my thighs. It wouldn't take much for me to sink down on it and let it rub me in all the naughtiest of places. "Tell me more."

"I . . . guess it is using my tail on you." After a moment, he adds, "In the furs."

I bite back a giggle. As if there were any question why he'd do that. "I might be into that," I tell him, and ease down, spreading my thighs wider. It means I'm no longer able to reach his ear to nibble on him from behind. Instead, I slide up against him and press my stomach to his back, and my pussy—already slick with heat—grips his tail as I move against him. "Oooh. I definitely like this idea."

Raahosh groans, the sound low in the cavern, and I feel his tail press up against me. It twitches, as if trying to thump, but I just rub up and down against him instead. I slide my hands lower and grip his cock from behind. He's still hard and aching, and when I stroke him, pre-cum soaks my hand.

"You know what I like?" I tell him, pressing a kiss to his back.

"What?" His voice is hoarse.

"Dirty talk." I let the fingers of one hand skate up and down the length of him as I grip the base of his cock with my other hand. "Filthy words."

I can feel him panting. "Filthy . . . words?"

"Yes." I flick my tongue against his back even as I rock my hips, rubbing up and down on his tail and letting it graze my clit. Oooh, God, I don't know if this is what people had in mind when they said tail play, but I know I'm liking it. He's thick at the base of his tail, and it's like riding his cock and letting it glide through my folds without ever penetrating me. Fuck, it's dirty and hot and I'm definitely a fan. "Like you'd tell me how you want to take this big fat cock and stuff it into my mouth." I stroke his length, then squeeze lightly. "How you'd want to push it so far into my mouth that you'd hit the back of my throat. How you'd watch as you feed it between my lips and how it's so big and thick that it makes me have to stretch my mouth open wide just to take it all—"

His loud groan echoes around us. One big hand covers mine and then he's using my hand to jerk off even as I ride the base of his tail, rocking against him. A few seconds later, the breath hisses between his teeth and then I feel his hot release splash over my fingers. I keep stroking, squeezing lightly to try and wring every ounce of pleasure out of his climax that I can. I love that he just came so hard. I grind down against his tail and my pussy clenches on nothing. I didn't come again, but that's okay.

I have no doubt that won't be the case for long.

Raahosh sags against me, his head falling back as he takes a deep breath. He shudders, and then lifts his hand from where he's covering mine. "I came on your hands."

"I noticed." I press a kiss to his back again. "I liked it. It was dirty and hot and I liked watching you lose control. I love watching you come."

Laughter rumbles in his chest. "I love watching you come, as well." He moves forward, the motion making his tail slick through my folds, and I suck in a breath. Mama like. But then Raahosh is wiping my fingers free of his release with a soft fur and tending to himself.

I remain where I am, drowsy with contentment, my cheek pressed against his broad, rippling back. "I love you."

"I love you as well, my Liz."

"You know what I love best, though?"

"What is that?"

"I love that I can be me around you. I love you for who you are. I don't want you to be anyone but Raahosh—my Raahosh. You can be as grumpy as you want, because I know I can be a pain in the ass." I ignore his snort and continue, because I'm having a sappy moment, dammit. "I know I can go on far too long about Star Wars and I've never met a cussword I didn't like, and I know I can be bossy. But I feel like that's all okay with you and I love that. I don't have to try to be someone else." I snuggle up against him from behind, pleased. "And I'm not alone. You have no idea how alone I felt for so, so long."

He wraps his arms around mine, as if hugging me in that small way. "I no longer feel alone, either. It is the best feeling. Thank you, my mate. You know you have my heart."

"You have mine, too," I tell him . . . and then add, "But not my butthole. That's off-limits without prior discussion."

He snorts with amusement.

Raahosh

Liz sleeps next to me, curled up. Her bottom is pressed against my groin and my tail is between her legs, the tufted end gripped in her hand. Her head is propped up on my upper arm and her mouth is open, which means she is drooling a small river, but I do not wake her. Instead, I pull her closer to me and press my mouth to her pale shoulder.

My fierce, determined mate.

When I felt foolish, she did not let me retreat. She will not let us walk away from each other in anger, but keeps talking until I must acknowledge why I am angry or upset. When I first met Liz, I thought she would never cease her endless conversations, and it annoyed me. Now, I am glad for it. I kiss her skin again, thinking of all the bold things she said to me as she sat and rode my tail and stroked my cock from behind.

I worried I would not be interesting enough for her. Now I am starting to think there is no one that can keep up with her wild, creative mind, and that pleases me.

She can be the bold one. I will be the rock, the protector, the shield. She can be the arrow, launching itself forward. I will be the bow—the brace, the stability that the arrow needs to speed ahead.

In this, we are a good pair.

Liz smacks her lips and rolls onto her belly, releasing my numb, drool-covered arm and presenting me with her backside. I ease out of bed, though I am reluctant to leave her side. I want to curl up in the furs with her forever, but that will not stoke the fire or make warm tea for my frequently cold, thin-skinned female who needs heat. It will not put food in our bellies, and so I get up and tend to the fire, putting on a pouch of fresh snow to melt and heating cubes of frozen meat on a skewer until they sizzle and blacken at the edges, the way Liz prefers them. She still likes raw, but now that she carries our kit, her favorite is the crispy bits, so I make sure she has the best bites of food.

Once it is all ready and prepared, I pour a cup of tea, put the food in a bowl, and approach my mate where she is still curled in the furs of the storage area. She did not leave my side after I retreated last night, and we spent the nighttime hours mating with all the feverish intensity of first resonance.

I move quietly into the storage area and then crouch by her side. I flick my tail against her hand to wake her, and she blinks up at me with a sleepy expression.

"I made you food." I set it down next to her and wait, feeling awkward. She is beaming up at me as if I am all good things in the world and it is . . . pleasurable. I do not know how to handle that.

"Breakfast in bed? This honeymoon's just getting better and better," Liz says, sitting up and taking the bowl. "Oooh, and you crisped my meat. You are so getting laid again."

I snort, amused at her words. "There is a thick snowstorm today. You cannot see past your hand."

She nibbles on a chunk of meat with her small teeth. "So . . . does that mean no travel for you and me today?"

I reach over and touch a lock of her soft golden mane. "We stay here this day. Perhaps we will stay in the furs by the fire and you can tell me all about a Star War."

Liz giggles. "Oh my God, you are so cute."

The base of my horns grows hot. "I am a hunter. We are not cute. We are strong. Brave. Fearless. We—" I pause as she lifts her small foot into the air. "What are you doing?"

"Can you rub my foot? It's cold and your hands are warm."

I take her foot and begin to rub it, caressing the small whitish-pink toes and kneading the sole. "As I was saying—"

She closes her eyes and shakes her head. "This is awesome. Just like this. You can rub my feet, I'll eat in bed, and it'll be the best honeymoon ever."

"It is already the best of honeymoon ever because I am here with you," I admit to her. "I am thankful you are my mate and no one else's."

Liz grins at me, wiggling her other foot into the air, and I hold them both, massaging as she pops another piece of meat into her mouth. "I was going to give you bow lessons, though. I guess we can't do that while it's a blizzard outside. Are you disappointed? You're not getting much out of this honeymoon and here I'm getting a massage and breakfast in bed." She props her arm behind her head and looks up at me. "Is there something you want to do?"

Other than drag her into the furs and rut into her like a wild beast? But Liz is always as eager for playing in the furs as I am. She means something else. I think in silence as I rub her feet, considering. "Are there certain things that are done while honeymoon?"

Her lips twitch as if she wants to laugh again. "Most people go on a trip and do sightseeing. They look at old places, visit ruins, or just hang out at the beach and swim."

I consider this. "I guess we can go to the beach, but I do not think you will like it. It is on the far side of the mountains, in the opposite direction of where we are headed, and you cannot swim. These pink toes will freeze." And I nip at one, because I like seeing her eyes light up.

"I will pass on the frozen beach, thank you." Liz eats another piece of meat and gives me a hot look that tells me she is not thinking about beaches much at all. "It's bonding time. What do you want to do? What would make this special for you? Something you wouldn't want to do with anyone else?"

Immediately, an idea springs to mind. I almost discard it, because it feels too open, too vulnerable. But she is looking at me with eager eyes, and I can refuse her nothing. "I would," I say carefully, "like to go fishing."

"Fishing?" She gives me a look of confusion. "We've fished before, Raahosh."

I shake my head. "There is a place my father used to take me, back when he was alive. I remember that spot, and I would sit on the banks of the shore with him and we would wait for the fish to creep close. And we would just talk. It is my best memory I have with my father."

Her expression grows soft. "Then of course we'll do that. I'd love to. Do you know how to get to the place?"

"I do." I have passed it many times since my father's death, but I never approached. I never wanted to, because I wanted to keep those memories as they were. I wanted to see the place in my mind's eye as a kit holding my father's hand as we headed toward the lake with nets and fishing poles.

But I want to share this with Liz. I want to make new memories with her. I am tired of living in the past.

"I can't wait," she says, and puts her bowl aside, licking her lips. I offer her the cup but she shakes her head. "Not thirsty. Okay, so we'll go fishing once the weather clears up, yes?"

"Not today," I agree. "Today is a day for staying in the furs."

"I'm glad you said that," my mate tells me, breathless. "Because I'm totally thinking about sex right now. Raw, raunchy sex with you on top of me and my ankles on your shoulders."

Now I am thinking of this, too. I stop massaging her feet and place them on my shoulders even as I move into the furs to join her. "I think that is a fine idea."

It snows for two days straight, and I spend those days curled up in the furs with my mate. We mate. We play foolish word games. We discuss names for our kit. We talk of others in the tribe and who we think will resonate next. Sometimes we talk of nothing more than the weather, and even that is enjoyable. I like sharing everything with Liz, and I have never shared so much with another person before. Vektal is as a brother to me, and yet there are things I have never confessed to him that I readily tell my mate because I feel safe in telling her even the smallest of things.

I am almost sad when the snows let up and the suns peek out from the thick cloud cover, because it means we must move on once more.

"Fishing day!" Liz announces happily as we pack.

Her excitement makes me less sad. With her, all things are enjoyable, and when we leave the cave behind, it is hand in hand, talking of the best kinds of birds to eat and what herbs to use when stuffing the cavity before roasting it. Silly things, but I just like hearing Liz talk.

It takes maybe half a day of walking off of the familiar path before I see a familiar mountain peak, and a familiar purple-edged rock cliff. We are close. I hold Liz's hand tightly as we head into the valley, and nestled amongst the cliffs I can see the lake. Warm water bubbles out of the rocky cliffs above and trickles down to the surface, but because it is so cold, it freezes before it makes it into the pond. The result is a glassy cascade of frozen strands that tumble down the rocks in a frozen waterfall to the tepid lake below. The edges of it are crusted with ice, but the interior is warm. And near the frozen waterfall itself, I spy my father's favorite perch.

"It's all so pretty," Liz breathes, clapping her gloved hands. "I'm glad we came here."

I point to the small overhang of rock. "My father and I would sit there. This is not a good lake for spearfishing, because the ice on the edges will not hold weight. So we would use something called a 'pole' and put a bit of meat on a barb to trap the fish into biting . . . Why are you looking at me like that?" I scowl down at her, because as I speak, a mischievous grin crosses her face.

She reaches up as high as she can and taps my chin. "You are so cute. Humans fish with poles, too, silly."

"Do they?" I grunt. "Perhaps you are not as primitive as I thought." I keep my voice gruff, and love when she makes an outraged squawk.

"We are not primitive!"

"Says the people that burn their perfectly good meat."

Liz laughs and gives me a hard nudge. "You suck!"

I smirk at her. "Come. Let us climb up and claim our seat."

I remember scaling the steep, icy cliffs as a young kit and the ease my father climbed with. It is different with my human mate at my side, though. She does not have the size I do, and her hands are covered to protect them from the cold so she cannot grip as she should. My heart thunders in my chest when she slips once, and I decide that I will carry her down.

My hands go to her waist to help her to the top, but she slaps my grip away. "I can do it. I'm not fragile, Raahosh."

She thinks she is not fragile. I snort and keep my hands on her anyhow.

Up at the top of the ridge, Liz puts her hands on her hips and draws a deep breath. "Wow, this is beautiful. I love the view."

I keep my hand on her arm and my tail wrapped around her leg. "Do not lean so close to the edge."

"You'll catch me," she says, and leans over the lip of the cliff. "Oh, we're right above the water."

I pull her backward gently. "Sit. Let us prepare our fishing poles."

She sits obediently and I move closer to her than I probably should, and I keep my tail latched tightly to her leg, just in case. We are higher up than I remember as a kit, or perhaps I am just worrying about Liz and the kit in her belly. Either way, I will not get comfortable this day.

Even so, it soothes my spirit to be here with her. She watches as I tie a long length of sinewed cord to one end of my spear and tie a bone hook on the other. Liz takes the hook and baits it with ease, making sure to work the barbs through the meat so it will not fall off once it hits the water, and it shows me she has done this before.

"I used to go hunting with my dad," she says when I glance

over at her. "And sometimes fishing, though we mostly just caught turtles or snakes instead of actual fish. Do we need a weight of some kind attached to the line?"

I toss the hunk of meat down into the water below, and sure enough, it bobs on the surface and does not go farther. "We can use a rock." It is not a bad idea, and I am pleased she is so clever. "You are smart, Liz."

"Nah, just something I remember from before."

We adjust the lines with weights, tying a small oblong stone near the bait on the line to keep it under the water, and then drop one line into the water. I hand the "pole" to Liz while I work on my own. I watch her as I work on the line, the easy happiness in her face. I think of the other human females and try to imagine them out here with their mates and I cannot picture it. They do not like the wild. They would not be thrilled to be exiled with me.

Truly, I am the luckiest to have Liz. She is perfect in every way.

"You're watching me," she says, gazing down at the water.

"I am thinking how happy I am," I admit.

Liz glances over at me and a shy smile curves her mouth. "Me, too. This place is perfect . . . and you're awesome. I didn't think I could be so happy on an ice planet like this but . . . it's amazing and I can't imagine being anywhere else. I'm looking forward to the rest of our lives together." Her hand brushes over her stomach, and I know she is thinking of our kit.

Impulsively, I lean over and kiss the top of her head, then hold her closer to me, pulling her into my lap. I have a sudden vision of one of the large fish biting down and then pulling my mate off the ledge and into the water. "Perhaps we will fish together."

She chuckles. "All right, if you want."

"I do." I settle her on my thighs as she holds the pole. "You can tell me another Star War."

"There's only one," Liz says, exasperated. "And I've told it to you already."

"But you love it, so tell it again."

Her eyes flare with pleasure as she glances back at me. "You want to hear it again? Really?"

"I like the things you like," I tell her simply, and hold her tight.

"All right," Liz says, leaning back against my chest. Her head fits just under my chin. Perfect, really. "A long time ago, there was this guy named Anakin, and he was the chosen one . . ."

AUTHOR'S NOTE

Hello there!

I'm super excited that you have the special edition of *Barbarian Alien* in your hands. I don't think anyone could be more thrilled than me to have these extended versions out in the world, but I know Liz and Raahosh are the OG couple for so many Ice Planet Barbarians fans, so maybe not! Maybe we're all sitting at home, biting our knuckles so we don't scream so loudly the neighbors hear.

(And maybe that's just me! Who can really say?)

I don't know if you've noticed this about my books, but I have an *intense* love for secondary characters. Growing up, I loved nothing more than an ensemble cast in a book series, because then I would quietly pair them up in my mind. I just knew that Pern's F'nor needed a queen dragonrider, Samwise Gamgee needed to get his ass back home so he could marry Rose Cotton, and Dragonlance's Tika Waylan deserved far more screen time. Maybe it's because I grew up reading comic books, where characters like Wolverine were the stars, but I personally was dying for one single solitary panel of Gambit gazing longingly at Rogue.

Either way, I ship secondary characters, and I ship them hard. The moment Liz came on-screen, I knew she had a book. I didn't initially plan on her being mouthy. I wanted someone in the group to be a fighter. Kira was the brains, Georgie was the everygirl, and so Liz was my brawn. The moment I started writing her, though, she became The Mouth. Liz had something to say about everything, and it was all sarcastic and awesome, and I loved, loved, loved her. I figured either everyone would love her along with me or I would get hate mail if I wrote her book. Which is okay! As a writer, I try to make my characters have different personalities and goals, and if they don't hit the mark with every reader, that's all right. I like to think that every cast of characters is like a group of coworkers in an office. Someone's the peacemaker. Someone's the suck-up. Someone's the person who takes too-long breaks and gets everyone else to do their work. Someone's that weird guy in the back clipping his toenails at his desk.

(Okay, so I generally try to avoid writing that guy, because blech. Why do some men think being at the office is the perfect time to groom? Men, if you are reading this, leave your damn clippers at home. You are grossing the women out.)

So Liz is the obnoxious one in the office who has something to say about everything and everyone, and she doesn't care if you like her or not. I love the audacity of someone who absolutely gives no shits about whether you like her or not. I'm far too much of a people pleaser to be like Liz, but I wish I was!

I'm far, far more like Raahosh. He's the one who doesn't feel as if he fits into the group, despite having been there all along. He hangs out on the fringes, watching everyone else have a great time and wishing he could, too. He's a hard-ass and impatient, sure, but he also has a sensitive side that just wants everyone to like him. That's why it hits him so hard when he's exiled (spoiler? Can I spoil my own book?) and why he worries that he's not enough to make Liz happy. His parents were a mess, and he's scarred (both inside and out) from childhood trauma. He knows it's absolutely wrong to steal Liz from the group and that there will be hell to pay, but in his head, he feels that it's the only way he can get a mate. So he does it anyhow. Raahosh is the one full of emotions and longing in this pairing, and maybe that's why it works so very well? They're obviously one of my favorite couples to write, and I know they're the favorite of a lot of other people, too.

Liz and Raahosh's book was initially released as a serial, the second one I did, after *Ice Planet Barbarians*. By the time this one wrapped up, I was planning ahead. Everyone was loving my big blue cinnamon rolls (me included), and I just wanted to write books for *everyone*. I figured if I got lucky, I'd be able to write up to Josie's book and finish things. That'd be a nice, tidy ending, right? So that's why there's a quick mention in the story of people who resonated and why we don't see them on camera in this book. I figured I'd never come back around to them or I'd kill some of them off.

(Early Ruby did not know she was so soft and would have a hard time killing anyone. Also, Early Ruby really, really underestimated how well the books would do.)

At the end of this book, Liz and Raahosh are in a very mild state of exile, and so many people were very mad at me for doing that, and for making Vektal the unrelenting one. Raahosh and Liz were in love, right? And if they weren't upset, why should they be punished? To me, though, it makes perfect sense. We'll go back to the office analogy (you know me and my analogies) and compare the kidnapping to . . . cigarette breaks. Let's say that you're Vektal and you're the boss of IPB Inc. Your employees take a lot of smoke breaks, so you tell them they can only have one a day. Raahosh is your best employee, but he takes five smoke breaks a day. You notice. Everyone else in the office notices. Now, Raahosh might be kicking ass at getting his work done, but he's absolutely not paying attention to the rules. If you do nothing about it, you run the risk of everyone taking a million smoke breaks a day (because if you're not going to punish Raahosh, then why punish someone else?), so you have to say something. You can't ignore wrongdoing just because it's your friend. If you do, you're not a good leader. You're just a good friend. Likewise, Vektal hates to punish Raahosh, but he knows he has to, because if he doesn't, everyone else is going to decide to snatch a woman.

I hope that makes sense (and that you don't want a cigarette now). Long story short—sometimes being the chief/boss sucks and you have to make uncool decisions.

I hope you like the new cover of the book! The first cover for *Barbarian Alien* (another on-the-nose title, am I right? Just call me a marketing genius) absolutely does not match the story at all. It features a very pretty, very brunette woman hugging the back of a blue mopey-stanced guy. Which is great, and my cover creator, Kati Wilde (also one of my best friends ever and the person I would secretly love to be), did an amazing job with what I gave her. Back in the early days of *Ice Planet Barbarians*, I searched for cover art that would show a sexy couple (gotta keep those science fiction bros away from the girl cooties) and that would still work if we hid the guy's face. I wasn't sure how well it would come across if we had HORNS! TAILS! PLATING! GLOWING EYES! on the cover. I didn't want to scare anyone, so that's why on the old cover of book one Vektal is artfully facing away from the camera and the model really doesn't look like Georgie, and why two rando (but sweet-seeming) strangers are on the original cover of *Barbarian Alien*.

So . . . now you know.

Enjoy the special edition, and thank you for reading. Most of all, thank you for being a fan!

—RUBY DIXON

THE PEOPLE OF
BARBARIAN ALIEN

THE CHIEF AND HIS MATE

VEKTAL (Vehk-tall)—Chief of the sa-khui tribe. Son of Hektar, the prior chief, who died in khui-sickness. He is a dedicated hunter and leader, and carries a sword and a bola for weapons. He is the one who finds Georgie, and resonance between them is so strong that he resonates prior to her receiving her khui.

GEORGIE—Unofficial leader of the human women. Originally from Orlando, Florida, she has long, golden-brown curls and a determined attitude. Newly pregnant after resonating to Vektal.

FAMILIES

RAAHOSH (Rah-hosh)—A quiet but surly hunter. One of his horns is broken off and his face scarred. Vektal's close friend. Impatient and rash, he steals Liz the moment she receives her khui. They resonate, and he is exiled for stealing her.

LIZ—A loudmouth huntress from Oklahoma who loves Star Wars and giving her opinion. Raahosh kidnaps her the moment she receives her lifesaving khui. She was a champion archer as a teenager. Resonates to Raahosh and voluntarily chooses exile with him.

ARIANA—One of the women kept in the stasis tubes. Hails from New Jersey and was an anthropology student. She tended to cry a lot when first rescued. Has a delicate frame and dark brown hair. Resonates to Zolaya. Still cries a lot.

ZOLAYA (Zoh-lay-uh)—A skilled hunter. Steady and patient, he resonates to Ariana and seems to be the only one not bothered by her weepiness.

MARLENE (Mar-lenn)—One of the women kept in the stasis tubes. French speaking. Quiet and confident, and exudes sexuality. Resonates to Zennek.

ZENNEK (Zehn-eck)—A quiet and shy hunter. Brother to Pashov, Salukh, and Farli. He is the son of Borran and Kemli. Resonates to Marlene.

NORA—One of the women kept in the stasis tubes. A nurturing sort who was rather angry she was dumped on an ice planet. Quickly resonates to Dagesh. No longer quite so angry.

DAGESH (Dah-zzhesh; the *g* sound is swallowed)—A calm, hardworking, and responsible hunter. Resonates to Nora.

STACY—One of the women kept in the stasis tubes. She was weepy when she first awakened. Loves to cook and worked in a bakery prior to abduction. Resonates to Pashov and seems quite happy.

PASHOV (Pah-showv)—The son of Kemli and Borran; brother to Farli, Salukh, and Zennek. A hunter described as "quiet." Resonates to Stacy.

MAYLAK (May-lack)—One of the few female sa-khui. She is the tribe healer and Vektal's former pleasure mate. She resonated to Kashrem, ending her relationship with Vektal. Sister to Bek.

KASHREM (Cash-rehm)—A gentle tribal tanner. Mated to Maylak.

ESHA (Esh-uh)—Their young female kit.

SEVVAH (Sev-uh)—A tribe elder and one of the few sa-khui females. She is mother to Aehako, Rokan, and Sessah, and acts like a mom to the others in the cave. Her entire family was spared when khui-sickness hit fifteen years ago.

OSHEN (Aw-shen)—A tribe elder and Sevvah's mate. Brewer.

SESSAH (Ses-uh)—Their youngest child, a juvenile male.

KEMLI (Kemm-lee)—An elder female, mother to Salukh, Pashov, Zennek, and Farli. The tribe's expert on plants.

BORRAN (Bore-awn)—Kemli's much younger mate and an elder.

FARLI (Far-lee)—A preteen female sa-khui. Her brothers are Salukh, Pashov, and Zennek.

～

ASHA (Ah-shuh)—A mated female sa-khui. She is mated to Hemalo but has not been seen in his furs for some time. Their kit died shortly after birth.

HEMALO (Hee-mah-lo)—A tanner and a quiet sort. He is mated (unhappily) to Asha.

THE UNMATED HUMAN FEMALES

CLAIRE—A quiet, slender blonde with a pixie cut. She finds her new world extremely frightening.

HARLOW—One of the women kept in the stasis tubes. She has red hair and freckles, and is mechanically minded and excellent at problem-solving.

JOSIE—One of the original kidnapped women, she broke her leg in the ship crash. Short and adorable, Josie is an excessive talker, a gossip, and a bit of a dreamer. Likes to sing.

KIRA—The first of the human women to be kidnapped, Kira has a large metallic translator attached to her ear by the aliens. She is quiet and serious, with somber eyes.

MEGAN—Megan was in an early pregnancy when she was captured, but the aliens terminated it. She tends toward a sunny disposition when not abducted by aliens.

TIFFANY—A "farm girl" back on Earth, she suffered greatly while waiting for Georgie to return. She has been traumatized by her alien abduction. She is a perfectionist and a hard worker.

THE UNMATED HUNTERS

AEHAKO (Eye-ha-koh)—A laughing, flirty hunter. The son of Sevvah and Oshen; brother to Rokan and young Sessah. He seems to be in a permanent good mood. Close friends with Haeden.

BEK (Behk)—A hunter generally thought of as short-tempered and unpleasant. Brother to Maylak.

CASHOL (Cash-awl)—A distractible and slightly goofy-natured hunter. Cousin to Vektal.

EREVEN (Air-uh-ven)—A quiet, easygoing hunter.

HAEDEN (Hi-den)—A grim and unsmiling hunter with "dead" eyes, Haeden formerly resonated but his female died of khui-sickness before they could mate. His current khui is new. He is very private.

HARREC (Hair-ek)—A hunter who has no family and finds his place in the tribe by constantly joking and teasing. A bit accident-prone.

HASSEN (Hass-en)—A passionate and brave hunter, Hassen is impulsive and tends to act before he thinks.

ROKAN (Row-can)—The son of Sevvah and Oshen; brother to Aehako and young Sessah. A hunter known for his strange predictions that come true all too often.

SALUKH (Sah-luke)—The brawny son of Kemli and Borran; brother to Farli, Pashov, and Zennek. Very strong and intense.

TAUSHEN (Tow—rhymes with "cow"—shen)—A teenage hunter, newly into adulthood. Eager to prove himself.

WARREK (War-eck)—The son of Elder Eklan. He is a very quiet and mild hunter, with long, sleek black hair. Warrek teaches the young kits how to hunt.

ELDERS

ELDER DRAYAN—A smiling elder who uses a cane to help him walk.

ELDER DRENOL—A grumpy, antisocial elder.

ELDER EKLAN—A calm, kind elder. Father to Warrek, he also helped raise Harrec.

ELDER VADREN (Vaw-dren)—An elder.

ELDER VAZA (Vaw-zhuh)—A lonely widower and hunter. He tries to be as helpful as possible. He is very interested in the new females.

THE DEAD

DOMINIQUE—A redheaded human female. Her mind was broken when she was abused by the aliens on the ship. When she arrived on Not-Hoth, she ran out into the snow and deliberately froze.

KRISSY—A human female, dead in the crash.

PEG—A human female, dead in the crash.

ABOUT THE AUTHOR

RUBY DIXON is an author of all things science fiction romance. She is a Sagittarius and a Reylo shipper, and loves farming sims (but not actual housework). She lives in the South with her husband and a couple of geriatric cats, and can't think of anything else to put in her biography. Truly, she is boring.

VISIT THE AUTHOR ONLINE

RubyDixon.com
RubyDixonBooks
Author.Ruby.Dixon

Ready to find
your next great read?

Let us help.

Visit prh.com/nextread

Penguin
Random
House